Stephanie Lehmann graduated from University College Berkeley. She attended the New York University Graduate Program in Creative Writing. A playwright and a novelist, she lives in Manhattan with her husband and two children. To find out more about her novels, visit Stephanie's website at www.StephanieLehmann.com

Also by Stephanie Lehmann

Thoughts While Having Sex (New American Library)
Are You in the Mood? (New American Library)

the art of

undressing

stephanie lehmann

HODDER

Copyright © Stephanie Lehmann 2005

First published in Great Britain in 2007 by Hodder and Stoughton
A division of Hodder Headline

The right of Stephanie Lehmann to be identified as the
Author of the Work has been asserted by her in accordance
with the Copyright, Designs and Patents Act 1988.

A Hodder paperback

1 3 5 7 9 10 8 6 4 2

A CIP catalogue record for this title
is available from the British Library.

ISBN 978 0 340 89956 4

Typeset in Giovanni Book by
Palimpsest Book Production Limited,
Grangemouth, Stirlingshire

Printed and bound by Clays Ltd, St Ives plc

Hodder Headline's policy is to use papers that are natural, renewable
and recyclable products and made from wood grown in sustainable
forests. The logging and manufacturing processes are expected to
conform to the environmental regulations of the country of origin.

Hodder and Stoughton Ltd
A division of Hodder Headline
338 Euston Road
London NW1 3BH

acknowledgments

Writing about a stripper means doing all sorts of grueling research, and since I couldn't do it alone, I want to thank my friends who went with me on field trips to enjoy, complain, giggle, analyze, and turn down lap dances: Wendy Walker, Andrea Schell, Shannon Mullen, her friend who hurt her back falling off a bar, and Franny Silverman. I also want to thank my husband for staying home.

The following people had the less enjoyable task of reading early drafts and giving me invaluable feedback: Julie Carpenter, Anne Galin, Leah Pike, Elizabeth Audley, and Minnette. Thank you, thank you.

The following people were an important part of my research on stripping and/or the sex industry: Annie Sprinkle, Sky London, Elisabeth Eaves, Lily Burana, Matt Sycamore, Heidi Mattson, Tim Keefe, Leah Stauffer, Sheila Kelley, Jill Nagle, Shay Stephen, Merri Lisa Johnson, and Katherine Frank. Their inspiring and informative books, performances, classes, and conversations helped me immensely in my imaginings.

I also want to acknowledge the following food experts who have written about and shared their experiences in restaurant kitchens: Andrew MacLauchlan, Jeremiah Tower, Anthony Bourdain, Michael Ruhlman, Helen Studley, and Karen Hubert Allison. Also, thanks to Lisa Hazen for loaning me those books. And Simon Feil for the last-minute read.

I want to express my appreciation to Elaine Koster for teaching me so much about the publishing business, Rian Montgomery for her enthusiasm and support, and Elizabeth Kandall for helping me think *again*, as always, and especially for that conversation about 'sex objects.'

I also want to thank my daughter, Madeleine, and my son, David, for tolerating me when I'm grumpy about having a lot of work to do. Because you constantly distract me from my writing to watch Austin Powers on DVD, to shop for clothes, to remind me to call the dentist, and to defrost frozen meals, I'm always able to return to my work with a fresh sense of urgency. What more could a mom want?

And, finally, I want to express gratitude to my agent, Stephanie Kip Rostan, and my editor, Kara Cesare, for joining me on this project. Thanks for seeing what this could be from the beginning, and for being so great to work with.

chapter one

'**S**o you all think I'm a whore!'

Thirty-three students of all ages, shapes, and sizes had shown up for my mother's beginner class on how to strip. 'And you all wanna be whores too!' An ex-stripper who goes by the name Coco Winters, my mom was well of aware of the irony. She'd always been considered a slut, and now it was fashionable to be a slut. Women flocked to her classes so they could learn from a professional.

It was my job to start the Madonna CD when she did her demo and sell the products when class was over. Feathery fans, hot pink boas, plastic pearl necklaces, vibrators, autographed copies of her self-published book *How to Strip for Your Lover*.

I really did not want to be there.

But her assistant Sunny was on vacation in Greece, and when Coco asked me to fill in for July, I couldn't say no. Then Sunny kept extending her vacation, and now it was almost September. As I stood in back watching, I couldn't help but feel foolish. The good little daughter – helping her mom sell vibrators.

I was feeling especially sensitive about it because that day, I'd moved back in with her. Yes, moved back in with my mom. Hired a 'Man with Van named Stan' and driven from One Hundred and Fifteenth Street to Forty-eighth Street with all my stuff. Boom. There I was. Twenty-five years old. Back in my childhood bedroom.

'So,' Stan had asked me, 'you're shacking up with your mom?' We were speeding down Broadway catching one yellow light after another. 'I hope you get along.'

'We do okay.' Coco and I had our problems, but nothing I couldn't handle. At least I wouldn't have to pay rent.

'I'd live on the streets before moving in with my mom,' Stan had said. 'But she's uptight.'

'My mom is the opposite of uptight.' Familiar stores slipped past. 'Which does present its own problems.'

At the huge intersection across from Lincoln Center, we stopped for a red light. That's when my bureau, which was stacked on top of my other stuff, slid forward and bumped me in the back of my head. Not hard, but it was disconcerting. I turned around and pushed it back. The light changed. Stan sped up only to brake quickly for another red light, so I leaned forward to make sure I didn't get hit again. 'You sure this stuff is packed in okay?'

'It's fine. Everything is under control.'

I had no reason to believe him, seeing as he didn't appear to be under control. Unshaven, greasy hair, red-rimmed eyes. It didn't take a degree in physics to figure if he slammed on his brakes, the bureau would shoot forward and smash into perhaps both our skulls. I could've gotten out of the van, wounded his pride, and let him get decapitated by himself. But maybe he'd decide to ride off with all my belongings, and I'd never be able to track him down. Not that it would've been the worst thing. My most valuable possession was my set of knives. I was particularly fond of my eight-inch Global chef's knife. It was Japanese-made – cheaper but more user-friendly than the heavy, high-carbon, hard-to-sharpen Henckels and Wusthofs. It had become like a natural extension of my right hand. Most exciting of all, it had a spiffy stainless steel handle.

I get excited by stainless steel the way most women get excited about diamonds. Its solid silver shine makes me feel so secure. I love the way every time you wipe it down it looks all new again.

I checked to make sure my knives were okay. Yes. There they were, right behind me, wrapped inside a thick piece of blue canvas that rolled up like a pirouette cookie. I could just grab them and get out, couldn't I?

But no, I wanted to be polite. So I sat there and silently pleaded with the powers that be to allow me to make my sixty-seven-block journey without a spinal cord injury.

'So may I ask why you're moving?' Stan asked. 'I like to hear people's stories. Usually it means they're going through a major change for the better – or worse. Sounds like you're on the downhill side.' He chuckled. 'Am I right?'

I'd gotten his name off a flier stapled to a telephone pole, but I still felt the need to defend myself. 'My roommate's boyfriend is moving in. She has the lease, so I have to go. And I'm about to start at a culinary school that's just a few blocks from my mom, so it made sense to move back in with her. After graduation, I'll get a job somewhere and move on. It's just temporary.'

There was something reassuring about making a 'pit stop' in the apartment I grew up in before getting back out in the race. Even if Coco did drive me crazy, it was a familiar kind of crazy, and there was something comforting in that.

'That's cool. Those cooking schools are expensive, aren't they?'

'Yep.' When I'd first looked into it, I couldn't *believe* how expensive. The one that seemed to have the best program for me (and wasn't even the *most* expensive) was ten thousand dollars per semester. They had a scholarship that knocked off some of that, but still. Coco was on a budget, and I didn't want to ask my father for help, so it wasn't clear how I'd be able to pull it off. My parents had been divorced since I was a baby. Coco had always been too proud to take alimony, and, other than college, I'd never asked for anything beyond my child support. But I gritted my teeth and asked, and he said yes, even though I could tell he wasn't thrilled to finance my decision to get a 'degree' (certificate) that would only help me get a 'substandard' (crummy-paying low-status) job.

'That's something I've thought of doing too,' Stan said.

It seemed like everyone (other than my dad) wanted to go to cooking school when they heard I was going. Even Coco. I could still hear her voice in my head when I told her. *That's not fair. I want to go too!* When I told her I was thinking of specializing in pastry, she was even more jealous. Desserts, she liked to say, are 'sex on a plate.' In my opinion, sex was 'dessert in bed.'

When we were ten blocks from my building, I called my boyfriend, Ian, on my cell. He was supposed to be stationed in front of my building.

'I didn't forget,' he said.

'So you're there?'

'On my way. I got stuck downtown.'

'How long will you be?'

'A half hour?'

'We need you there now!'

'Start without me. I'll get there as fast as I can.'

I hung up on him and tried not to be angry. No one wants to help you move, right? That's why you pay a complete stranger to do it. Still, I knew it wasn't just that. Our relationship was dying a slow death, and neither of us was able to put an end to it.

I called my mom to see if she was around, but just got her voice mail. I didn't leave a message. 'My boyfriend is late,' I confessed to Stan, 'we'll have to start without him.'

'One of us has to stay in the van or I'll get towed.'

'We can take turns taking things up.'

I could tell he was annoyed. And really, twenty dollars an hour did not seem like enough to compensate him for having to do this. We pulled in front of my building. Coco had inherited the apartment on the third floor from my grandma, who got it at an insider's price in the seventies when the building went co-op. Even though it was just a crummy old tenement on a noisy street in midtown, that was too good a deal to pass up. The totally central location made it convenient to everything.

There was no legal parking on the street. If a cop came by, we'd get a ticket. 'Let's do this fast,' Stan said. The apartment was in one of four walk-ups that had managed to escape being torn down for office buildings. At the eastern end of the block there were huge, modern high-rises. Rockefeller Center was right around the corner. But as you headed west towards Eighth Avenue, the street became more run-down, with lots of small businesses catering to the people who flooded the area on weekdays. On my block alone there was a theater, a parking garage, a nail salon, a Duane Reade Pharmacy, a tarot card reader, a pawn shop, and a guy who sold ties and baseball caps against the side of a building under an awning. Plus almost every variety of food: Chinese, Indian, an Irish bar, a small grocery. On the ground floor of my building was a deli where they made fresh bagels. The street was totally congested with traffic, and police cruised the area like crazy.

We propped the back door open, loaded up, dodged through the never-ending pedestrian parade, and got everything we could up the front stoop stairs. I stayed in the van (feeling guilty) while Stan took it all up. Then we had to deal with the bureau. It was too bulky for him to take by himself, so we both had to carry it up, and it was heavy, even with the drawers out. Then we ran down to see if his van was still there. Thank god it was. No ticket. We'd done it!

I thanked Stan profusely and gave him three twenties plus a ten-dollar tip. He wished me luck and drove away. That's when Ian sauntered up the street in his baggy green khakis and navy blue T-shirt. Tall, tan, wiry, and slightly grungy-looking with his unshaven face and spiky, short dirty-blond hair. Looking at him still had the power to make me go soft inside.

'I'm here! How can I help?'

'Your timing is amazing.'

Ian's reason for being late: He was at Tower Records on East Fourth Street. 'I was listening to some tracks and lost track of time. Sorry!'

We went up to the apartment, a small two-bedroom with one hallway running the length of the apartment. The kitchen faced the street. A big blue sign for HOT BAGELS was right outside the two front windows. Then there was the living room, my room, then the bathroom, then Coco's room in the back. The place was run-down and cramped and a perpetual mess. Home sweet home.

My room was unchanged from when I'd left for college. Same collection of stuffed Tweety Birds lined up on a shelf, a poster of Alanis Morissette, and my worn-out old braided blue rug on the floor. One thing I'd always loved about growing up there was how all that life and activity was going on right outside, while inside, in my quiet windowless room, I had my own cozy, safe and serene little world.

I shut the door and began to unpack. Ian stretched out on my childhood bed, a twin, and neither of us spoke of the fact that I was moving in with my mom instead of, say, my boyfriend, who had his own one-bedroom in Washington Heights. I'd suggested the possibility, but he'd nixed it. He was a musician, that's where he worked, he needed the place to himself . . . His instrument? A computer. He was obsessed with mastering this program where he composed on his PC and could 'play' all the instruments himself. I'd been prepared to give him his space. I wouldn't be demanding. After all, I'd be busy with school. The idea was incredibly attractive to me. Without actually being newlyweds, we could pretend to be newlyweds. Play house. Be there for each other at the end of the day. Didn't that sound fun?

Evidently not.

Still. He was so damn cute. Maybe there was hope. Maybe he would come to appreciate me. I stretched out next to him on the narrow mattress. I wanted to rest my cheek on the soft T-shirt of his chest. Wrap my legs around his legs. But I was feeling insecure. Wishing he would touch me first. 'I wish my mom didn't have a class tonight.'

'Can I come?'

'No.' I'd let him come once before. Always regretted it.

'What's the big deal?'

'I just don't enjoy watching you watching my mother take her clothes off.'

'Don't you think it's kind of funny . . . how different you are from Coco?'

He was referring to my modesty. In the beginning of our relationship, I'd made sure to get into bed before all my clothes were off and wanted the lights out by the time I was naked. I was better now. Could actually, for example, make it across the room naked in front of him. Still, I had to pretend to both of us that I felt casual letting him see me 'in all my glory.'

'You wish I would do a striptease?'

'That would be fun.'

'Forget it.'

'Why?'

'If only I could be more like my mother, then we'd all be happy.'

'No one expects that.'

'You do.'

He chuckled. 'You are not by any stretch of the imagination like your mother.'

The front door of the apartment opened and closed. Had to be her. 'Hello!' she yelled, coming straight back to my room. I sat up. 'Knock, knock! Can I come in?'

Coco opened the door without waiting. I was just getting off the bed.

'Whoops! Sorry. You two aren't having sex already, are you?'

I gritted my teeth and went to set up my bureau. If she knew how infrequently we were doing it these days, she'd be sadly disappointed. 'Hi, Mom.'

Mom. Forty-three years old. Tall and gorgeous. Long, thick auburn hair with flaming red highlights. Pale, milky skin lightly salted with freckles. Luscious lips, big green eyes. I was a slightly plainer or should I say understated version of her. Not very pleasant to witness Ian enjoying my mother's ultratight burgundy stretch top with implants spilling out all over.

'Hi, Coco, how are you?'

'Great! So how's it going here? The move went okay?' She lifted a foot and unstrapped a hot pink sequined T-strap sandal.

'Yes.' I pushed my bureau up against the wall.

'Ginger's a little annoyed. I was supposed to help, but I was too late,' Ian said.

Coco removed her other sandal. 'As long as she's mad at you and not me.'

'She's not mad,' I said, sliding an empty drawer back into the bureau.

'Okay. Well then, come 'ere!'

She opened her arms to me. I went to her.

'Welcome home!' She gave me a big hug and our breasts collided. 'Mwah!' She gave me a big, sloppy kiss on the forehead. I caught a whiff of her Chanel.

'Thanks, Mom.'

It did feel good to hear her say that. I was aware that she might not be completely thrilled to have her space invaded.

'So if you'll excuse me, I'll leave you two alone. Gotta get ready for class.' She hooked both sandals on the crook of an index finger. Ian checked out her toned, bare legs as she left the room.

I closed the door behind her and went to the closet. It seemed smaller than I remembered. Good thing I didn't have many clothes. Some of my old games were still in there. Life. Risk. Sorry. Trouble.

Ian sighed. 'I can see how it must be hard.'

'What.' I knew what he was going to say, but I had to hear him say it, like cream calls out to be whipped.

'To compete with your mom.'

'Because she's so sexy.' I zipped open my suitcase. 'And I'm not?'

He sat up. Put his feet on the floor. Sighed. 'Look, maybe I should go.'

I pressed my lips together. Removed a stack of T-shirts from the suitcase. I had to get over this fast. Of course he didn't prefer my mother.

Of course he loved me just the way I was, even if he didn't want to live with me.

'I should let you unpack.'

I put the T-shirts in a drawer. I was being overly sensitive. And really, this apartment was much closer to the school, so it would've been ridiculous to move in with him all the way uptown.

He stood up. 'I'm gonna get going.'

And really. What was the big deal? Why not do a striptease? *Where do you think you're going? Sit back down on that bed, honey, and I'll show you what I've got.*

'See you later,' I said.

'Bye.'

He left without touching me. I closed the door behind him.

At least he wasn't there to see Coco when she emerged from her bedroom all done up for class. She was wearing tight red short-shorts that zipped all the way down the front and a tight, low-cut leopard-skin top. With 'her face on,' she looked about ten years younger.

'How's the unpacking going?'

'Done.'

'Great. That was easy.'

We stood next to each other in front of the hallway mirror. I redid my ponytail while she fluffed out her long, thick hair.

'It almost feels like I never left.'

She frowned into the mirror. 'Except now I have more wrinkles.'

'Are you kidding? You look great.'

'But it takes a helluva lot more work. Ready?'

I considered putting lipstick on, and decided not to bother. I didn't look as glorious as she did, but at least youth was on my side. 'Let's go.'

She slipped on her red stilettos. I put on my white sneakers. We both grabbed a handle on each side of a trunk filled with sex toys and striptease accessories, and lugged it out the door.

chapter two

'Okay, ladies, the first thing you need to do is get rid of that pubic hair!' She paced back and forth in the front of the room. The wall behind her was all mirror. The students sat cross-legged on the floor in three crowded rows ready to get up and try out her moves. I stood in the back watching everyone else watching her.

'Get rid of it! Men don't like a furry bush! They have a hard enough time knowing where to go down there – why confuse him with a jungle he's gonna get lost in? He'll need a machete to find your clit!'

The women laughed. I took a moment to straighten out the 'table of wares.' I liked to line up the vibrators in descending height, like a row of soldiers standing at attention. I had my own personal favorite. The Hello Kitty Vibrator. Forty dollars. Battery-operated. Gentle stimulation. Totally cute. It was pink, and the kitty sitting on top nestled against a little brown plastic teddy bear.

Maybe I was becoming a little too personally attached to my own. But when Ian and I did get around to having sex, I tended to take a backseat when it came to my own pleasure. Please him – take care of myself later. Just seemed easier that way. Even when we were in the middle of sex, I didn't particularly like being on display.

Coco loved having people admire her body. She was slim but curvy in all the right places. Small waist. Born a B, like me, but got the implants when she was twenty-five. Yeah. She was the fantasy. I suppose I could've been that too. I did resemble her. We were both tall, five-nine, same frame, and I inherited at least some of her good looks. But that fantasy thing takes so much effort! The makeup, the accessories, the dieting, the exercise regime . . . Coco worked out every day at the gym. She was toned, and had great thighs and rippling calf muscles. I had more cellulite than she did! I hated the gym. That smell. Sweat mixed with wheatgrass juice. It made me want to vomit.

She went on about the necessity of getting a Brazilian wax. Yeah, right, the more pain and suffering you go through the more you're ready to present yourself to the man – that was the not-subliminal message. I refused to shave my pubic hair. I hated shaving my upper thighs. It always itched like crazy the next day and got little red marks. Who needed that? In college, I went one year without shaving my legs. That was great. My college boyfriend said hairy legs are sexy. Not that I needed him to give me permission. Well, maybe I did. Because after we broke up, I started shaving my legs again. Anyway, hair just shows we're animals, right? Why pretend otherwise? Isn't animalness sexy?

'And,' my mother said, 'very important . . .'. She strutted across the room in her six-inch stilettos. 'The fuck-me pumps.' Coco loves the pumps. 'You can tell I'm a stripper,' she said proudly, 'because I can dance in these things.' Big deal. Good for her. To me, no man was worth being uncomfortable for. My favorite shoes? Currently, lime green Nikes with orange trim dressed up with purple laces.

I just could not understand why men wanted women to be uncomfortable. Wouldn't they really show they care by pleading with their dates not to wear those crippling shoes? *Here, honey, I want you to wear these moccasins tonight. You'll feel so much better.*

'If you think you're going to feel embarrassed,' my mother continued, 'remember to keep it simple. You don't really have to do much. Take it slow. And pick out music that makes *you* feel sexy, not him. You're the one that's got to feel it. This is a performance. An act. And – very important – always keep eye contact with him. Keeps him involved. Because men have very short attention spans, and he's gonna be ready to fuck you long before the dance is over.'

Some of the women giggled with a mixture of amusement and discomfort. The blunt language was part of her act – an act that often spilled over into her 'real life.'

'Every once in a while, lick your lips. Don't do it all exaggerated.' She flicked her tongue like a lizard having an epileptic fit. 'Do it like you're saying *Ummmm*. Like you're imagining his cock in your mouth, and how that really turns you on. Believe me, that'll turn *him* on.' A pair of gorgeous twins in the front row exchanged amused glances. They had matching skinny model figures, olive skin, and identical dark shoulder-length hair. I couldn't help but wonder if they were planning on doing a lesbian act for some rich man.

'Very important,' Coco was saying as she touched herself all over, 'don't be afraid to touch yourself. Use your hands to draw attention to your tits, your hips, your pussy . . . As you do a few moves . . . take something off. Do a few more moves, and take something else off . . .'

Even if I did manage to get my body to look as good as hers, I knew I could never be as good a sex object. Because I didn't have her grace as a dancer. She just had it. And I didn't. Ever. I couldn't move like she moved, all smooth and feline and feminine. I didn't even need to try it to know that those moves – they were not in me. And yes. I was jealous of that. I wished I had it. But I didn't.

As a matter of fact, I felt like an oaf whenever I felt anyone looking, *really looking* at my body. Naked? Forget it. Suddenly there were a million things wrong with me, and I just wanted to disappear. Ridiculous, considering I was the daughter of a woman who loved to be naked. Even more ridiculous considering I had a feminist point of view on the whole thing. I'd read my Naomi Wolf. I knew all about how society makes women feel like they should be skinny, perfect, airbrushed ideals, and I knew I should've known better than to inflict those impossible standards on myself. But no matter how many small-press books written by angry feminists I read, I still felt like there was something intrinsically wrong with me. And it really pissed me off.

When I was in high school, I thought my modesty problems would go once I moved away to college. I figured I was overwhelmed by my mother. Too worried that I couldn't measure up. Everything would work out once I put some distance between us.

I applied to schools as far away from New York as possible. Got into UC Santa Cruz, the University of Michigan, even Reed, where I really wanted to go. Oregon just sounded so wonderfully idyllic. But none of those schools offered me any money. Coco was barely making ends meet. I didn't want to ask my dad for help. So when SUNY at Binghamton, my total backup school, offered me a full scholarship, I took it. Not as far away as I wanted, but far away enough, I hoped.

'I like to use the fan,' my mom said, taking out a big red feathery fan. 'It feels good. Fan yourself. Fan him. Hide your pussy with it. Bend over and put it up behind your ass. Throw it and catch it. Simple stuff you all can do, right?'

I could see the women thinking *Yes. I can do that. I'm gonna buy a fan!* We got the fans wholesale for fifty cents each and charged seven dollars.

In college, I did have that one really good relationship with the guy who didn't mind my hairy legs. We dated for a couple years, and it was with him that I had my first non-self-induced orgasm. I wasn't comfortable getting naked around him, but we had a routine where he'd undress me when we were already in bed, so I managed to skirt the issue. I loved how he would take off each article of clothing as we got more and more aroused.

But we gradually grew away from each other and moved on. Maybe the routine was getting a little stale. A year after moving back to the city, I met Ian. He was dating a friend from high school at the time. He broke up with her and started going out with me. Now she and I weren't speaking. Sometimes I wished I'd stayed friends with her and dumped him.

Coco got the women to stand up and follow her lead. I observed one chunky woman in a purple T-shirt and gray sweatpants swiveling her hips. From my rearview angle, I could see the flab on her back bulging up out of her bra. Her thighs were flabby, varicose veins sprayed down the back of her knees, and she had cankles. Her hair looked like it was cut by a blender. Why did she think she wanted to do a striptease? There was no way she'd be able to pull it off. I cringed imagining her husband sitting there watching with a fake smile on his face wondering when he could get out of the room to watch Howard Stern.

'Move those hips, ladies! You look like you have rigor mortis!'

On the other hand, I took my hat off to her. That woman wanted to affirm to herself that she was sexy no matter how much she departed from the ideal, no matter how many bikinied twenty-year-olds her husband saw in a typical television-watching day. By god, more power to her. I could learn something from her. Right?

Except . . . she looked ridiculous!

Except . . . she was having fun! They all were!

Maybe I was really just the slowest learner. Taking her class over and over again. Never passing.

Coco would certainly tell me to loosen up. Sometimes she called me a tightass. I hated it when she said that. Who wants your mother calling you a tightass?

Was I a tightass?

I looked at my watch. I wanted to get home. Home to my cozy twin bed and a good night's sleep.

'Another thing I love are the beads,' Coco went on, taking out a long string of pink plastic pearls, twenty-five cents wholesale, five dollars for our customers. 'Just like you can get at the Halloween Store if you want to be a flapper. They come in all sorts of fun colors. And the boa. Very important to have the accessories.' Two dollars wholesale, fourteen dollars for them. She wrapped it around her arms and shoulder and gave everyone her *Playboy* pinup pose. 'It gives you something to work with,' she said, taking it and pulling it through her legs, then snapping it at a woman in the front row. Everyone was mesmerized. It's no wonder she loved this.

How many of those women actually did go through with doing a striptease for their guys?

'And start out in something sexy, okay? Don't start in a pair of jeans. Please. And do not, under any circumstances, laugh or giggle while you strip. You've gotta make him forget it's you.'

Forget it's you? Why? Because you're not good enough?

'If you laugh and get all self-conscious,' she concluded, 'you'll ruin it.'

After leading the women through a routine, Coco ended the class with a little performance. The women were really curious. Most likely, many of them had never been in a club. This was their first chance to see what got the men so excited.

I put on the Madonna CD. 'Open Your Heart.' The song that has the video where she's working in a peep show. I loved it before I got sick of it from hearing it so many times. Coco got quiet, and very serious, as she did the moves.

Bump. Grind. Undo shirt. Fling it to the side. Squat. Get down on knees. Gyrate hips. Lean all the way back. Open legs. A few pelvis pumps. Bring crotch up. A few more pelvis pumps. Then she was on her stomach doing a little pinup pose with her knee bent, foot up in the air. Submissive. Then on her knees like a dog. Crawl. Lick lips. Roll her head back and forth. Flounce her hair. No one in the room made a sound. Finally, she sat with her legs apart in a wide V and tucked the spandex cups of her black lace bra down under her breasts. They were gigantic, of course. Even though they were done in her twenties, they still looked like new. Her face was full of confidence. Power. Down to business. It was a look that scared me. *I know you want me,* it said. And the men certainly did want her. *Do you dare?* There was nothing for me in that look. No room for me.

A woman in the back row whispered to the woman next to her, 'How old is she?'

I wanted to tell her my mom was forty-three. I couldn't help but feel proud of that. With her makeup on, she could easily pass for early thirties.

She finished off with a backward somersault into the splits. Just a final little move to make everyone in the room feel inadequate.

Or was it just me?

I turned off the music. She put her cups back up. 'And that, ladies, is the deal. Unfortunately, we don't have time to do it justice. If you want more detailed instruction, come back for my advanced class. It meets here same time next week. I have fliers . . .'

Everyone applauded.

She put her top back on and gave them her closing spiel. 'You have to give 'em what they want or they're gonna find it somewhere else. With someone like me. Because we're out there ready for 'em. And if they have money, they're gonna spend it. And who'd you rather have them spending money on? Us? Or you? You, that's right! So make it fun!'

Like she was going to solve their relationship problems. Like she'd ever been seriously involved with anyone. Even my father, Ben, had been fleeting. She was a senior in high school. Her one and only marriage. It didn't last past my first birthday. They never even lived together. Other than a monthly check, the only thing I got out of that was his last name, Levine. Coco was not into monogamy or commitment. To her, marriage was a financial arrangement, nothing more, and since she was perfectly able to support herself, why bother?

Class was ending. The women gathered around her, competing for her attention, asking questions as if she knew the secrets of the universe. Soon enough they would migrate over to check out the stuff on the table. One woman around my age was approaching. She had a pixie haircut, flat chest, good legs.

'That was fun,' she said. I wondered if she had a boyfriend and if she would do a striptease for him that night. Her eyes swept over the vibrators, but I could tell. Even if she was curious, she was too embarrassed to buy one right at that moment. 'That Coco. She is so cool.'

I nodded and tried to look pleasant.

She took a pink boa and wrapped it around her neck. 'How much?'

'Fourteen dollars.'

She handed me her money. I took it with a smile.

chapter three

With six years' experience working in restaurants, I knew more than most of the others in the new batch of students at the New York School of Culinary Arts. Still. That first day, standing around the butcher-block tables as Jean Paul passed out the silly white paper chef hats, I felt like an imposter.

When I began college, I thought I was going to become a lawyer. My father is an estate lawyer and my stepmother used to practice environmental law. I was going to do something intelligent and respectable too. I was determined not to make my mother's mistakes. I was going to save all the poor women working in the sex industry from being exploited and abused.

I did great in my ethics class and was a whiz at my volunteer job at the Broome County Battered Women's Hotline. But I could barely stay awake during 'Introduction to the Legal Process.' Constitutional law? Dry as flour. I switched to anthropology. Maybe not useful in any practical sense, but at least it wasn't a struggle to keep my eyes open.

At the time, I was a waitress at a place near campus called JD's Luncheonette. I liked working where people went to relax and have a good time – just like my mom. Except being nice to abusive people and relying on tips felt like underpaid prostitution. What I really wanted to do was work with the food.

So I asked the owners if they'd ever let me cook. But it was family-owned, three sons divvied up the shifts, they just didn't need me. A few months later a job opened up at a crepe restaurant in town. The owners, a couple from Ukraine, weren't comfortable with the fact that I lacked experience and was female. But I'd been there a few times as a customer, and I told them how much I *really loved* crepes, which was true, and *really wanted* to learn how to make them. They took a chance.

I loved that job. There was something so satisfying about pouring the batter out on the grill, spreading it out into a beautiful large circle, smelling that wonderful combination of cooking eggs and flour, flipping it at just the right moment of light golden brown, then filling it up with bits of ham, grated cheese, chunks of spinach or sautéed mushrooms. But the very best part was folding it up like a little gift, putting that dollop of sour cream on top with a sprig of parsley. And the dessert crepes were so beautiful! I was really generous with the strawberries and the whipped cream. The grill was out front, so I could actually see peoples' faces light up when the waitress served their food. Then to see the plate come back scraped clean . . . what could be more satisfying? I was only earning ten dollars an hour, but I was happy.

The place folded after I was there about two years. That happens. Restaurants come and go all the time. The profit margin is very thin, especially if you don't sell liquor, and people get tired of the same old menu and décor. It's almost expected that, like a beautiful woman, a restaurant's power to attract customers is only a fleeting thing. The closing coincided pretty much with my graduation, so when the owners told me they knew someone in the city who was looking for a prep cook, I took the bus in for an interview. Before I knew it, I had a job at Chantal.

Back to Manhattan I moved. After a major search using roommates.com, I found a psychology major at City College who let me move into her small two-bedroom. My portion of the rent was a thousand dollars a month – not bad for the neighborhood, but a hefty chunk of my paycheck.

The Upper West Side has never been known for its 'cuisine,' and Chantal was not anything spectacular. I assisted Carlos, the garde manger chef, basically prepping the cold appetizers on the menu. I got very fast at chopping parsley, peeling carrots, and tearing lettuce. I'd heard that the guy who did the job before me was an illegal alien from Mexico who spoke no English and went on to get a better job – delivering dry cleaning – but I was determined to learn everything I could and move up in the hierarchy there.

I found I really didn't like working with cold things. Turnips, carrots . . . very standoffish, those foods. I was attracted to warm, cuddly ingredients like butter, cream, and flour. I started to hang out a lot with the pastry chef, trying to pick up what I could. He was a middle-aged ex–real estate agent who'd given up his Volvo to study at Le Cordon Bleu, and it was from him that I got the idea of going to a cooking school.

So here I was, at the New York School of Culinary Arts, standing with my new classmates around six butcher-block tables shoved together in the middle of a huge, fully equipped kitchen. My uniform – black-and-white houndstooth pants and white cotton double-breasted jacket – was brand-new. I'd worn jeans and a baseball cap at Chantal, so it felt like I was dressing up for Halloween. Coco would've hated it except as a costume to be flung in someone's face. But I liked it. The black-and-whiteness. The way it made us all look the same. Except the hat. The hat was just silly. Not that I had any right to complain. I knew going into it about the hat.

'Now we will go around the room,' Chef Jean Paul said in his thick French accent, 'and introduce ourselves.' He was tall, about six-three, in his fifties, with pale skin, a round face, and thinning, sandy brown hair.

There were twenty of us total. A plethora of pimply-faced boys who looked like they were just out of high school, or the army, or prison. A few middle-aged second careerers. Four women other than me – one very pretty blonde, one short brunette named Priscilla who I thought I could be friends with, and one who reminded me of the older ladies who used to work in my school cafeteria. Then there was the one cute guy. He had this clean-cut look with a strong jaw, short brown hair, surprising blue eyes, a rosy glow and, most important, he was taller than me and had a very nice build. When he introduced himself, he said he was from Iowa. Or was it Ohio? Some small town with a name like Grand Junction. He looked so solid, so reliable, so steadfast! His name was Tom Carpenter.

Then Tara introduced herself. The blonde. I really wanted to make friends with the other women in the class. We gals had to stick together! But Jean Paul fussed over her like she was an honored guest. 'Miss Tara Glass is the daughter of Jonathan Glass, who owns L'Etoile.' L'Etoile was one of the most successful restaurants going in Manhattan, and Jean Paul was obviously delighted to have her in our midst.

'My father has owned restaurants since before I was born,' she announced. 'My dream is to own my own restaurant one day.'

'Welcome,' he said with a slight bow, 'to our class.'

'I'm honored to be here.'

How long had it taken her to bobby pin her hair so beguilingly under her hat?

When it was my turn, I only fleetingly referred to college, as if it had been a waste of time. In this world, brains were only of interest sautéed with a little butter. Desired attributes were brawn and stamina as demonstrated by the ability to function under pressure while drunk, stoned, cut, and burned, along with the facility to speak fluent Spanish with the immigrant dishwashers and prep cooks in virtually every establishment in the city. Classes in human evolution? Definitely not helpful. I mentioned the crepe restaurant in passing, and then made my job at Chantal sound more impressive than it really was.

After we'd gone around the room, Jean Paul went over the drill. 'You will rotate back and forth between the main kitchen here with me, and the demonstration kitchen with Mr. Robert Kingsley, where you will have lectures on the history of cooking, restaurant management, and the difference between a Burgundy and a Bordeaux.'

My pulse revved at the mention of Robert Kingsley. He was a guest instructor this semester, somewhat of a celebrity in the foodie world, and one of the big reasons I'd picked the school.

'Of the twenty students who begin,' Jean Paul continued, 'only ten will be chosen to move upstairs for the Master Class to have the privilege of cooking in the school restaurant.'

Three of those ten students would specialize in pastry. It would be up to Jean Paul to choose who made the cut. Nancy Riviere, one of the most highly regarded women pastry chefs in the world, was going to be visiting from Paris to teach. It would be so incredible to study with her.

Meanwhile, there was Jean Paul to contend with. I was hyperaware that I really needed him to decide I had that extra glimmer of talent to move me into the Master Class. He began our first lecture, or should I say rant, about *mise en place*, which is the French term for having all your ingredients ready before you cook. 'You must prepare your station! You must be ready for the shit that is going to hit the fan! You must have your pots, pans, ladles, side towels, salt, pepper, parsley, oil, butter, wine, tomato *concassé*, chopped shallots . . . everything you need positioned around you, so that you know exactly where it all is the moment you need it. Why? Because! Once you start the service, and everyone sits down at the same time, and orders off a menu of ten or twenty or thirty different things that all must be ready together, there will be no time! So! We will now chop the mirepoix for our first stock!'

After we'd all settled at our respective cutting boards, I peeked at Tom Carpenter. He was chopping onions. His sweet, serious dash of a little mouth was set with determined concentration. His eyes were really watering, so you'd almost think he was truly upset. He paused to wipe his tears with the back of his hand. Chopped some more. Paused to wipe them again. Then looked around, self-conscious, and caught me spying. He shook his head at how ridiculous it was that his eyes were watering so much. I realized he was embarrassed. It wasn't 'manly' to cry, even if it was just from onions. So I nodded my head and frowned with sympathy, trying to let him know that it was okay. He nodded and smiled. And I smiled. And I went back to peeling my carrots. And he went back to chopping his onions.

'What is more important,' Chef Jean Paul asked, 'taste or presentation?'

It was the end of the day. We were all once again standing around the butcher-block tables. Everyone gaped at him, stumped and stupefied. I tried to blend in to the bank of reach-in refrigerators behind me. But his finger was pointed at . . . *moi*.

'You?'

I thought of one of my mother's favorite sayings: *You can make a living displaying your naked bod, but you won't earn the big bucks unless you actually make 'em come.*

'Taste?'

Jean Paul sneered at me like I was curdled cream. 'And why is that?'

'Because the whole point is to make food that people will enjoy eating.'

Tara's hand shot into the air. He called on her.

'Presentation,' she said.

'And why, Miss Glass, iss presentation so important?'

'Because,' she said, 'it is with your eyes that you first taste.'

Did she just sneak a smile at Tom Carpenter?

'Yes! You see eet first! *Zen* you decide whezer to eat it. Zee first impression – that iss the most important one.' He turned to me again. 'So tell us. Why will they eat your food if eet looks ugly?'

I wanted to answer. I wanted to say it didn't matter how anything looked if it tasted lousy. But I already knew that Jean Paul was always right about everything because he learned from the bottom up interning at the Hotel de Monte Carlo when he was fourteen while we were wasting our time in school. On my way out of the kitchen, Jean Paul muttered to me that I might want to 'stick to toasting *le Pop-Tarts*.'

I stood in the lobby in a daze. What just happened?

'What he just did?' a male voice came from behind. 'That was so not fair.'

I turned around. It wasn't Tom Carpenter. It was a guy who looked a bit like the Pillsbury Doughboy. Blond, apple-dumpling cheeks, cuddly body, adorably gay.

'Was that not a rhetorical question?' I asked.

'They're both too important! You can't choose one.'

'No matter what I said, it was going to be wrong.'

'He just wanted to make her look good.'

'Or me look bad.'

'He doesn't even know you. Does he?'

'No. But he can tell.'

'What?'

'I'm an imposter. And I'm destined to fail!'

'Oh, my god.' He took both my hands. 'That's exactly how I feel. Chef Jean Paul is so scary!'

'You feel that way too?'

'I'm terrified!'

Tom Carpenter was approaching. He looked at both of us with a teeny smile, then looked down at the floor as he passed by. Such a drag he had to see Jean Paul pick on me. Doughboy and I followed his ass with our eyes until the door to the men's locker room shut behind him.

'I'd stay and commiserate,' Doughboy said, 'but don't want to miss the show.'

'It's not fair the locker rooms are segregated.'

'What's your name?'

'Ginger.'

'Ginger? Spice Girl! I love it.'

'And you are?'

'Ralph. As in Lauren, not Kramden. Now I really must go or I'll miss all the fun.'

chapter four

i have always been intimidated by my father. A handsome man. Tall. Broad shoulders. He was currently wearing his dark hair very short, almost a buzz cut, very fashionable. He liked expensive clothes. Expensive restaurants. I was in awe.

It sucked. Good-looking men can get away with a lot, especially if they have money. He didn't deserve my awe. The man lacked warmth. But I couldn't help myself. When I was around him, I was on my best behavior. Polite. Hoping, constantly, for some little token of his love. All it took to melt me was the tiniest bit of attention. Like the question: 'How are you?' It didn't matter if he didn't bother to listen to my answer. It didn't matter if there wasn't even one follow-up question. He had deigned to look at me, just me, if only for a moment, and ask. I knew that I wasn't really supposed to tell him how I was. I knew that it was important for him to believe I was doing great, and important for me to let him think I was doing great, and the true communication during that question was that he was confirming that I was not going to be making any demands on him. But still. He'd asked.

My father was not a talkative man, but he liked to think of himself as an expert on everything. Wine, food, movies, theater, literature. His name was Ben, but long ago, Coco had given him the nickname 'the Sheriff.'

I sat across from him at a good table by the wall at a new restaurant a few blocks from his townhouse on the Upper East Side. I felt, as usual, honored to be in his presence. The food was a combination of French, Italian, and Mediterranean. We commented on the frescoes painted on the walls and the huge mosaic pizza oven. It was extremely noisy and lively and everyone around us seemed to be having a great time.

Emma, my half sister, was not invited along because it was understood that this was my 'special time' with him, whereas she got to live with the guy. Part of me would've liked her there with us, if only to help sustain the conversation. Leah, his second wife, had always been the expert at keeping the conversation going. But she wasn't there to help either.

My state of awe was a real impediment. It made it really hard to get mad at him. You need to be able to get mad at a person every now and then if you're going to be able to be close. And I think many objective people would agree that I deserved to be mad. Not that I wasn't mad. I just couldn't show him.

I was probably that way because I'd never actually lived with him. I hardly even saw him when I was little even though he'd always lived in Manhattan, just a bus ride away. But he left my mom when I was a year old, and he never even tried to get custody, and they didn't speak for a long time. It wasn't until I was in high school, after my grandmother died, that Leah made him make the effort to get to know me. She was the one who engineered dinners out every few months to help us build more of a relationship. I always felt happy to see Leah, at those meals, and honored that he showed up.

As a matter of fact, Leah was the one who convinced me to swallow my pride, go to my father, and ask him to help me pay for cooking school. He'd always been reliable about child support, but this felt different. It was like I was saying, okay, I'm not going to hold a grudge against you all these years because you were a shitty father. I'm going to get over that, accept your help, and hope it brings us closer.

But still. He never felt comfortable with me. I always knew, on some level, that as far as he was concerned, I simply wasn't supposed to exist.

'How are you?' he asked, after the waiter filled our glasses from a bottle of Pouilly–Fuissé.

'Good. How are you?

He was wearing his usual Egyptian cotton three hundred thread count white shirt and blue silk tie. I was dressed up (though he may not have been able to perceive that) because I was wearing some black stretch bellbottoms and a short-sleeved button-down flower power print shirt and spanking new hot pink Converse sneakers. I waited for him to pour his heart out to me about how he always wished he could've raised me himself, and even if Coco was a 'trip,' she was a really fun person, wasn't she, and why don't you move in with me now and we can make up for lost time?

'I'm good. How's cooking school?'

'Great. How's the law?'

'Keeping me busy . . .'

'Emma?'

'Doing really well.'

'That's good.'

'You know.' He smiled. 'Under the circumstances.'

'Right.'

Emma was born when I was in middle school. There I was, plagued with greasy hair, acne, and a growth spurt so intense it should've qualified as an extreme sport. Emma? She was so little, so precious, so perfect, so adorable you just wanted to kill her. Okay. I was the only one with the homicidal thoughts. It just didn't seem fair. She got to grow up in their beautiful East Side apartment. She went to posh private schools, fancy summer camps, deluxe hotels in Europe. It seemed like she had every benefit of living in the world that I did not, crowned by the fact that she got to grow up in the perfect nuclear family.

When I wasn't hating them, I used to wish that I could live with them. And it made me feel so guilty to betray my mom like that, even if it was just in my head.

But Leah was a wonderful person. She worked part time as a lawyer trying to save rain forests. And she didn't care if her apartment was messy. And even though she was way too obsessed (in my opinion) with things like designer clothes and interior design, I excused her for it. Because she was a really great listener. She always encouraged me talk about my problems without giving me condescending advice. And she never tried to put Coco down either, even though it must've been tempting. She just let me talk about her. So I could bounce back and forth between being angry and defensive and then realize all my contradictory feelings made some sort of sense. Because, god knows, my mother was confusing. For obvious reasons, she wasn't like other mothers, but I didn't completely realize that for a long time. I just assumed all daughters had some sort of problem with their mothers and mine was just a variation. It wasn't until I went to college that I started to think this was not variation, this was Bizarro World. All the more bizarre because it felt normal to me. But Leah never tried to turn me against Coco. She just tried to help me get some kind of grip.

And then, two years ago, Leah found a lump.

There was a year of chemo and radiation and that whole nightmare and of course when she got through that we all hoped she could put it behind her. But it came back, and spread to her liver and lungs. She had another round of chemo, but it continued to spread. She got weak. And skinny. It began to affect her breathing.

She died at home. She'd just turned forty-five.

Right after it happened . . . right after my father called to let us know she had passed away . . . I suddenly felt so grateful to have my fun, crazy but loving, never-been-sick-a-day-in-her-life mom!

On the day of the funeral, after the services, my dad's living room was crowded with people wiping tears off their cheeks and shoving hors d'oeuvres in their faces. I sat there on the sofa feeling like an outsider. Coco told a joke about someone who calls the hospital and asks how Mrs. Jones is doing in room 420. And the nurse says her blood work came back and everything looks fine and she's going to be released the next day. And the caller says good, because I'm Mrs. Jones calling from room 420 and the doctors don't tell me anything! And I laughed. I laughed good and loud at her stupid joke. Because I wanted poor ten-year-old Emma to know that for once I didn't have to feel jealous, because even if Coco was a freak and a slut, she was alive.

I didn't say that out loud. But the fact that I thought it and laughed . . . It made me feel hideous, even then. I still cringe at the memory.

I probably don't have to mention that Emma and I had never been close. Sometimes I got this really strong wish that we could be. I'd get it in my head that we really should hang out together and get to know each other and I should really get over all this stuff between us, and it was my responsibility to make this happen because I was the older and therefore more mature one.

But then, especially when I was actually around her, I got overcome with this stupid insecure feeling that she thought she was better than me. I was the poor relation from her father's weird past. An aberration that should never have happened. Ridiculous I gave her so much power over me considering she was younger, but I did. Just couldn't break the barrier.

That night at the restaurant, with my dad, I wondered if I'd break the barrier with him. It was about three months after Leah's death. I couldn't help but wonder if our relationship might change because of it. And we'd get closer. Maybe he'd begin to confide in me in some way. Or at the very least, we could have some intimate conversation about how sad it was. This had not yet happened. But maybe, I thought, maybe it would happen that night.

'I hear the chef here studied with Wolfgang Puck,' my father said.

'Really. His frozen pizzas are surprisingly good.'

'Wolfgang Puck is a famous chef in LA,' my father said. 'You know, trendy restaurants for the stars?'

'Right.' Did he really think I didn't know that? 'He also has a line of frozen pizzas.'

'Oh.' My father took a sip of wine.

Or was it that he couldn't appreciate the irony that a famous chef known for using fresh foods sold frozen pizzas?

'So have you had any interesting cases recently?' I asked.

'Two sons contesting a will. The father died in a plane crash. He left all his money to the dog.'

'That's cruel.'

My father shrugged. 'People have their bones to pick.' He took another sip of wine. There was no pouring out of hearts, only that crisp, white Chardonnay. I ordered a chestnut fettuccine with wild boar ragu that turned out to be incredible. He got calamari. And then we shared a slice of pear almond tart with caramel sauce. God, that was good. Sure I was stuffed, but it was research. Coco was not mentioned (as usual) and neither was Leah (as usual). He picked up the check (as usual) and why was I, a grown woman, craving an invitation to live with my father? It was bad enough I was still living with my mother.

But he did surprise me at the end of the meal. We were standing out on the sidewalk in front of the restaurant about to part ways. I saw him hesitate, and then he said, 'Can I ask a favor?'

My father needed something from me? 'Sure.'

'Maybe this is unfair to ask. But . . .'

Anything, I was thinking. Anything at all . . .

'Since Leah died . . .'

He was actually bringing her up?

'I've had a hard time . . .'

He was admitting to having a hard time? Out here on the street with a hundred people walking by while we were in the middle of saying good-bye?

'I haven't been able to take care of her things.'

Things. Leah's things. 'Her things.'

'Her things. In the closets. They're still in her closets.'

I actually thought I saw him tear up. Or maybe a piece of dust had blown into his eyes.

'Yes.' I nodded.

'I was wondering if I could ask you to help me to sort through it all. Figure out what we should keep, what we should give away, what things Emma might want. I know this is unfair of me to ask . . .'

'I'd be happy to.'

'Are you sure?'

'Of course.'

'I would do it myself. But . . .'

I waited for him to finish. I really wanted him to say he couldn't do it because it was too hard because he missed her like hell and could barely function without her, and you know what? Life sucked!

'I've been really busy,' he said.

'It's totally understandable.' I looked very deliberately and compassionately into his eyes and wanted to say this was the most human he'd ever shown himself to be, but kept that to myself since it would've sounded critical at the very moment he was finally being at least a little bit vulnerable.

'And Emma is still in shock, so I can't ask her. But I think it's time.'

If Coco died, I don't think I'd ever get rid of her things. They'd stay in the apartment gathering dust, and I'd stay on with them – a weirdo spinster woman hoarding her mother's vibrators as if they were gonna be collector's items someday.

I wondered if Leah owned a vibrator.

'When should I come?'

'Call me. We'll set up a time.' He reached into his pocket. 'Let me give you a key so you'll be able to come and go at your convenience.'

'Okay.' I'd never had a key to his place.

'I really appreciate this. I know it's not an easy job.'

He pressed a shiny Medeco in my hand. And kissed me. A drier kiss could not be planted but it was, at least, a kiss.

'It was good seeing you,' I said.

'You too. We'll do it again soon. So call . . .'

'I will.' We went off in our different directions. I was still gripping the key in my hand as I walked down Fifth Avenue. How would I tell Coco? I knew she would disapprove. But I didn't have to tell her. I put the key in my backpack in a special little secret zippered pocket that even the stealthiest mugger would not be able to find.

'So he's giving you the privilege of cleaning out his wife's shit?'

I really tried to keep it to myself. And I was doing really well. For about an hour. She'd rented season four of *Sex and the City*, and we were having such fun watching it, and I was feeling so warm towards her, because we really could have a good time together, just doing nothing but eating Chinese takeout and crabbing about who Sarah Jessica should've ended up with, and I thought maybe she'd see that this was a good thing, a positive thing, and say something warm and encouraging and hopeful about the possibility of me having some kind of closer relationship with my father. So when the credits came on, I blurted it out. And immediately regretted it.

'I knew I shouldn't have told you.'

'What business does he have asking you to do that?'

'I knew you'd try to turn this into something bad. For once he needs me!'

'It's not like he can't afford to hire someone!'

'Don't you think it's kind of a personal thing to have someone go through your things like that?'

'So why should he ask you?'

'I'm his daughter!'

'But you aren't *her* daughter.'

'I think it's nice that he asked me.'

'Ginger, come on. Don't let him take advantage of you, honey. Call him back and tell him you changed your mind.'

'No!' I thought of the key safely tucked away in my backpack. 'I want to do it.'

'Fine.' She dumped the greasy remains of our chicken with broccoli into the bag it came in. 'But don't come crying to me when he disappoints you.'

'How can he disappoint me? I'm doing him the favor.'

'Right.'

'I am!'

She paused before going into the kitchen. 'You think it'll make him appreciate you more? Good luck.'

Just because he'd never appreciated her.

'I'm going to bed,' I said, and went into my room and shut the door.

Fights with my mother about my father had a way of putting me in an extra special bad mood. I knew she'd never really forgiven him for getting out of the marriage and going off to college and leaving her with me. They were high school seniors at Wagner, a gigantic public school on the Upper East Side, when she got pregnant. It was 1978 and she should've known better than to become a teen bride, if you ask me. He was ambitious, and had already been accepted into Cornell, and I know she saw him as a pretty good catch. But she'd never described it as being in love. My grandma liked to tell me she was crazy about him, but I was never sure if she just said that to make me feel better. I wasn't sure if it *made* me feel better. He seemed to see her as an impediment. When he went off to school, he didn't take us. We stayed on with her mom. In this apartment. Her dad, my grandpa, had died in Vietnam, so it was just us girls.

My mom was always wild. She started dancing 'professionally' soon after my father left for college. My grandma, Mimi, taught social studies in an elementary school, and she took care of me when my mom was working. Coco's first job was at the Pussycat Lounge downtown. Lots of Wall Street guys went there to chill after work. It was a pretty seedy place, or so I'm told, and she danced in a bikini for all the horny drunk men who either felt like big shit because they'd just made a killing, or needed to be reminded they had big dicks because they'd just lost their life savings. But she didn't mind. She told me she liked it. The stage was set back behind the bar, so actual contact with the customers was pretty minimal. And she loved to dance. And she loved to be admired by men. So in a way, it was Coco's ideal job. Well. As much as it could be 'ideal' because obviously it did have its downside. But I'd guess she preferred that scene to being stuck at home with me.

When I was two, Coco left the Pussycat Lounge and became a circuit dancer, and she was really raking it in then. She traveled around from city to city as a featured performer. Her idol was Lili St. Cyr, who was famous for routines like draping herself completely with gardenias and slowly plucking them off until none were left. Coco developed her own specialized dances – one involved a bathtub and lots of bubbles.

When my father found out what she was doing, he used that as an excuse to ask for a divorce. Or so I've been told. I don't think that was the actual reason. I think it was just the excuse for what he already wanted. It's not like I ever heard that he tried to get custody of me because she was an unfit mother or anything like that. He just wanted to get away. So she let him get away. Not that he'd ever been there.

In any case, she was not about to quit dancing. The money was too good. And the attention. As far as she was concerned, my father could go to hell. That's how it had been ever since.

chapter five

*i*t's not easy rolling croissants with Chef Jean Paul breathing down your neck like a drill sergeant. *'Vite! Vite!* No deellydallying!' I pretended I was GI Jane at boot camp. Head down, face blank – I will roll up my dough triangles better and faster than anyone goddamn it or die trying. 'The customers!' he yelled, 'they are fast asleep now, but in a few hours, they will drag themselves out of bed thinking only of your croissant! Your croissant with a nice cup of hot coffee! That is all that will keep them going until they get to the pastry shop and stand in line and wait to pay for your pastry. Are you going to disappoint them? No! Your pastry must be ready! And it must be delicious! And it must be the same! Every day, exactly the same!' I was rolling as fast as I could. But a Band-Aid on my index finger (a recent onion-slicing incident) was hampering me. As he paused to look at my work, his proximity to the back of my head caused me the worst kind of anxiety. My hands started to shake. Damn. I hated that!

'What is this?' Jean Paul picked up the croissant I had just rolled and held it out for all to see. It hung out of his hand like a limp dick. 'It is an insult to the baking profession!' He threw it into the garbage.

'Miss Levine!' he yelled at me. There was an ugly silence. 'Why do you waste our time here?'

Everyone stopped rolling and looked at me.

'If I were you,' he said, 'I would go to the office and see if you can still get a refund. Because in my opinion, you do not have what it takes!'

I fumed silently. It was the third week of the semester. How could he know what I could or couldn't do? Everyone around the table was looking at me with pity – even the second-career wimps who'd never set foot in a restaurant kitchen – and I knew I would never live it down. Even if I stayed in the program, they would all know Jean Paul thought I was no good.

I should just quit. Ditch this torture chamber. Remove myself from the room, the school, the sight of all these people forever, but then Jean Paul yelled at everyone, 'What are you staring at? Get back to work!' And everyone looked back down at the tabletop and continued rolling dough like nothing had happened. No. Make that with more efficiency, since they didn't want Jean Paul to say the same things to them. 'The dough sits out too long,' he yelled, 'it will get too soft!' He looked at me. I was still standing there trying to figure out what the protocol would be for quitting, how much of a refund I could get, and what I was going to do for the rest of my life, when he yelled, 'Get me the bones I have roasting in the oven. And the vegetables we will need for the mirepoix. When we are done with these, we will make a brown stock!'

I took the opportunity to collect myself in the walk-in while I gathered some onions, leeks, celery, and carrots, put them on a sheet pan, and brought them to Jean Paul. I was missing his lesson on stocks, catching only a few comments as I came and left.

'From your stock, you will create those five mother sauces,' Jean Paul said as he distributed the vegetables around the table to be coarsely chopped. 'Your mother sauces are the key to all the sauces you will ever make. So! The three basic elements to the stock include the *flavor* base, the *aromatics*, and the *liquid*, water. Occasionally,' he went on, 'there is a fourth element . . .'

But I missed that as I went to retrieve the huge, ten-ton roasting pan filled with bones from the oven. I noticed Tom looking at me with sympathy as I slid the pan onto the table in front of Jean Paul.

'The stock is perhaps the most important thing you will make! It is like raising a child. *Oui?* You must be patient so that you will end up with the best flavor possible!' And then, with barely a pause, he said to me with an accusing tone, 'Tomato paste?' I went to the storeroom, got a large tin, then opened it with the temperamental can opener that was mounted on one of the counters. When I got back he received it without comment. I took my place at the table. He was saying the bubbles should be 'simmering at a smile,' not 'belly laughing at a boil.' I imagined everyone at the table was getting a really good chuckle out of my humiliation.

Ian and I were supposed to meet after school for coffee at this place on Fifty-seventh Street. When I got there, it was packed. He wasn't there. No surprise. I took my place in line. There were six people ahead of me. As I heard the counter person bellow, 'Next guest in line!' I descended into one of my 'one day I am going to move out of New York' trains of thought.

A girl behind the counter steamed some milk. I bet people who order cappuccinos when there's a big line have no problem taking their sweet time coming to orgasm. Or maybe they do, and they're taking it out on the rest of us. As the line barely moved, I had plenty of time to consider where in the world I would choose to live. The Midwest sounded good. Someplace where nice people lived. I could open a bakery café on Main Street. It didn't matter which Main Street. Any one would do.

Finally. First in line! This could very well be the high point of my day. I stood tall, ready to order. One of the girls behind the counter was talking to the other about hair extensions. When she finally asked what I wanted, it was as if she was doing me a big favor. I asked for my iced coffee in a pleasant way. She got it for me, and I gave her the three dollars and fifty-five cents, and she yelled, 'Next customer!'

Why can't counter people in New York City say 'Thank you'? It's such a simple thing. Counter people around the world are saying 'Thank you' after every transaction, but not in New York. They slam the register shut. 'Next!' You don't matter. 'Next!' And then you have to decide whether to say 'Thank you,' because that's your way, but it becomes a hostile gesture – I mean they're the ones who are supposed to be thanking you for the business, right? But you tell yourself, hey, I recognize the fact that she's underpaid and overworked so maybe it would be nice of me to go the extra mile and say 'Thank you' to her, just as a show of support to help her get through the day. And then maybe she'll say 'Thank you' back. So you say 'Thank you!' And she says, 'Next!'

I prayed for an empty table. A piece of luck! Someone was just leaving. I nabbed it. She'd even left a couple magazines. One was a *Cosmo*. There was an article on how to give a blow job. Coco always liked to say, if you want to keep your man, just give him a blow job now and then.

My cell phone rang. Ian. 'Ginger?'

'Yes?'

'I don't think I'm going to make it.'

'Don't worry about it.'

Come to think of it, I hadn't given him a blow job in two months. Or was it three?

'I'm really sorry,' he said. 'I just can't get away from the computer right now. I'm in the middle of this song . . .'

After we hung up, I looked out the window at a woman pulling a screaming child down the street. Maybe a blow job would solve all our problems.

Right.

I tossed aside *Cosmo* and opened the *Travel & Leisure*. '50 Spa Resorts That Will Make You Happy.' They were missing the subtitle: 'That You'll Never Get To.' Well, at least I had my table. My table made me happy. I took a sip of coffee and was reasonably content for about five minutes. Then a really happy couple sat down at that table next to me.

Yes, they were a young and happy couple in love, sharing a piece of carrot cake with a little rosette of cream cheese frosting on top, and they were kissing and cuddling and soon enough they were making out and couldn't keep their hands off each other, and let me just say, I hate public displays of affection. They always make me feel weird. Maybe because Ian and I had a problem with private displays of affection.

The make-out girl giggled. I did not look up. I tried, I really tried to concentrate on the amenities at the Enchantment Spa of Sedona, Arizona. I tried not to feel uptight about the fact that they were making slurping sounds with their kisses and I was mildly aroused even though I was mildly disgusted, and I just wanted to mind my own business and read about the benefits of hot stone massages.

The make-out girl purred with delight. It was clear they weren't even going to eat their cake. I put down *Travel & Leisure*. Took a last sip of coffee. Said a silent good-bye. And left them forever. Sorry. But this relationship was not working out.

chapter six

bacon. I followed the smell into the kitchen, where Coco was micro-waving some slices out of a box. She was in boxers and a T-shirt, back from the gym. 'Hi, honey! You want some? I really shouldn't be eating. Jack is in town, and we're going out to dinner, but I started to think about bacon and just couldn't get it out of my head . . .'

Jack.

I've been avoiding the subject of Jack. He was her 'boyfriend.' Sixty-five years old. Too old for my forty-three-year-old mom, as far as I was concerned. A retired button manufacturer originally from Long Island, Jack was silver-haired, tall and lean, but with a belly that hung over his belt. He had very tanned skin with that cooked-red-meat look that people who spend too much time in the sun get. His main home was in Palm Beach, where he lived with his wife, but he kept a place on Central Park South too. Sixteenth floor, views of the park, in a white brick postwar building right down the street from the Plaza Hotel. This was just eleven blocks away from us – but a completely different income bracket. For the past year, he'd been in the process of divorcing his wife. Coco didn't care. She had no interest in marrying him, not even for his money. She liked her independence too much. In the meanwhile, they seemed to have a good time together. So I tried not to disapprove of the relationship. At least, out loud in front of him.

'Those Atkins people,' she said, putting the box back in the fridge, 'they better know what they're talking about.'

'You don't need to lose weight.'

'I don't need to lose weight because I'm dieting. If I wasn't dieting, I'd be overweight, and then I'd need to lose weight.'

'Whatever.'

The microwave beeped. 'You sure you don't want some? You know you can't resist that smell . . .'

'No, thanks.' My mother will microwave for me, but she doesn't cook. When Coco makes a hamburger, she knows it's done when the smoke detector goes off.

I settled in at our tiny kitchen table and looked at the blue and white HOT BAGEL sign mounted in the space right between our two front windows. It messed up our view of the street, but at least we were rewarded with the heavenly smell of baking bagels wafting up, though Coco claimed she'd been smelling it so long she couldn't smell it anymore.

'So, Ian flaked out on me again.'

'Surprise, surprise.'

I pried the heel of a sneaker off using my big toe. 'We were supposed to meet for coffee, but he calls and cancels. . . .'

She pulled out a giant thing of Diet Coke from the fridge. 'Don't you think it's about time you expand your horizons?'

I got a glass of milk from the fridge and two Fig Newtons. 'I know you're sick of hearing me complain about him . . .'

'That's got nothing to do with it.' She pulled up a chair, sat right in front of me, and looked into my face. 'I want you to be happy!' It always got to me when she gave me full-force attention like that. 'You've been with him what, two years? Why do you have to be so serious? You're young. You should be out there meeting other guys. Getting experience. Having fun. Getting laid. Why do you have to be so monogamous?'

She said it like I had a disease. Well. She was right about one thing. That bacon did smell good. I tore off a piece. That hickory smoke flavor – it really brought out the carnivore in me. Fat. Gristle. Blood. Lust. Rage. Murder. 'I'm sure you're right. Ian cares more about you than he does about me.'

'If you really think that's true, then dump him. Ian's not the only sperm in the jism.'

'But then I'll have absolutely no social life. Seems like all my old friends either moved away or we're not talking, and I can't meet anyone new.'

'Any cute guys at school?'

I thought of Tom Carpenter. 'Maybe.'

The warm spray of the shower felt good. School was not only nerve-racking, it was physically demanding, and I was beat. Instead of expending the effort to towel myself off, I got right into bed. I liked to dry off between the soft sheets. And I took a little nap. They say naps are one of the best ways to relieve stress and stay healthy. So even though part of me felt guilty about getting into bed so early in the evening, another part of me felt like if I didn't, I would crack up.

After dozing a bit, I considered getting my vibrator out. Yes, I wasn't completely monogamous, even if my other boyfriend needed batteries to get going – at least he was always there for me and didn't care what I looked like. It was hidden in the bottom drawer of my bureau. I hadn't used it since moving in. Coco was in the bathroom on the other side of my wall. The shower went on. Maybe a little Hello time with Kitty would make me feel better . . .

The doorbell rang.

'Ginger?' she yelled through the wall.

'Yes!'

'Jack is here! Can you let him in?'

I sighed. Good-bye Kitty.

I slipped on my favorite pair of drawstring jersey pants with little poodles on them, a tank top, and a sweatshirt.

'Hey!' he said as he stepped in the door, 'long time no see!' Jack's thick Long Island voice was so loud it was as if he was shouting to me from across the street.

'Mom's in the shower. She'll be right out.'

I turned, trying to make a quick escape back to my room, but wasn't nimble enough.

'So how are you?' He went directly to the refrigerator for a can of beer. 'Come talk to me!' He took the beer into the living room, plopped down on the couch, and seemed to expect me to join him. Jack wore blue jeans, and his long legs sprawled out in front of him. I hate older men in blue jeans. Not that his body was that bad, not that I wanted to think about what his body was like.

'I'm good.' There was an easy chair angled next to the couch to make a cozy conversational corner, and lots of room next to him.

'Come!' he said. 'Sit!'

I stood back near the doorway and stared across the room at three prints on the wall that Coco had gotten at the Museum of Sex downtown.

'That's okay,' I said. The pictures were very cheesecake-y, from the 1940s, and each one featured a woman with a pair of underwear that had just fallen down to her ankles. Each woman's moment of exposure took place in a different setting. One had just gotten on a bus. One was on the street holding groceries. And one was bowling. Each one looked back at the viewer with surprise.

'So!' he said. 'The prodigal daughter! Back home with Mom!'

'Back home with Mom.'

'So talk to me! Sit down! How ya doin'?'

'Good.' I remained standing near the doorway.

'So what are ya doin' with yourself?'

'I'm going to a cooking school.' I knew he knew, but if he was gonna ask, I'd pretend like he was as dumb as he looked.

'What for?'

'To learn more skills. So I can get a better job.'

'What, you wanna be, who was the famous chef, what's his name . . . with an E? The one who's got that show on TV?'

'Emeril?'

'Yeah. That's the guy. You want to be like Emeril?'

'No.'

'That guy makes a lot of money.'

'I know.'

'You should be so lucky.'

I inched my way back so I was actually under the arch of the doorway.

Jack had made a lot of money in his button business, and he was proud of the fact. He couldn't imagine having any other goal in life. He took a swig of beer. 'He's not just a cook. He's a personality. An entrepreneur! He does everything, that guy! You see him everywhere.'

'Uh-huh.' If you spend your entire day watching television.

'So what makes you think you could do what he does?'

'I don't want to do what he does.'

'I thought you said you're taking a class on how to be a chef!'

'Well,' I said, making it into the hall, 'if you'll excuse me . . .'

'You ask me,' he said before I managed to turn, 'you should get a job. You shouldn't be living with your mother at your age! My kids? They've all got families! Good jobs!'

This little attack was so typical of him. I wanted so badly to ask him how his wife was doing. 'Good to see you, Jack.'

'My son? He just bought a house in Boca.'

'Great.'

He picked up the remote. 'So let's see what's on the idiot box.'

I escaped.

Back in the safety of my room, I lay back down on my bed and listened to Coco's shower. She had the radio going and was singing to that old U2 song, 'I Still Haven't Found What I'm Looking For.' My mind turned to Jean Paul's attack. *You do not have what it takes.* Maybe Jack was right. I was wasting my father's money, and really should quit school. Surely they'd refund the money, or at least part of it, especially if Jean Paul told them I didn't belong there.

But the thing was, I *did* have what it took. Didn't I? And why didn't he ever yell at Len, who'd been an ad executive for years and, as far as I perceived, spent most of his time at school sharpening his Wusthof knives? Was it because I was a woman? He didn't pick on Tara. Or Priscilla. Or even Miriam, the sixty-five-year-old grandmother who took a half hour to julienne one carrot.

Maybe he just didn't like me.

After I heard the shower go off, I went back to Coco's bedroom thinking I'd complain to her about how annoying Jack was, not that I believed she'd be sympathetic. I sat on her bed and looked at the elaborate display of boas and fans on the walls. The boas, black and lavender, were draped horizontally on little hooks, so they dipped around the room like swags of icing around the perimeter of a birthday cake. The fans made a pyramid over her bed.

'You have plans for tonight?' she asked as she stepped into a short black skirt with slits on the side.

'Yeah. To chill out.'

She pulled a matching black top over her head. No bra was involved in this outfit. The top had a slit down the front that went past the southern end of her boobs and a slit coming up that went past her belly button. I could never pull off an outfit like that.

'We'll probably go to his place later.' She stuck a gold hoop earring the size of an onion ring through her ear.

'Okay. Have fun. And never leave me alone in a room with him again.'

'Was it that bad?'

'Yes.'

'Should I talk to him about it?'

'There's nothing he can do. It's his personality. Just let me continue to avoid him as much as possible.'

'You should know . . .' She put the other earring in. 'His divorce came through.'

'What?'

'He's making noises about us, now.'

'He asked you to marry him?' There was nothing I wanted less than to have Jack as a stepfather.

'Not yet, but I can see it coming.' She noticed the look of panic on my face and laughed. 'Don't worry. I have no interest in changing his bedpans.'

'Thank god.'

'But we should figure out a way for you two to get along.'

'We do get along,' I said. 'Badly.'

'So why do you think he's wasting his time on us?' I asked Ralph. We were in the demo kitchen waiting for Robert Kingsley to honor us with his presence. It was a small, sterile, windowless room with three rows of chairs on three levels of ledges so everyone could have a good view of the countertop up front, which was equipped with a stove and a sink and a large butcher-block surface on one side and a marble surface on the other. Ralph and I were in the back row in the corner. Tom Carpenter was front row center. Tara was in the second row, directly behind Tom.

'Must've made some sort of error in judgment,' Ralph said under his breath. 'Maybe he was soused when he agreed, and then he couldn't get out of it.'

The man certainly did not need to teach. He was famous. In demand. Had his own show on the Food Network. Speaking engagements all over the world. A deal with Perdue. His cookbook memoir was a best seller. He owned Zin, which was considered THE best restaurant in Sonoma, California. He was not your typical celebrity chef.

In general, there are three basic types. There's the educated, bourgeois ones. They never actually cooked in restaurants. They have a beautiful, fully equipped kitchen in their home, and they know how to talk on camera while neatly combining premeasured ingredients.

Then you've got your clog-wearing Europeans, who trained in hotel and restaurant schools under medieval conditions and want to spread their suffering throughout the world. If we wanted to worship them, we were free to do so.

Then you have your Vin Diesel 'I'm a macho line cook' kind of guys. Until you've pulled all-nighters with a broken limb, burned every square inch of your body, dripped your own blood on someone's sirloin, and gotten through a dinner service for five hundred while stoned, you're a sissy who hasn't earned the right to stand in your shit-kickers behind a Wolf stove.

Robert Kingsley went to Stanford, where he got a degree in philosophy. His first job? Chez Panisse. He worked up to sous chef before taking off to travel, cooking in hotels and restaurants all around the world. Then he opened Zin. He was a genius at using fresh regional ingredients with an international flavor and was also one of the world's experts on wine.

So why was he bothering with us? He certainly didn't need the money. Whatever the reason, I'd lucked out. I didn't have to hide the fact that I'd been to college, or feel I had to 'make up' for the fact that I was female. He'd worked for Alice Waters, after all, and his sous chef at Zin used to be Charlotte Wilcox, who was now a celebrity in her own right. Kingsley was definitely woman-friendly.

'One thing's for sure,' I said. 'I'm glad to get out of Jean Paul's kitchen for awhile.' I could only hope that Jean Paul hadn't briefed Kingsley on the students and polluted his mind against me.

Everyone sat erect when he walked into the room. One more way he was unlike most celebrity chefs – he looked like a movie star.

The man was thirty-four years old. Healthy, California tan. Thick brown wavy hair combed straight back. Handsome, clean-shaved face. No chef's whites for him. He wore a dark tweed suit and a white shirt. Black leather dress shoes. 'So I was just at the airport,' he said immediately. His voice was silky and rich. 'What do you think I saw?'

Everyone was quiet. I just stared.

'I was sitting at a table in the restaurant, if you can call it that, waiting to board my plane.'

I waited for Tara to open her mouth but even she stayed quiet.

'I was starving. What were my choices? Dried-up pizza. Burgers in foil sitting under a heat lamp. Fruit salad in plastic cups. And what else?'

Ralph raised his hand and then said, 'Hot dogs?'

Ralph was flirting. But Kingsley was not gay. His book had detailed two affairs. One was with the daughter of a French vintner. He wrote all about learning the 'pleasures of wine' with her while picnicking on Stinson Beach and hiking on Mount Tamalpais. And he'd almost married Carole Binchy when he did segments on her morning show in London.

'There was a sign,' he continued, 'that said "Gourmet Sandwiches." '

The class was silent.

'Gourmet sandwiches!' He laughed a bit maniacally. 'Do you know what was in them?'

'Sun-dried tomatoes?' someone said.

'Black Forest ham?'

'Bologna!' he yelled with indignation. 'Egg salad, tuna, ham, processed American cheese, soggy iceberg lettuce, mustard, mayo – now I ask you. *Is that gourmet?*'

That was a safe enough question. The class answered more or less in unison. 'No!'

'But the sign said "gourmet." '

'It's false advertising,' Tara said.

'Was it?' he asked. He looked around the room. No one spoke. I slowly raised my hand. He nodded at me.

For the first time ever my class in linguistic anthropology was going to come in handy. 'It *is* gourmet.'

'Go on,' he said. The way he lifted his chin and his eyebrows and the corners of his mouth all at the same time let me know. This man accepted me.

' "Gourmet" used to mean the food was of the highest quality in the French tradition,' I said, 'but now it's been appropriated by business people. They want to use what it *used* to mean to sell products . . .'

He pointed at me. 'Exactly. And what does that tell you about the restaurant business?'

No one answered.

'It means nothing lasts. What was considered stylish last year is boring now. Asian Fusion? Nobody cares anymore. Fresh, local ingredients? Ten years ago the concept was revolutionary. Now it's expected, for god's sake. Then we saw a shift to the exotic, the foreign. Today? It's all available overnight on the Internet! It's all been done! Everyone keeps wondering what the next wave is going to be. Some people think there's nothing new left to do. No new way of eating to be discovered. No new combinations to be tried. Do you think that's true?'

No one dared answer.

'Of course it's not true! But *you* are the ones who will have to come up with the new ideas. And in order to do that, you've got to travel the world.

Work in different restaurants. Become intimate with every nationality of food. That's the only way to become a brilliant chef. Not from sitting in a classroom.'

Great. So he thought we were fools for being here too.

'It is not your job to serve them what they *want*!' he proclaimed. 'It is your job to teach the customer to want what *you serve*!'

Everyone was totally still. This was good. This seemed profound, even, despite the fact that he was basically promoting himself and his own success story. A man like him never needed anyone else to tell him he was good. He just knew it. Was he born with that confidence? Or was it instilled by his parents? I'd read he'd been very close with his mother, who took him traveling to Europe a lot when he was a kid. God, it would be so incredible to have an affair with a man like him. Not that he was my type. Too old. Too put together. He would never go for someone like me. Not that he could know anything about me, since I was dressed like everyone else. But he most certainly knew everything there was to know about making love to a woman. In a vineyard. With the smell of grapes and wood and smoke and the hot sun beating down . . .

'So, if you could open whatever restaurant you wanted, what would it be like?' He paused and looked around the room. I shifted in my seat. Didn't really want to put my fantasies out there in front of my classmates. Evidently, no one else did either.

'How many of you plan to own your own business?'

Tara's hand shot up. Sure. She would have no problem. Her father would set her up. Me? How would I ever get the money? The idea of going to my father again was depressing.

Evidently, I wasn't the only financially challenged one there. Tara and a couple of the second-career people were the only ones to raise their hands.

'Really,' he said. 'I'm surprised. Well,' he continued, 'you still need to understand how a restaurant is run. And that's what we'll be talking about in here. How to plan a menu. How to make a wine list. How to hire a staff. How to make a profit. Because even if you're drawn to this business because you have a love for food, and for cooking, and you love, as we all do, the theater that is part of creating your own restaurant . . . if you don't know how to make money, you're going to fail.'

With that, he dismissed us. I walked out to the elevator with Ralph, and we went to get lunch. As soon as we hit the street, Ralph started to swoon. 'I'm in love.'

'He's not gay.'

'He can evolve.'

'He's out of our league.'

'A guy can always dream.'

We went into a deli. And got ourselves a couple gourmet sandwiches.

*m*y father let me in. His apartment was a floor-through in a nineteenth-century townhouse on East Sixty-sixth Street. Not the biggest space in the world, but it was beautiful.

'Thanks for coming,' he said. He was still in his suit, but his tie was undone.

'I'm happy to. Can I put this here?' I set my knife roll down on a small table by the door.

'Sure. Can I get you something to drink? A soda?'

'Maybe just some water. Thanks.'

'No problem.'

Why did we have to be so stiff with each other? Every time we saw each other it was as if we'd just met.

He went to the kitchen, and I noticed Emma. She was sitting on the couch watching TV. Catatonic. 'Hi,' I said.

'Hi.'

Her voice was cold and her gaze didn't leave the screen. Still, my heart went out to her. She looked so all alone and innocent swallowed up in that couch wearing a T-shirt that said BLONDES HAVE MORE FUN. She had brown hair. Her face was splotchy. Her twelve-year-old body was just starting to grow curves. She needed her mom. Her mom wasn't here. It was too sad! Yet there was so much of Leah's essence in the room. She'd loved going to auctions and dealers and antique stores, and she'd managed to create a home that was luxurious but also laid-back. Earth tones. Thick wool rug. Huge, soft golden brown sofa. New York could be such a harsh place to live. It had to be a comfort to come home to a place like this. At least, it must've *been* a comfort. But now?

My father returned with the water. 'Emma, did you say hi to Ginger?'

She didn't respond, just seemed to sink deeper into herself.

'She said hi before,' I said.

He led me to his bedroom. 'Sorry. When she gets in front of that thing . . .'

I'd rarely been in his bedroom, except for passing through quickly on the way to use the bathroom when the one near the kitchen was occupied. Now I stood next to the queen-sized bed with its thick, eggplant-colored goose down quilt and looked around. Faced with the reality of this task, I was wondering exactly why I had agreed to do this.

'I really appreciate this,' my father said. 'I know it's asking a lot. But everything's been sitting here, and I put it off, and put it off, and realized I just couldn't bring myself to touch anything. Maybe I just should've hired someone.'

'No, I'm glad to do it, really.'

'And I admit, I had an ulterior motive.'

I raised my eyebrows at him. Maybe this was his clumsy yet well-meaning way of getting closer! Maybe his plan was to do this along with me. We could work side by side, and as we put Leah's things into boxes, we could talk about her, and then us, and finally really get to know each other.

'My work schedule is crazy,' he said. 'And Emma is alone so much. I wish she had more friends. I'm worried about her. I thought maybe you two could get to know each other better.'

I shrugged. 'I'm sure it hasn't been easy for her.'

'Yeah, at her age especially, it's hard to open up to me.'

I wanted to say it would be hard to open up to him at any age, or had he not noticed I'd never opened up to him, or maybe he had – just didn't think that was a problem. But I kept my mouth shut. I wasn't a child. (Though I sure felt like one around him!) Emma was the one who'd just lost her mother. My hurt was nothing compared to hers. 'I'll try,' I said. 'Though I don't think she really likes me very much.'

'I'm sure she'll open up to you.'

I wanted to ask why he thought that. Because I was such a warm, engaging person? Then why hadn't he ever opened up to me? Okay, I was regressing again, and my father was on to showing me around, giving me instructions. He had a meeting to get to.

'There are Hefty bags in the kitchen, under the sink. And please feel free to keep anything you want. Maybe you should check with Emma first, in case it's something she might want. But obviously there's a lot here, and most of it's way too old for her anyway.'

'I don't think the clothes are really my style.'

'Well, you never know.' He looked in the mirror and retied his tie. 'So. You have the key. Feel free to come by whenever you want to.'

'Okay. Thanks.'

'Don't thank me. Thank *you*.'

As soon as he left, I sat down on the edge of the bed. There was so much to do! Where to begin? Why had I said yes to this? I decided to take inventory. The top of her bureau was crowded with stuff: hairbrush, jewelry box, books, papers. It was true, he had not touched a thing. Her walk-in closet was double-hung and packed with lawyerish skirt suits, summer dresses, dinner dresses, winter coats. Two shelves along the top were crammed with storage boxes and shopping bags. Treasures? Junk? The floor was covered with shoes. She had obviously not been a neat person. I liked her for that.

Emma. She was out there. I was supposed to bond with her. I made myself go to the living room.

'So,' I said, 'I'm just gonna start. If you want to come in and help . . . I mean, you don't have to, but if you want to . . .'

'I'm watching *TRL*.' Her jaw required a concerted effort to be moved. Her eyes did not leave the TV. Some curly-haired guy was interviewing J-Lo.

'They say she has a big butt,' I said, 'but it doesn't look that big to me.' It looked to be about the same size as my own butt. Or how I imagined my butt to be. It's hard to have perspective on your own butt. In any case, Emma was not weighing in on J-Lo's butt size, so I went to get a garbage bag.

I started with the underwear drawer. It was a jumbled wad of cotton Jockey underwear, black and white cotton socks, and nylon bras with no padding. Death meant I knew Leah wore no thongs. I shook my head and fought back a sudden attack of tears. Dumped it all into the Hefty bag. Told myself I was not going to get all emotional about this, was just going to do the job, do the job, do the job. Then, on the bottom of the now empty drawer, I found a folded piece of paper.

I smoothed it out on top of the bed. It was a child's crayon drawing of two stick figures wearing triangle skirts, one taller than the other, holding hands. In a child's crooked printing, it said, 'I miss you at lunch today my Mommy, luv Emma.'

My eyes stung. Should I show it to Emma? I certainly couldn't throw it out. She had to know her mother was saving this in her underwear drawer. It would make her feel good. Miserable, but good.

I went to the living room. Looked at the screen. The camera was panning out the studio window at screaming fans in Times Square. 'I found something.' I sat next to her. 'In your mom's drawer.'

Everyone was clapping and cheering for J-Lo.

'Would you like to see it?' I held it out. 'It's very sweet.' Her frown just turned into a deeper frown. Maybe I'd done the wrong thing.

But maybe not.

'I'm going to put it on your desk, okay? You should have it.'

'Would you please leave?'

'What?'

'You shouldn't be going through my mother's things.' It took her such effort to say the words, I thought her face was going to crack. I appreciated that she'd managed to say anything. I remembered when Coco once confessed that she'd read my journal. I remembered her sitting on the edge of my bed apologizing and all I would do was stare straight ahead, silent, with such anger tensing up my face I thought my eyeballs were going to explode.

'Your dad asked me to do this,' I said. I hated how it came out like that. As if he wasn't my dad too.

'She's not your mother.'

I suppressed an urge to walk out of the apartment without saying another word. Or remind her that even if Leah wasn't my mother, I certainly did miss her. But there was no point telling her that. My loss didn't begin to measure up to hers, and I was still lucky enough to have my mother. I couldn't imagine losing Coco. For that matter, I couldn't imagine Coco dying. She was too much a life force. It was bad enough when Grandma died my senior year of high school. Man. It wasn't fair. Mothers shouldn't be allowed to die. I went back into the bedroom, put the drawing in Leah's jewelry box, and started in on the next drawer down.

chapter nine

It was a Sunday night, and I'd prepared a leg of lamb for Coco, Ian, and well, Jack was there too so I suppose I had to allow him to have some. It was such a good dish, and so simple. Just rub the lamb with garlic, salt, pepper. Coat with mustard and bake. Ian was raving about the Strokes' most recent CD when I set the platter on the middle of the table. Jack was watching me. When I returned with the salad he said, 'Did Coco tell you?'

Coco was spearing a piece of lamb, unusually quiet, with a guilty smile.

I took my seat. 'Tell me what?'

'I am treating her to have some work done. As a birthday present.'

'On the apartment?' I said, knowing full well what he meant. 'That's a great idea, because the bathroom, as you well know, is disgusting. The old tiles are so grotty.'

'I'm not talking about the bathroom.'

'I didn't think so!' Ian said, stabbing a piece of meat on the platter and bringing it to his dish.

'You mean the kitchen? I can't tell you how much I would love a new refrigerator . . . can I pick out some new wallpaper?'

'Work on her face!'

'What?'

'I know you disapprove,' Coco jumped in, 'but I'm psyched, so please don't make a big deal – '

'Mom, don't do it, please?'

Ian drizzled oil on his lettuce. 'Ginger, come on. Everyone does it these days.'

'I don't care if everyone is doing it. Mom looks great, she doesn't need to hack up her face to make it look better.' God, she wasn't even that old. I'd always figured this would become an issue one day, but so soon?

'She's not hacking it up,' Ian said, drizzling vinegar. 'There's nothing sacred about nature. Nature doesn't mind being altered. Look at it this way. It's like turning yourself into a work of art. The same way you carve a sculpture out of a piece of wood.'

'What the hell are you talking about?'

'Savages do this stuff all the time. It's part of their culture. And at this point, it's part of our culture.'

'Then the culture is stupid. People die from going under the knife. Anesthesia is dangerous.'

'It's less dangerous,' Jack said, 'than crossing Broadway, let me tell you.'

'Okay, we aren't going to argue about this,' Coco said. 'I want to do it and that's that. The lamb is great, by the way, honey. You've done it again.'

'Why can't you love her as she is?' I glared at Jack. 'She's not a commodity, she's a human being.'

'This is my idea, not Jack's. He is generously offering to pay, so would you please shut up?'

I stared at my meat. When Coco had her boobs done way back when, I was too little to really understand, other than thinking that for some reason she'd blown her breasts up like balloons. I remembered telling her, 'Don't float away!' By the time I hit my teens, though, I was infuriated and let her know it. *How could you? So disgusting. Pandering. Where's your self-respect?*

My mother's response had driven me crazy. 'Don't you get it?' she'd said. 'I'm more valuable this way.'

She'd never even used them to breast-feed me, only to seduce men. 'Forget the aesthetic crime against nature aspect,' I said. 'People go into comas during these operations. They die! I saw something on TV about this woman who had them do her eyelids and then she couldn't close her eyes! Can you imagine? No one should do surgery unless they have to.'

Jack cut up his lamb in this annoying way that made his knife scratch against the plate. 'No one is forcing her to have surgery. This is something she wants to do.'

'Because you pressured her.'

'He did not! I want this. Okay? I hate these wrinkles here.' She pointed to her eyes.

'I love laugh lines,' I said. 'I can't wait till I get laugh lines.'

'And these jowls.'

'You don't have jowls.' Maybe she was starting to get jowls, but who cared?

'If she feels like she's getting jowls,' Ian said. 'it's her right to get rid of them.'

Coco started pulling the skin back on her face with the palms of her hands. 'I'm just thinking cheek lift, forehead lift, and some laser work around the eyes. We're not talking major overhaul here, just a little tinkering.'

'Everyone knows, once you start doing it you get addicted. And then you have to do it here, and there, and keep it up because it all starts to sag . . .'

'Don't you think you should stay out of this?' Ian again. 'She's a grown woman. She can make her own decision.'

'Me? Why don't you stay out of this?'

'Because I don't see anything wrong with it. And you, as usual, are taking it personally, as if she's somehow doing it to you.'

'Are you suggesting that you and Jack have more say about this than I do? She's my *mother*.'

'It's her decision.'

'So why should you be voicing an opinion?'

'I am merely trying to be supportive of your mother.'

'So you admit she's *my* mother!'

'What the hell?'

'You think you can just hang around here, like my mom is your mom, but she's not!'

'Oh, Jesus, do we have to do this now?' Coco took a large gulp of wine.

'I have a mom,' Ian said. 'I don't need your mom to be my mom.'

'That's right. You need her to be your girlfriend. That's what you really want, isn't it?'

Now Jack was interested. 'What the hell is she talking about?'

'Nothing. Ginger, would you calm down?'

'I am calm!' I screeched. 'I am perfectly calm!' I stood up. My appetite was gone. 'I'm not hungry.'

'Fine,' Ian said. And he sat there, and I realized that I was about to leave, and he was going to stay, and then they would all enjoy dinner together. The dinner I had made. I turned to Ian. 'Go.'

'What?'

It tore my heart out to say it. 'I want you to leave.'

'*I'm* hungry. I'd like to have my dinner.'

'I am asking you to leave my kitchen. My kitchen in my home where I live.'

Ian looked at Coco. 'If she wants you to go' – she shrugged – 'I think you should go.'

It took Ian a moment to digest that. 'Fine,' he said. 'But this is ridiculous.'

He tossed his fork on the table, stood up with his eyes on his food, as if he was considering asking for a doggie bag, then left. There was silence except for the sound of Jack's chewing. It was horrible. I could feel Ian's humiliation. I didn't want him to suffer, even though he'd made me suffer. I hated to see him leave like that, in defeat.

I went after him, almost tripping down the stairwell trying to catch up. I heard his feet hitting the stairs. 'Ian?'

No response. I heard him cross the lobby and open the front door to the street. I sped up, pushing open the front door a moment after it slammed shut. Why did I need to apologize? It was just one more dumb fight. We would get back together in a few days and pretend nothing had happened. 'Ian!' He was at the bottom of the stoop stairs. 'Can you wait up?' He paused, and I caught up with him on the sidewalk. Fresh air, traffic, people rushing past, a whiff of bagel.

'I'm sorry.' Why was I apologizing? 'But this . . .' Our eyes met. 'We both know it's not working.' I hadn't meant to say that. Had I? Why did he suddenly look so young? So vulnerable? His skin so soft. Little boy lost. No. Don't think that. We were blocking people trying to get past, but we didn't move. Let them circle around us. 'It seems like we just . . . don't . . . make . . . a very good couple.'

'No,' he said. 'We don't.'

Some man in a pin-striped suit skirted around us. 'Can you get out of the fucking way?'

We moved to the side. 'I think,' I said, 'we should take a break from each other.'

A woman walking a golden retriever heard and looked at us while her dog sniffed a hydrant. I glared at her until she passed.

'Maybe we should,' he said.

I paused. 'So I guess this is it.'

'Yes.'

'Well . . . good luck.'

'You too.'

He turned and walked away.

I stood there for a moment and braced myself for feeling miserable. My body got hot. I trembled. Tears stung my eyes. I turned to go back inside, inhaled a whiff of fresh warm bagel, and exhaled with a surprising sense of relief.

'*e*dible flowers,' Kingsley said, 'are a wonderful way to dress up a dish.'

Though I was usually happy to be in the demo kitchen with Kingsley, I was exhausted and looking forward to getting home. 'We know that Romans used roses to flavor wine. Aztecs mixed marigolds with chocolate.'

I took notes, thinking how the flower stand outside my corner grocery had a truly impressive selection of flowers. I'd never even considered using them to cook with.

'I like to add nasturtiums to my salads; they add a wonderful spicy flavor. You've probably all seen those candied violets they like to use on cakes, but they're expensive. You can take fresh petals and arrange them on your icing for a beautiful effect.'

When Kingsley dismissed us, I headed to the locker room intent on getting home and taking a nap. Unfortunately, I had to help Coco with a class that night. A good night's sleep sounded much more attractive. I looked forward to that moment of getting into my bed.

The locker room was really just the end of a hallway. They'd walled it off and put up a door. Installed gray metal lockers on both sides of the wall and put a bench in the middle. In other words, it really was too small to be a locker room. (And obviously I'm using the word 'room' broadly.) But, as usual in Manhattan, space was at a premium. We girls struggled to get into our street clothes without elbowing the next person in the ribs.

I couldn't help but notice Tara's annoyingly cute, tight, curvy little body and flawless tanned skin. Whereas my transition from chef's uniform to civilian was always brief and efficient, she liked to prolong her state of undress for as long as possible. She pulled off her clothes while blathering on to Priscilla about a benefit her father's restaurant was hosting at Lincoln Center that night. 'We're serving braised squab with figs in a vinaigrette, rabbit with polenta, and this incredible goat-cheese cheese-cake with blackberry purée . . .'

I tried to navigate within the six inches of space I had claimed on the edge of the bench so I could put my sneakers back on. Some of the guys, and even women, wore heavy black work shoes. That's what the school tried to get us to wear, and it did offer more protection in case a heavy pot or the point of a stray knife happened to fall on your foot. But most people wore sneakers since they were more comfortable. And this was a job where you're on your feet all day, so comfort was important.

In other words, no fuck-me pumps.

Tara stood there in a black bra and a skimpy little black G-string with a row of rhinestones running up the back. To think all that was hidden under her unisex houndstooth chef's pants all day. Her big dilemma was whether to wear her hair up or down. 'It's so much more elegant up, but honestly, I think I look prettier with it down. And I do want to look hot,' she said, 'because guess who's coming with.'

Priscilla was in her pants and bra brushing out her long sleek brown hair. 'You aren't asking me, I take it?'

'You can come if you're willing to be a third wheel. I asked Tom Carpenter.'

I concentrated on tying my left shoe. Damn. Of course she was after him. But that didn't mean he was into her. Maybe she'd asked him to go, and he'd felt obligated to say yes because he didn't want to hurt her feelings, and he would be curious to see all the glitz at the benefit. Who could blame him?

'Tom is definitely the cutest guy here,' Priscilla said.

'Tom is the *only* cute guy here,' Tara said.

Except for Robert Kingsley, but he wasn't a guy, he was a man.

'Up?' Tara gathered her locks to the top of her head and admired herself in a little mirror she'd hung in her locker. 'Or down?' She let them cascade around her shoulders. 'What do you think, Ginger?'

I shrugged. 'Either way seems fine.'

'I feel so bad for you,' Tara said. 'The way Jean Paul treats you? I'm impressed you still show up.'

Her voice was wooden, and there wasn't an ounce of sympathy in those ice blue eyes. I ignored her thinly veiled putdown. 'See ya.' I grabbed my knife roll and left.

Tom was in the lobby waiting, presumably, for Tara. I hit the button for the elevator. We gave each other a nod. Something in his expression made me think it was more than just friendly. It was such a teensy-weensy communication, but it charged my body with electricity. As I stepped onto the elevator, I treated myself to the thought that he'd rather spend the evening with me.

chapter eleven

Coco and I lifted the trunk out of the back of the cab and lugged it into the lobby of our building. Strip class that night had been very well attended, and we'd sold a lot of stuff. I was more than ready to get to bed, but Coco was looking at the elevator like it was a one-way express to hell. She had a hard time coming down after her gigs. 'Don't you want to get a cup of coffee?'

'I do have class in the morning.'

'Just a quick bite?'

'Okay.'

I could be totally annoyed with her, feel claustrophobic and smothered, but if she asked me out for a bite to eat, I could immediately switch to feeling flattered she wanted to spend an hour alone with me.

We left the trunk in the lobby closet and went down to this cutesy fifties retro restaurant on the corner called Betty's Diner. It had the typical chrome details, white Formica tables, and nostalgic posters of freckled kids and housewives in ads for Carnation milk, Nestlé, and Pepsi. The hostess tried to seat us at a depressing booth in the back. Coco nodded to a table by the window. 'How about that one?'

The hostess gave Coco a disapproving once-over, then looked at the window table as if it was being saved in case Queen Elizabeth happened to pop in. 'That one?'

'Looks good to me,' Coco said.

We followed the hostess back to the front table. She put the two menus on it without looking at us or saying anything and went back to her little podium at the door.

Someday, I swore, I was going to move out of this city. If not the Midwest, maybe California. Southern California, where it's sunny all year round. Except there were all those blondes with perfect bodies walking around trying to make everyone else feel bad. Maybe Oregon. The Pacific

Northwest. Trees. Rain. Perpetually cold weather. Pale people who wore lots of clothing and went to bakeries. My kind of people.

Coco went to use the bathroom while I looked at the menu. I seemed to have a much larger bladder than she did. Plus she always needed to redo her makeup. Even with the day almost over, she had to 'fix her face.' I didn't get it. Who was going to see her? I generally only wore lipstick, and I only put it on in the morning. After that, I avoided looking at myself during the rest of the day so I didn't have to worry. It drove Coco insane.

I closed the menu. I knew everything on it, and liked pretty much everything they had. I wasn't in the mood for a burger. They had good soups, which seemed to be 'homemade,' though they were probably delivered in big vats from somewhere in Queens. Or maybe I would throw caution to the wind and get dessert. Diner desserts, done well, are my favorite, I have to admit, even though it's blasphemy when you're learning traditional French pastry. This place had a mean apple brown Betty.

When Coco returned, I was staring down the dessert menu. It was extra tempting because I'd been fighting the temptation to call Ian all week and I needed some kind of comfort for my new single status. Devil's food chocolate cake. Banana cream pie. Strawberry shortcake. Ice cream sundae. But it was late. I wasn't hungry. Who needed the calories?

'Get the brown Betty,' Coco said. 'And I'll get the Cobb salad. We'll share, okay?'

'Deal.'

With the heavy decisions behind us, we relaxed into our seats. The waitress came and took our order. That's when I saw Robert Kingsley walking by out on the sidewalk. He happened to look into the glass when he was right next to us and saw me telling Coco, 'That's Robert Kingsley!' Coco, who had no idea who Robert Kingsley was, motioned for him to come in.

'Mom, no!'

But it was too late.

'What?'

'I don't want to have a conversation with him.'

'Well, I do. He's cute.'

Damn! The idea of making stupid small talk with one of my instructors was bad enough. But I really didn't want him to meet Coco. He'd never look at me the same again.

Not that it mattered. He was out of reach. Fantasy material.

'Hello there,' he said as he approached our table, 'Ginger, right?'

He knew my name! 'Hi.' His gaze turned to Coco. She had her glamour smile on. His eyebrows went up. Damn. 'This is Coco. She's my – '

'Sister.'

I glared at my mother. This was not the first time she'd pulled this. 'And this is Robert Kingsley. He's teaching at my school.'

He smiled politely. 'Ginger's sister. Nice to meet you.'

'And it's very nice to meet you!'

Obviously Coco did not find him out of reach. Of course, no man was out of her reach as long as he had a functioning penis and wasn't gay. He'd already taken a good look at my mother's breasts. I did a quick calculation. I was twenty-five. She was forty-three. His age was exactly halfway between ours.

'So would you tell me something?' Kingsley looked at me. Which I appreciated. Men's eyes don't always find their way back to me after taking in my mom.

'Sure.'

'Am I a horrible teacher?'

I smiled. 'No.'

'I think I must be very boring.'

'Not at all.' I wanted to explain to him that it didn't matter what he said up there. We were all perfectly happy to sit there and observe the graceful way his forearm bent into his wrist when he wrote on the blackboard. The tender way he let wine trickle into the sauté pan when he was doing a reduction. You just knew, he had the touch.

'Why don't you stay?' Coco said. 'Have a bite to eat.'

'I'm not hungry, thanks.' Did Kingsley find diner food below him? He eyed the space next to me. 'Maybe just for a second.'

I moved. The shoulder of his gray tweed jacket bumped lightly against mine for a moment as he landed. It was just a tap, but the wind was knocked out of me. Luckily he and my mother were maintaining the conversation.

'You both have unusual names,' he said.

Of course, my mother got to pick her name. She was born Elaine – totally wrong, Elaine Wineberg. She called herself Cinnamon when she started at the Pussycat. But then she decided Cinnamon was too long and hard to get out, and she switched to Coco. Coco Winters. I liked it better too. I wished she'd named me Coco. My next choice would've been Cinnamon, then Ginger.

'That's cute,' he said, 'how they're both food.'

'Chocolate's supposed to be an aphrodisiac, or so I've read – not that I've ever noticed that actually working, have you?'

The waitress brought our drinks and asked Kingsley if he wanted anything. He hesitated, and then said no thanks.

I poured some half-and-half into my coffee.

'They say people who eat chocolate live longer,' he said.

'Oh! Now that's something I could endorse. Eat me! Live longer!' Coco laughed. She could make almost anything a dirty joke. I glared at her to no avail. Time for me to speak up.

'I was named after Ginger Rogers. *Not* the movie star on *Gilligan's Island*.' I always feel it's important for people to know that. Ginger on *Gilligan's Island* is so totally not me. And Ginger Rogers had a lot of spunk.

'Don't you just love those old Fred Astaire–Ginger Rogers movies?' Coco went on. 'She could make you believe she was falling for him even though he was so unattractive.'

Like a stripper, I thought, stirring in another creamer.

'He was a great dancer,' Kingsley said. 'When I was growing up, I saw all his movies at the Pacific Film Archive in Berkeley. They had a wonderful restaurant there, the Swallow. Ruth Reichl worked there' – he turned to me – 'did you know that? They had the most wonderful cranberry orange scones, before scones were the new muffins. I lived for them.'

'Ruth who?' my mother asked.

'A food writer,' I explained. 'She used to review for the *Times*.'

'I have a restaurant in Sonoma,' he said to Coco, downplaying the level of his celebrity. 'I'm here in New York teaching a class at your sister's school, but I'm afraid the students want to be cooking, not sitting at desks.'

'That's not true. I'm sure we all dream of having our own restaurant one day. And we're really honored to have you of all people . . .' He was looking straight at me, and I started to blush.

'So, Robert.' My mother stepped in (thank god). 'How do you like New York?'

'I love it,' he said. 'That's part of why I accepted this job – just to have an excuse to be here. Have you ever been to Sonoma?'

'No,' Coco said, 'but I'd *love* to go. Drive around all day and go to wine tastings . . .'

'How about you, Ginger? Does a place like Sonoma appeal to you?'

'I would *love* to live someplace like that.' I beamed as I launched into my daydream. 'Open a little bakery on some Main Street. And live in a cute little Victorian house. I would paint it pink. Or yellow. Or maybe lilac. I bet the people there are really nice.'

He looked amused. 'It's boring, really. A sleepy little town.'

'Are you kidding? It's one of the most beautiful places in the world. I mean, I've never been there, but I bet it is. And the people out there really appreciate good food. They know how to relax and enjoy life.'

Northern California. Yes. That's where I should move. Find a Main Street in California and open my café.

'Well' – he smiled indulgently at me – 'they aren't sitting around in the sun consuming wine, pâté, and biscotti *all* the time.'

'Right. I'm sure there's crime and misery and loneliness out there too.'

'Absolutely! Well.' He sat up straight, nodded politely to each of us. 'I should get going.' He slid out from the booth. 'Enjoy your meal, ladies. See you in school, Ginger. It was very nice to meet you, Coco.' He looked back and forth between us. 'I see the resemblance. Your mother must've been quite beautiful.'

'Aren't you sweet!' Coco fawned.

I just smiled.

When he walked away, Coco and I both watched him go. Even through his suit, you could see his ass was a definite ten.

'Gorgeous,' Coco said.

The waitress brought our food. My apple brown Betty was really good. Tart, chunky apples. A thick brown-sugar crust. Real whipped cream. How could you go wrong?

'Yum.' I dipped my fork into the whipped cream.

'He seemed to be very into you.'

I savored the soft sweetness as it melted on my tongue. 'Are you kidding? He only came in because he saw you through the glass.'

'Maybe I'll have to enroll for next semester.'

'Don't even think of it.'

I ended up eating the entire apple brown Betty. And my mom had her Cobb salad. And we didn't share a bite.

'*a* re you still determined to be a pastry chef?'

Jean Paul looked straight at me.

'Yes.' I looked straight back at him.

'Then you may put away today's delivery.'

While everyone else practiced cake decoration, I lugged huge sacks of flour and sugar into the storeroom.

During the lunch break, I stayed inside and practiced piping frosting on the butcher-block table. I was trying to get my script to look beautiful. Jean Paul had told us how he'd written 'Happy Birthday' a thousand times every afternoon when he was apprenticing. He could do it with his eyes closed.

Jean Paul walked by. 'Your script looks like shit.'

I ignored him and kept at it. I wanted to give the appearance that this was not affecting me. But inside, I was dying.

About twenty Happy Birthdays later, Ralph came by. 'Hi, Your Cuteness.'

'Jean Paul hates me.'

'No, he doesn't.'

'Then why does he always give me drudge work?'

'You're good at drudge work. I wish I had your muscles.'

'It's not funny.'

'I'm serious!' he said, nodding at my work on the table. 'Your piping looks good.'

It's true. I was improving. And where was Jean Paul to see? Nowhere. 'I should quit. He's never going to put me in the Master Class. This is a waste of money. Doesn't he pick on me more than anyone? Why is he so mean to me?'

'Tough love?'

'I'll tell you why.' I picked up my bag and piped out, 'Because he's a shithead.'

'Well done!' Ralph said. 'Your script looks quite professional.'

'Your script,' I suddenly heard from behind me in a thick French accent, 'looks like crap!'

I froze.

'Shitfuck!' Ralph said. 'You gave me a heart attack!'

I turned around. It was Tom.

'Sorry,' he said, sheepish.

'Funny,' I said, trying to remain cool. But, I noticed immediately, Tom's presence made my blood warm as if someone had just turned up the gas. I turned back to the table and finished off a 'Happy.' But now my hand was shaking and the tail of the y looked more like an unraveling lasso.

'I didn't think my French accent was that good,' Tom said.

'Good enough,' Ralph said as he winked at me and walked away. I felt a moment of panic. Don't leave me alone with him! What will we say?

'So.' Tom leaned on the edge of the table and peered straight down at my handiwork. My palms were wet against the pastry bag, which I was gripping too tightly. This was hopeless. I put it down and made a big deal out of stretching out my back.

'You're from here, right?' he said.

'Born and bred.'

'That's cool.'

'You're from Ohio?'

'Iowa.'

'Right. Sorry. So you must be having major culture shock.'

'It's pretty intense. Especially because I don't really know anyone here.'

'That must be hard.'

'Yeah. I'm pretty much skating my wing. Take the subway home to Queens. Come back here in the morning. I spent Saturday wandering around the city but it's not so fun when you're by yourself.'

Was he suggesting something? I looked into his bright blue eyes and his little twitch of a mischievous smile. Something so adorable, how the top of his cherry red lips rose like delicate twin peaks. And here he was opening up to me. The poor guy . . . alone in the big city. My services were needed! 'Would you like me to show you around some?'

'That'd be great.'

'Okay. So . . . is there a good time for you . . . when you want to do it?'

He shrugged. 'Today?'

'Okay.'

'Great. So . . .' He nodded. 'Later!' He walked away looking sort of cheerily self-conscious. Was he nervous around me? Was it possible?

Maybe I didn't need to quit school quite yet.

As we walked up Sixth Avenue, I noticed that even though we'd changed out of our chef's uniforms, we were still dressed identically, as it happened, in blue jeans and white T-shirts. Though I was wearing a pair of my favorite sneakers – bloodred Pumas with gold laces – and he was in black work boots. I found that very sexy, to be dressed the same, though I wasn't sure if he did, so I didn't point it out.

It was a beautiful, sunny day and I wanted him to appreciate how gorgeous the city could be even if I was sick of it, so I led him north to Central Park. When we passed the Plaza Hotel, I confessed my secret wish. 'I'd love to stay in a room facing the park and order room service for dinner and then order room service for a midnight snack and then order room service for breakfast . . .'

'With so many great restaurants around?'

'I love being served food on a tray. With mini salt and pepper shakers. And those chrome covers they put on the dishes to keep the food warm. And an individual-sized pot of coffee.'

'And the Saran Wrap on the creamer so it won't spill when they wheel it down the hall . . .'

'Are you making fun of my fantasy?'

'No way I'd stay in the room. Too much to look at on the streets.'

'I've had enough of the streets. Give me a nice, cozy room any day.'

'With servants at your beck and call?'

'Exactly. I just want to be pampered.'

We strolled past the lineup of horse-drawn carriages for tourists. Tom took in a deep breath. 'Now *that's* a good smell!'

'Horse manure?'

'Yep!'

'You like that?' I wrinkled my nose.

'Reminds me of home.'

I laughed. 'You've got to be kidding.'

'I wish I was. I grew up in one of those towns with one main street with a grocery store, a diner, a gas station, and a shuttered-up shoe store.'

'Sounds kind of wonderful.'

'Kind of boring. Blink your eyes and you miss it. That's why this here is totally amazing to me.'

'It's hard to imagine how it must seem to someone who isn't from here. Sometimes I wish I could experience it as a tourist,' I said, eyeing an elderly couple stepping up into one of the carriages.

'You want to take a ride?'

'Way too expensive. And better to walk.' We took a path that wound around the lake. 'So where are you living in Queens?'

'Astoria. Been there?'

Astoria's a fairly decent residential area in Queens with a big Greek population and all the fresh feta cheese you could want. I'd been in Queens exactly twice in my life. The first time, it was to visit a strip club where Coco worked. Tom didn't need to know about that. So I told him about the second time. 'Years ago, to visit a friend of my mom's.' She was dying of AIDS. I decided not to mention that either. Coco had dragged me along, and I didn't want to go. My most vivid memory was of her friend lying in bed looking like a corpse. 'I remember having this incredible baklava, with this thick layer of custard.' I also remembered the stomachache I had because it was so damn filling. We'd gotten it on our walk back to the subway and ate it in the station as we waited for the train, as if we needed a quick fix that life could still be sweet.

'Yeah, that stuff is good. Filo dough. A pain in the ass to work with.'

'So good, though. Dripping with honey . . .'

'So you've lived here,' Tom asked, 'all your life?'

'Yep.'

'That's cool. Someday maybe I'll live in Manhattan.'

'So you plan to stay on after you're done with school?'

'Yeah, this is the place for me.'

Didn't he want to whisk me away from the big bad city, move back to Iowa (or was it Ohio?) to Main Street where we could open a bakery café?

Exactly how bad were his finances?

Astoria was not a good sign. But maybe there was a supportive relative ready to help finance his dream restaurant. An inheritance waiting to happen. You never knew.

'As a matter of fact,' he said, 'I'm looking around for a job. So if you hear of anything . . .'

'While you're in school?'

'I'm impatient. I want to learn everything now.'

'Won't it be exhausting working while you're going to school?'

And wouldn't that take away from our time to have fun together?

'Yeah, well, tuition is a killer and my parents are stretched to the limit . . .'

It seemed premature for me to say that I didn't want him to get a job because I was already planning my life around him. So instead, I suggested we take a seat on a bench just outside the Sheep Meadow. The huge lawn was heavily sprinkled with half-naked people soaking up the last rays of sun before fall turned into winter. The high-rises on Fifty-ninth Street loomed over the trees of Central Park. It was a beautiful sight except for the fact that Jack's apartment was on the sixteenth floor of one of those buildings. I'd looked down on this very spot a few times from his balcony.

'Can you believe sheep used to graze here?' I said idiotically. 'And it wasn't really that long ago. I mean, we're talking a hundred years, and everything has totally changed. There's this wonderful museum, the New York Historical Society. I should take you. I once saw these totally amazing photos of the Lower East Side from the 1800s. . . .'

Did he think I was a nerd, talking about taking him to a museum? He was a Healthy American Male. He wanted to get stoned, go to clubs, and have sex with strangers, right? I looked at him. We were sitting quite close to each other.

'You know where I really want to go?' he said.

'Where?'

'The restaurant supply stores. Down in the Bowery.'

'Oh, my god!' I put my hand on his arm, then took it away because he glanced down at it. 'I *love* the restaurant supply stores! I have this thing about stainless steel!'

'All those shiny new appliances . . .'

'You want to go this weekend?'

'I'd love to.'

'Let's do it.'

'Great.'

We sat back. Let the sun shine on our faces. Grew quiet. Now the sides of our arms were touching slightly, but I wasn't sure if it was by accident. I didn't move so we wouldn't lose contact. Would he put his arm around my shoulder? It was a sweet kind of torture to sit there feeling the warmth of his arm, wondering if this proximity meant something. Or was I just a cooking school buddy? Good for ogling napkin dispensers and sauté pans.

He nodded towards a new cut on my left index finger. This time a mushy tomato had made my knife slip.

'It's nothing.'

'You should get a Band-Aid on that, or it might get infected.'

'I had one, but it fell off.'

'Actually, I think I have one . . .'

He took out his wallet and started to look through.

'That's okay, really, I have some at home.'

'Where do you live?'

'About ten blocks away.'

'Really?' He pulled out a Band-Aid, somewhat scuffed but still sealed, and asked, 'Can I see it?'

'My apartment?'

'Yeah. I haven't actually been in anyone's apartment since moving here.'

Good. Then he hadn't been to Tara's. 'Oh. Well . . .' Would Coco be home? 'It's a real mess.'

'I don't care.'

He peeled open the Band-Aid. I held out my finger. He wrapped it around the cut and pressed gently but firmly on my skin. A thrill zinged my body.

'So what line of work are your parents in?' he asked.

'My father's a lawyer. My mother is a dancer. What about yours?'

'My dad's a plumber.'

'Really?' Coco liked to say sex is all about plumbing – so why does everyone make such a big deal out of it? 'And your mother?'

'My mother never worked at a job. I guess she's what you'd call a homemaker.'

'That sounds so lovely. Did she bake you cookies all the time? And forbid you to get piercings and tattoos? And ground you for staying out past curfew? Did she actually look at your report cards to see what grades you got?'

'Yeah, and worry incessantly that I'd get hit by a car or drown in the lake or have too much fun because she wasn't having any because she was just spending all her time worrying about her kids and cleaning out the bathroom and watching Oprah.'

'That's just the kind of mom I always wanted.'

I expected him to contradict me, but he got this tender look on his face. 'She's pretty great. That woman made meals for the family – and I've got three brothers – she made us three meals a day every day, and let me tell you, we were big eaters. Matter of fact, I'd say she's the one I got my cooking skills from.'

'For me it was my grandma.'

'Oh, yeah?'

'We used to bake together every Saturday night.' I didn't really want to go into it. How I basically grew up with her because Coco was on the road so much. But those Saturday night treats were a happy memory. We'd take whatever we made to the living room, gorge on it while it was still warm, and watch *The Facts of Life, T.J. Hooker, Comic Strip Live* . . . It was from Grandma that I learned to sift flour, crack eggs with one hand, and melt chocolate in a double boiler. She was the one who waved a dark little glass bottle under my nose and put me under the spell of vanilla, the most potent perfume in the world.

'You were an only child?'

'Uh-huh. Where do you fall age-wise?'

'Youngest.'

I liked the idea of him being a youngest. 'Did they always beat up on you?'

'My mom could probably qualify as an emergency room nurse.'

'I bet she entered contests that were in women's magazines, right? And collected points on Betty Crocker cake mix boxes so you could send away for free things, and clipped coupons. I used to clip coupons. Those little dotted lines used to call out to me – *Cut me! Cut me!*'

'She had a folder in the kitchen drawer that she'd file 'em in.'

'With a picture of a cow on it?'

'Um, I think a kitten.'

'My coupons always ended up in the garbage. The little grocery on our corner wouldn't take 'em. We had a Food Emporium a few blocks away, but the aisles were so skinny and the lines were so long you always came home in a bad mood. I still remember the first suburban grocery store I was ever in. A friend of my mom's had a car, and she offered to drive us to a Pathmark in Jersey City to stock up. I was so excited. Before we went, I sat down at the kitchen table and cut out almost every coupon in the supplement and stuck 'em in my purse and it was like a half hour drive once you got through the tunnel. When we pulled into the parking lot, I felt like I'd discovered the Promised Land.'

'Wide aisles. Better selection. Jumbo sizes.'

'All those things were good. But the most exciting thing was a surprise.'

'And that was?'

I grasped his arm. It was firmer than Ian's. He had real muscles. *'Double coupons.'*

Tom laughed. 'You're funny.'

He glanced down at my hand. Maybe he just didn't want me to touch him. I took it off. He looked at me very earnestly and swallowed.

'Living in the suburbs is not worth double coupons,' he said. 'City people are much more interesting. Like having a dancer for a mother. I can't even imagine . . .'

That was for sure.

'Where did she perform?'

'Oh . . . different places.'

'She had aspirations,' he said. 'She wanted to do something artistic.

She had something to think about other than you. And I bet she takes really good care of herself. My mom thinks whole-wheat flour is something fancy people eat, and she never exercises. I bet your mom still looks great, right?'

'Yeah.' He definitely wasn't coming over. 'She looks okay.'

The sun was going down and it was getting chilly. We made our way out of the park to Fifty-ninth Street. I didn't say anything about the concept of his seeing where I lived, just sort of pretended he'd never asked and herded him in a westerly direction to his subway stop. When we got there, we stopped at the top of the stairs leading down to the station. 'Well, here you are!'

'Here I am.'

'Thanks for the Band-Aid.'

'Anytime.'

'See ya.' I watched him descend into the subway, then headed home. When I stopped at the corner for the light, I pressed the Band-Aid against my lips and smelled the plastic. I didn't like to wear Band-Aids; I always felt like they suffocated my skin. But this one, I was leaving on.

chapter thirteen

*W*hen they invented 'Take Your Daughter to Work Day,' I don't think they were thinking of moms who worked in strip joints. I'll never forget the first time I visited Coco at the Platinum Club. I was seven years old, but it's one of the most vivid memories from my childhood.

The Platinum Club was a new 'upscale' place that catered to the more 'genteel' customers who resided in or decided to seek their entertainment in Queens. Sometimes Coco stayed with us and slept on the couch, but she also shared a place with another dancer near the club so she wouldn't have to take a cab across the Fifty-ninth Street Bridge in the middle of the night to get home. Grandma was the one who helped me with my homework and tucked me in at night. But one week she was away at some teacher's convention and the woman who was staying with me had some sort of emergency, so Coco ended up taking me with.

I was really excited to finally have the chance to see where she worked and exactly what she did. I knew it had to do with dancing. And taking some of her clothes off in front of men. I was pretty sure she let them see her breasts. I was so used to seeing her breasts at home, I didn't think that was a big deal. So I felt prepared, even though Coco didn't seem very happy about having to take me along.

We took the subway and walked a few blocks in a neighborhood that was mostly crummy, small office buildings and warehouses. I thought it was all surprisingly cruddy considering people went there to have fun. From the outside, the building – with THE PLATINUM CLUB written in silver script on a black awning – looked like a big black box. No windows. Really ugly.

But when I followed her inside, it was spectacular as a really good dream. Everything was glass and mirrors. The walls were painted silver. The carpet was gold. Whoever owned this place – they had to be rich!

And everyone was so nice to me. The woman at the cash register with the long red fingernails. 'Is that your daughter?' she asked my mom. 'She's so cute!' The woman selling cigars and cigarettes. She leaned on a glass case that curved around her like a horseshoe. Her metal bracelets clanked against the surface. The cigars looked like Grandma's pastels lined up so neatly in the box, except of course they were all brown. That woman didn't say anything, just smiled. There was something about her honey blond hair – the way she got it to flip up around her shoulders – it made me want to keep looking at her.

It was frustrating, though, because my mother was rushing me through, and my head was doing the twist trying to take it all in. We passed an Asian woman who was sitting in a closet behind a half door that reached her cleavage. What did she do? 'Hi, honey,' she said, and laughed. What was so funny? Her incredibly plump lips were dark red and she had acne scars on her cheek.

'Let's go.' Coco urged me on. 'I've gotta get changed.'

I glanced to my left through a doorway as my mom pulled my hand. It seemed to be a restaurant with white tablecloths and gold drapes. To the right was a white neon sign with fancy white script that said REST-ROOMS. The sign was so inviting, it seemed like there had to be something extra special happening in there, not just peeing. Straight ahead were two men in black tuxedos. They didn't smile. We went past them through double doors under white neon script that said SHOWROOM. Once inside, I tripped on a step down that had little lights on the edge so you wouldn't trip.

It was even darker in there. Front and center was a squarish stage. A woman with very tan skin and long blond hair danced to a Michael Jackson song. She wore a sheer white, fur-collared robe that went just past her hips, and sheer white stockings that went up to her thighs with two big bows on the top. Silver stilettos. Dress-up stuff like my mom had loads of at home. My eye was pulled by another neon sign. It said CHAMPAGNE LOUNGE. A tipsy neon glass was next to it. No one was sitting at the tables and chairs over there. On the other side of the room was a bar. Four or five pretty women wearing long evening gowns sat on high chairs, their legs crossed under tall round tables. They were smoking and looking very serious and glum. In front of the bar area was a cushiony bench with more pretty women sitting all in a row. They looked bored too. In their evening gowns. Beautiful. Waiting.

A couple more men in black tuxedos stood in the room. I felt their eyes on me. 'Who are they?' I asked my mom.

'Bouncers. Touch and bust.'

'What?'

'If anyone makes trouble, they get rid of 'em.'

Well, they didn't have to worry about me. I was not going to make trouble.

Only about four male customers were in there. They sat in comfy leather chairs next to low-to-the-ground, shiny-top tables, drinking and staring at the woman dancing. I wondered why the men were separate from the women, and why there were so many more women than men.

The room seemed vast, as if it went on forever, maybe because it was so empty. There was a row of chairs around the stage, and another area behind that, and then another area in the back, in the shadows, though I didn't know why anyone would want to sit so far away from the stage. Not one person was sitting near where that woman was dancing, and I felt bad for her having to perform for so few people. 'Why is it so empty?' Was business bad? Would Mom lose her job?

'It's early,' she said. 'Come on.'

I tried to catch a last glimpse of the dancer. She must've taken her little robe off, because now she was just wearing a G-string and her breasts were there for all to see. They weren't so big as my mom's. I myself had nothing up top and was not even quite registering the thought that breasts would happen to me. This woman's were so tanned, and she had these delicate, pink little nipples. Not like my mom, who was light-skinned but had darker nipples.

Back in the dressing room, at least ten more dancers were getting ready to perform. 'Look at your baby,' one of the women said. 'She's so cute!'

'She looks just like you!' another one said.

'She's learning young,' said another. That made them laugh. Which really made me mad. Were they laughing at me? Suddenly I wished I was home watching TV. It was so bright with all those bulbs around the mirror, and loud with all their yakking. Makeup everywhere. Vast amounts of pencils and lipsticks and pots of gels and little plastic cases that clicked shut and boxes of pink tissues and white cotton balls and Q-tips and tubes in piles, as if they'd washed up on a beach after a huge storm.

All the women were in different stages of being undressed or wearing full-length evening gowns and it seemed to me like this was the place where everything was happening, this was where the fun was. Even though music was blaring in the showroom out there, it was louder in here because of all the chatter.

My mom sat me down in the corner and got undressed. I'd seen her naked a zillion times. She liked to walk around the apartment without clothes. But other women's naked bodies had been a mystery. I was fascinated by how each one of them was different. And my eyes kept pulling in all the variations. So I gaped. And no one seemed to mind, either. No one said 'Stop staring.' It was nice to get to look at where you didn't usually get to look.

The evening became a blur of body parts. Straight hips, round hips, big breasts, small. Light nipples, dark nipples. Long waists and short ones. Calves and thighs made smooth with sheer stockings. G-strings in every color pulled up around hips like huge stretchy rubber bands. That little piece of cloth covering the little triangle area up front so neatly. The string disappearing back into the butt. Didn't that bother them? Probably not as much as those shoes. I heard complaints about those all night. Groans of relief when they slipped them off. Stretch the toes. Rub the soles. One black woman, one Asian woman, many blondes. At first, I couldn't tell all the blondes apart. Some had foreign accents. They were all nice to me.

It became like a game, back in that dressing room, to see the next body undressed, and the next, and the next. As if someone was constantly removing a blindfold. Lo and behold, the world was filled with pretty women's bodies. Each one a little different. But in the end, the same too.

My mom pulled a long, slinky pink and gold glittery halter-top dress out of her bag. It was quite thin and stretchy, and she stepped into it easily – pulled the top up around her neck, and boom, she was in. I looked down at what I was wearing. It was my favorite dress. Short-sleeved, navy blue with a row of white daisies across the front. Suddenly it seemed very plain.

When it was my mom's turn to go out and dance, she told me to stay there. She looked so beautiful, with her hair all swept up. She was prettier than the finalists on the Miss America pageant! 'I want to go with you.'

'You can't.'

'I want to see!'

'Sit,' she told me, as if I was a dog in training. 'And stay put.'

She went out to the front. And I sat there in the corner and listened in on the women.

'His breath smelled like vomit. What a jerk.'

'At least he wanted you. I'm not making anything out there!'

My mom came in every once in a while to redo her makeup. I asked her again, 'Can't I go out there?'

I saw the blonde with the long curly hair exchange glances with my mom. Was she laughing at me?

'No.'

'Why not?'

'You just can't.'

'I want to see the dancing!' Plus lots of these women smoked and the air was giving me a headache.

'No, and don't argue. Why don't you go to sleep? It's late.'

There was a little cot, but there were three women sitting on it smoking. They started to move over for me.

'I don't want to sleep.'

'Suit yourself.'

My mom went back out. One of the other blondes motioned for me to move to the cot. 'Come on, hon. You might as well make yourself comfortable.'

She patted the spot next to her and I moved to it. I sat upright and watched the women coming and going, putting on makeup, cussing and swearing, laughing at the jerks, commenting on some regular who'd just arrived. 'He's asking for you, Angel.' Angel was the one black woman. 'He wants you to wear your red dress.'

'He loves that damn dress.'

Angel rubbed baby oil all over her legs and chest before putting it on.

I realized those women who were sitting out there before, in the evening gowns, were there to sit with the men. To keep the men company. The men just hadn't arrived yet.

'He only paid me fifty bucks. I wasted an hour on him, listened to him complain about his wife for one fucking hour, and the jerk gives me fifty bucks! No wonder his wife won't have sex with him.'

Did men pay their wives to have sex? Then someone should tell him to pay her more.

Every time someone left the dressing room, I caught a look into the other room. Was that a naked body? On that man's lap? His clothes were on. He wasn't even touching her. So what was she doing? Was that allowed out in public? Was that my mom? No. She wouldn't do that. Only the others must be doing that. It was so frustrating. I couldn't get a good look. But I could tell it was getting more crowded out there. And as it got more crowded out there, fewer women were hanging out in the dressing room. Now the party was out there and I was stuck in the back. But I didn't dare venture out. At some point, my head started to get heavy. I lay down on the cot. Still, I tried to keep my eyes open, I didn't want to miss anything, and the dancers were still coming in and out to fix their makeup, have a smoke. Without really meaning to, I fell asleep.

My mom took me back to the apartment sometime during the night, so when I woke up in the morning, I found myself in my own bed. But all the sights and sounds were still spinning in my head. Belly buttons on flat stomachs. Nipples like bull's-eyes. That tipsy neon champagne glass. The empty seats that had not stayed empty.

I went to Coco. In those days, when she didn't stay in Queens, she slept in the living room on a fold-out sofa. She liked to sleep late; I knew that well. Always had to be quiet, and if I wanted to watch TV, I did it in Grandma's bedroom, eating cereal on Grandma's bed. Coco usually got up at one or two or even three in the afternoon. But this morning, I couldn't wait.

'Mom?'

'I'm sleeping.'

'Mom?'

'What, for god's sake?'

'Are you taking me to work with you tonight?'

'I'm trying to sleep!'

'Because I don't want to go.'

She didn't respond.

'When is Grandma getting back?'

I didn't like how some of the women laughed at me. I didn't like how they all knew stuff I didn't, but no one was about to explain anything. I didn't like it at all.

Coco's eyes were closed. 'Mom?'

'We'll see,' she said.

I wasn't sure if she didn't know when Grandma was coming back, or if I was going with her again. 'We'll see what?'

'Ginger!' Now she was angry. 'Go away!'

She put a pillow over her head. I went back out into the living room. One thing was for sure. If she made me go again, I was gonna find out exactly what she was doing out there in that room in the front.

But she didn't take me again. And I was relieved. I didn't really want to know.

chapter fourteen

i prepared myself for the smell before opening the closet. Impossible to identify, but you could bottle it and sell it as a perfume: *Leah*.

The walk-in was absolutely packed with stuff. Mind-boggling. Would Emma want any of it? The Ralph Lauren skirt suits. The Polo sweaters in assorted colors, all with that pretentious horse insignia. The Lacostes with the annoying alligators. What about the dresses? Donna Karan, Yves Saint Laurent, Oscar de la Renta. The collection was worth a small fortune. In the world of Leah's closet, Ann Taylor and Banana Republic – two more stores I never went to – were the downscale brands.

Her big weakness was shopping at Barneys. Once she'd taken me to the restaurant there. I had the best calamari in my life. Deep-fried with a light breading and just the right taste of lemon. Really good. The clothes? I'd rather hit a thrift store in the village. Urban Outfitters if I feel like being scalped. Why spend thirty dollars on a T-shirt just because it had some cute slogan on the chest? Once Coco got a T-shirt there with an orange half right on each boob, and underneath it said SQUEEZE ME. I imagined perverted men on the street grabbing my breasts. It made Coco laugh, though.

It seemed wrong to be giving away Leah's expensive clothes. One day, Emma might want some of this. Should I tell my father to put it all into storage so she could look at it later? He wasn't around to ask. Seemed like he was hardly ever home, and poor Emma had to hang out by herself. There was a housekeeper who straightened up and bought groceries, but she was only there sporadically and didn't seem very friendly. No wonder my father had asked me to come around. It was time to make contact.

Emma was in her room with the door shut and the new Coldplay album blasting. I'd ask her if she wanted to look through some of this stuff with me. Truth was, I wouldn't mind the company. This wasn't exactly cheering me up.

I knocked on the door. 'Emma?'

No answer.

'Emma!'

'What?'

'Can you come out here a sec?'

'I'm busy!'

'I just want to ask you something . . . !'

She turned the music up.

I started folding and stacking. Undoubtedly some broke but ambitious newcomer to the city would pounce on this stuff when she saw it hanging on a rack at the Salvation Army. Or maybe a homeless woman. I'd love to see someone sitting on the sidewalk begging in the eggplant Eileen Fisher full-length linen skirt.

My father had told me I could take something. Leah would've encouraged it. That day at Barneys, she'd tried to get me to buy a blue-jean jacket. Maybe she figured since it was blue jeans, I might go for it. There was leather on the collar and the cuffs. It cost eight hundred dollars. That was almost my rent for the month. It was really cute. But I couldn't. I just couldn't.

But maybe . . . if I found something basic among these things . . . something I'd get some use out of. It would be nice to have something of Leah's. I held up a Tommy Hilfiger white cashmere V-neck top. Would I use it? Without dripping food on it? White clothes scared me. Into the garbage bag.

I opened a drawer built into the wall. A jumble of belts. An orgy of leather, alligator skin, and metal chains. I got a Hefty bag and dumped them all in at once in a clump. Should I start on the shoes? There had to be a hundred pairs. How many pumps did a person need? Most of them looked unworn, and they all looked almost exactly alike.

I sat down on the edge of the bed. All these clothes! I just didn't get it. Somehow I had missed the boat. The boat that all women board in eager droves without thinking twice. Clothes, makeup, shoes, accessories. I just couldn't get interested. Didn't want to do myself up like that. What was wrong with me?

I got back up and tried to stick my foot into one of Leah's black pumps. Ferragamos. It had a two-inch heel, a rounded toe, and a little gold buckle on the top. Coco would scoff and call them frumpy, but they were all about good taste and respectability. Leah's feet were smaller than mine, though, so I couldn't even get my toes past the halfway point. When I was younger, my height and my big feet sometimes made me feel clunky. I'd get into funks that my body was failing me. I was female, yet my body refused to be feminine.

But if I was a female, wasn't I *defining* what was feminine – not the other way around? Did the differences between the sexes have to be all exaggerated? That's why I didn't get why people needed to lay it on so thick with all these differences in their clothes. Because when you have a man and a woman undressed next to each other, you aren't exactly going to mistake one for the other. So what was the big deal about making them appear so different? As if you'd forget once you're undressed which one was which. As if you'd need to go, oh, yeah, you were wearing those six-inch heels, so you must be the woman.

I did like being different from men. It did make me feel special. I did like the fact that my body was different from a man's body. And that there are two sexes, not one. Two that fit together. Exactly.

I looked at my father's closet door. The forbidden door. Dare I open it? Yes. It was dark inside. I pulled the chain for an overhead light. A row of dark suit jackets hung on wood hangers. Below that were neatly folded slacks. Below that was a chrome shoe rack holding almost identical leather shoes with those things inside that help them keep their shape. Up above was a high shelf with tan canvas storage boxes going up to the ceiling. And the smell. Tweed. Leather. Shoe polish. It brought tears to my eyes. What would it be like living with a man? I really wanted to know. It would've been so fun to live with Ian. Just to know there was a guy to come home to, there for me, and me only.

I returned to Leah's closet. Opened up a fresh garbage bag. I couldn't bring myself to get rid of the shoes quite yet. So I pulled some silk sweaters with matching tops off their hangers and stuffed them in the bag. I just needed to find one man who didn't expect me to have all this stuff. A man who would be attracted to me just the way I was. Was that asking for too much? Certainly, if I ever wanted to live in lavishness like this, I would need to dress better. No wealthy man would want me the way I was.

I grabbed some tailored jackets and took them off their hangers. Who cared. I couldn't be bothered with having all this. I just wanted someone who would treat me nice. Who would cherish me.

I thought of Tom's gentle touch when he was putting on the Band-Aid and was overcome with a sudden urge to bake cupcakes. Vanilla cupcakes with vanilla frosting. I went to see what they had in the cupboard.

The cupboard was bare!

No vanilla. No confectioners' sugar. No flour.

I went to Emma's door and yelled above the music. 'I'm going to the grocery store! But I'm going to be back!' For some reason, I really wanted her to know that. As if she would feel like I'd abandoned her if I just left. As if she cared whether I was there or not.

No answer for a moment. Then a stilted 'Fine.'

I walked over to Third Avenue, found a Food Emporium and bought all my baking supplies. At the last second, I grabbed a little glass container of rainbow sprinkles.

When I got back, Emma was, presumably, still in her room, but there was no music playing. I knocked. 'Emma?'

After a moment, with impatience: 'What?'

'Do you want to help me bake some cupcakes?'

After a moment, with grouchiness: 'No.'

I'd gotten disposable foil cupcake pans since there were no baking tins. I found a handheld mixer in the pantry and two bowls in the cabinet next to the stove. Measuring spoons, measuring cup, wooden spoon. I was all set.

I measured all the dry ingredients into one bowl. Then I microwaved the butter just enough to soften it. Added some vanilla. Started blending away. It was hypnotic. The buzzing sound. The circular motion to incorporate everything together. Round and round and round. It reminded me of my vibrator. Swirls of the yellow batter swelled up like plump rolls of fat falling into each other. Swirling, I knew, was the secret. Circles and swirls . . . around the clitoris. Teasing it. Coming close. Staying away. Circumnavigating. The direct approach just didn't work. There had to be that element of evasiveness. Once you knew for sure you had it coming . . . well . . . then it was over.

Finally the batter was beautifully smooth and silky. I tasted it. Yum. The best taste.

Emma was still in her room. Now Jessica Simpson was playing. Would she like to lick the bowl, or would she think she was too old for that? I didn't feel like being rejected again, but on the other hand, what was one more rebuff? I went to her door. 'Would you like to lick the bowl?'

After a moment: 'No. Thanks.'

Well. At least there was a 'thanks.' That was progress.

As I washed up the bowls, I wondered who was going to eat these. I could take some home, but Coco wouldn't touch the carbs and I didn't want to give them to Jack, who didn't deserve them, though if I got him fat maybe my mom wouldn't be able to stand having sex with him anymore.

Maybe my father would come home, and we could eat one while sitting at the kitchen table across from each other.

But I didn't really want that. It would ruin the cupcakes.

I went to the living room and stretched out on the sofa. The warm, sweet smell filled the apartment. Ummm. I had to make sure I didn't doze off, or they'd burn.

Time to make the frosting, anyway.

I used a very simple recipe that was just butter, vanilla, and confectioners' sugar. Just as I was done mixing, Emma emerged. She stood at the door to the kitchen, as if it wasn't hers. She was wearing a T-shirt that said LABEL WHORE. Her mother's daughter.

'You want to help me frost?'

'Okay.'

At least she didn't hate me enough to turn down the fun of frosting.

'Here's a knife. Let's do it at the table.'

We sat down across from each other and started spreading. It was just the right texture. Not so soft it wouldn't hold its shape, but not so stiff it would tear the cake. This was our most communal moment ever. I didn't want to ruin it, so I stayed quiet.

She licked her finger. 'Mmmm.'

I licked mine. 'Mmmm.'

I was tempted to say something about our father. Ask her what it was like to live with him. Say something about how he was hardly ever around. Mention how I knew what it was like to feel shut out by him. But I made myself stay quiet. For one thing, I sensed that I wanted to go there more because I'd get pleasure out of putting him down, not so much because I thought it would help her feel better. For another thing, she might not take to me being critical of the guy. She might just get defensive, and then we'd be at odds. Had to make sure I didn't lay my trips on her.

'So,' she said, 'there's this boy . . .'

I stayed quiet, hoping she'd continue.

'In my class . . .'

'Yeah?'

'I hate him.'

'Why?'

'He's always saying mean things to me.'

'Like?'

'Like saying I look like Kelly Osbourne.'

She did look vaguely like Kelly Osbourne. But skinny. 'You don't look like Kelly Osbourne.'

'He says I do.'

'If you do, you look like a skinny version. And she does have very pretty features. So maybe it's his way of complimenting you. You know. Boys are idiots. They can't say what they feel.'

'I don't think so.'

We frosted some more. I thought of Tom. How he'd been so open about his love and affection for his mom – without being too disgusting about it. Maybe not all boys were idiots. Then she said, 'This other boy . . . Eugene . . . I think he looks like Nick Lachey.'

'He's cute.'

'Yeah.' She dipped her knife in the bowl and slopped out a big glob. 'Whoops. Too much.' She put some back. 'So anyway, I don't know.' She sighed.

'You like him?'

'He's okay.'

That had to mean she was madly in love.

'Is he nice to you?'

'He doesn't know I'm alive.'

'So . . . are you going to do anything about it?'

'About what?'

'Why don't you bring him a cupcake?'

'It'll probably get mushed when I take it to school.'

'He won't care. Shall we put some sprinkles on top?'

'Do we have some?'

'Yep.' I pulled the little bottle out of the grocery bag.

'Oh, can I do it?'

'Sure.'

I let her shake them out all over the tops. When she was done, we admired them. It was like they were smiling up at us. How could you not feel cheered up? 'They're beautiful,' she said.

'Shall we?' I asked.

'Definitely.'

Emma and I each picked a cupcake, took simultaneous bites, swallowed in unison, and smiled at each other. 'They taste,' I said, 'as good as they look.'

'All I need is a nice, tall cold glass of milk.'

'Coming right up.'

As I went to the refrigerator, I felt a warm glow inside. We were bonding! She was accepting me! She was actually going to let me be there for her! It felt so good in a nice, wholesome, deep-down-in-your-gut way. I poured us each a tall glass. This had to be how people in helping professions felt all the time. Nurses. Social workers. Even strippers. There was no denying they made men feel quite happy to be alive, even if it was a very temporary and superficial kind of happy. I knew that had always given my mom a deep sense of satisfaction in her work. I brought the two glasses of milk to the table. That deep satisfaction feeling was part of the reason I liked to make pastries. But even that had its downside, considering they're unhealthy. Jean Paul had us adding butter and cream and salt to our food like there was no tomorrow. I picked up my cupcake. If people realized how lethal the ingredients were, they'd never indulge in restaurant food again. I took another lovely bite.

chapter fifteen

'*m*ake sure your boning knife is nice and sharp. Cut the flap of skin between the thigh and the body. And hold one leg in each hand.' Jean Paul demonstrated the proper way to bone a chicken. We had our own birds, and followed his lead. 'Bend the leg backwards until you hear the bone pop out of the socket.'

I've heard that butchers are the happiest people, and I could understand why. Carving through the flesh. Knife against bone. Finding just the right spot between the joints where the pieces gave in. Pop those legs off.

'Now we will do the breast. Place the bird on its back, breasts facing you.'

Ralph and I exchanged glances. This was sexy in an S and M sort of way. Dividing that soft, cold little chicken body up into neat little pieces.

'Slice through the skin and the meat just to the side of the breastbone. Using short, sharp strokes, cut close to the bone, using your fingers to pull the flesh away from the carcass . . .'

After we'd massacred our chickens, Jean Paul took aside most of the other students to give them a chance to make chicken picatta. He told me to slice carrots. Very challenging. As I got out my cleaver, I watched Tom and Tara stand next to each other pounding breasts. He was laughing about something she'd said. What was going on here? This wasn't right. Tom laughing with Tara. Me stuck with a crate of carrots. I wasn't sure what to do. If Tom was attracted to her, no way he could be attracted to me. Tara and I were different as sugar and pepper. Nothing I could do about that. Losing battle.

And Jean Paul? Why was he still so down on me? Seemed like he was purposely keeping me from the more creative projects and relegating me to grunt work. Was it because of my scholarship? Was that what was going on? If he really knew me, he'd realize I had lots of potential. I had to make him see that.

At lunch, I went up to the school office. Robert Kingsley happened to be walking out just as I was walking in.

'Hi, Ginger.'

'Hi.' I had to accept the fact that the guy knew my name.

'How's your sister?'

'Good, thanks.' Also had to accept the fact that she was the one he was attracted to.

Jean Paul was talking to the secretary. I sat on a chair by her desk and waited while they quibbled over a huge order of produce that had failed to arrive that morning. Not a smart move on my part to attempt to speak to him when he was in a bad mood, but I was determined to make contact. Maybe he thought I'd come to this school impulsively. On a lark. He could have no idea that I already knew that this was going to be my life. If I could make him understand that . . .

But how could I, without sounding too sappy? It's not like I was about to go into anything too personal. It was more important that he didn't know anything too personal.

Finally, he was done talking with the secretary. I realized he was about to leave the room even though he knew I was sitting there waiting for him. I stood, but I didn't know what to call him. Chef? Jean Paul? Neither seemed right, so I didn't call him anything. 'Excuse me. Do you have a minute?' I trembled. 'I'd like to speak to you.'

He reluctantly turned towards me. 'Yes?'

'I just want you to know. I'm determined to do well. And this is what I really want to do. And I'm very eager to learn everything you have to teach. And I just . . . want you to know that.'

He shrugged. 'It's your money.'

The secretary, a chubby woman in a flower print dress who'd obviously been indulging in too many student lunches, was eavesdropping.

'Yes. And I'm paying tuition that is very high, even if I did get some scholarship money. Does that have something to do with the way you're treating me?'

'I know nothing about scholarships! I treat you the same as everyone else.'

'Do you?'

'Okay. You ask me? I will tell you, Ginger Levine. You may be able to learn zee craft of cooking. But will you ever have zee subtlety, zee finesse, zee *refinement* to perform zee *art* of cooking? Zat is zee question.' He looked at me with disdain and walked out of the room.

Refined. Yeah. My mother was not refined – I knew that. So maybe I wasn't refined either. Maybe I came off like she did and didn't realize it. I'd grown up with her, after all. Well, maybe I didn't want to be refined. Refined wasn't far off from uptight.

But could I make refined pastries? Pastries that looked refined?

The secretary took pity on me. 'Don't take it personally. He enjoys torturing his students.'

'Thanks.' I frowned. 'Then I must be giving him a lot of pleasure.'

*i*t was the usual pandemonium at the bachelorette party where my mom was doing her 'How to Have Sex Like a Pro' class. We were now into October, but Sunny was still in Greece, so I was still helping sell vibrators. The party was being held in the huge loft of the bride-to-be's best friend, who'd spotted Coco's ad in *Time Out*. About twenty women were yakking and giggling and barely able to keep their mouths shut while they waited for Coco to do her spiel and I really wished I'd brought my earplugs.

When you get a room full of women talking about sex toys, I've found they inevitably become hysterically giddy and loud. Put them in front of some Chippendale's dancers, they turn into hyenas on speed. I'm not saying men don't get rowdy, like at topless mud-wrestling bars, especially if they're drunk frat boy types out to prove what 'men' they really are. (And, in the process, show what boys they really are.) But in general, you look at male strip club clientele: They're fairly quiet. Much more likely to be looking at the women in a kind of dumbstruck awe than screaming their brains out.

We were all set up and ready to begin. Last-minute guests were still arriving. The partyers were all in a tizzy at the sight of the rainbow cavalcade of penile representations displayed on the coffee table in the middle of the room.

'Oh, my god!'

'Look at that one!'

'It's so big!'

'It's so intimidating!'

'I better have a drink.'

There was wine and cheese on a sideboard, but everyone was so riveted by the display barely a cracker was crunched.

'How do you pick one?' was the inevitable question from a typically overwhelmed customer.

'Why are there so many kinds?' asked another.

'We'll get to that, don't worry!' Coco said, trying to calm everyone down. 'We'll go over everything.'

Since the room was crowded, I'd stationed myself in a small kitchen where the wall had been cut away to make a pass-through. I sat on a stool semiremoved from the action and watched, ready to take the money at the end. The host's black cat was trying to knock over the silicone dildos, which could've caused a disastrous domino effect. I made eye contact with Coco and signaled she'd better do something about it, because I wasn't about to set everything up again with everyone sitting there watching. 'Can someone get the cat?' she asked. 'Thanks. Those are a little big for her. Ouch. Okay. Maybe we should start. First, I want to give you all a little basic sex ed. I'm assuming everyone knows where her clitoris is. Does everyone know what it's attached to?'

A latecomer was ringing the doorbell. I almost went to let her in, but the woman who was hosting got up. I heard her leading the woman in and offering her a glass of wine.

'Are you kidding? I want to be sober for this!'

The voice sounded familiar. I craned my neck through the pass-through to see. As the late person came into view, my stomach almost collapsed into my lower intestine. It was Tara. Tara Glass! I felt like Humphrey Bogart must've felt when Ingrid Bergman walked into his bar. 'Of all the vibrator parties in the world . . .' I wanted to disappear into thin air. But Coco needed me. I was trapped.

'The clitoris has thousands and thousands of nerve endings . . .'

Tara had so far not taken a look around the room. She was too busy settling in and listening to the lecture. I moved my stool back and tried to make myself small, but apart from actually sitting down on the floor to literally hide myself there was nothing much I could do. It was futile anyway, since she would see me at the end. Unless I just fled and left Coco to deal with everything herself.

'Except for pleasure, the clitoris has no function whatsoever. Nothing else on the human body is like that. So it's all about you having fun.'

Of course, Coco the saleswoman didn't really care if they were enjoying their bodies. She just wanted them to buy the equipment after her spiel was over. Which irked me. I mean, did they really need to *buy* something in order to enjoy their bodies? Did they really need the appliances? Sometimes I suspected mine was taking the place of relating to a real live guy. Like Tom. I'd been shy around him after our day in the park, and he'd been shy with me too. But instead of suggesting we get together, I expressed my affections to my vibrator – while thinking about him – because it was easier. Less risky. Your vibrator never rejects you.

Meanwhile, I'd noticed Tara becoming more and more chummy with him. I had to do something. Maybe ask him to visit the restaurant supply store, like we'd talked about.

'Okay, the G-spot you've all heard so much about.'

I saw Tara look around quickly, but she almost immediately focused back on my mom. Still didn't see me.

'How many of you know where your G-spot is?' Only a few raised their hands. (FYI, Tara was not one of them.) 'Your G-spot has a million nerve endings. How, you may ask, can women stand giving birth if there are all these nerve endings there? Well, it's on the bottom third. The top two thirds don't have nerve endings, so that's how you can have a baby without dying of pain. It must be true, because, as my daughter back there will tell you, I have a very low pain threshold.'

Coco nodded towards me. Everyone looked. No way to hide! Sure enough, Tara was now looking at me with her jaw hanging open.

'If you had nerve endings up there,' Coco concluded, 'you would probably die.'

Tara mouthed the words, 'That's your mom?'

'So once you know where it is, you can get your guy in the right position to get to it. His penis can go in different directions inside of you, so it's getting it to go the right way.'

I gave Tara a fake smile without showing any teeth, then stared at Coco as if she was lecturing on the threat of global warming.

'So if you look at dogs, and the way doggie style works, you'll see that's the best way your guy can make contact with your G-spot. That's not uncomfortable for the female dog, that's hitting the spot. So find it for yourself, figure out your body, then you can maneuver him to go the right way. He'll be glad because you're happy, and he'll think it's because he's such a good lay!'

Everyone laughed.

Coco started demonstrating some of the different novelty items, like the waterproof vibrating glove with massagers on each finger. 'Wear this, ladies, you'll have him in the palm of your hand.'

The small lipstick-shaped vibrator.

'So you can get through customs at the airport!'

The Allstar. A hefty vibe inspired, perhaps, by a basketball player? Coco held the thing with its thick shaft for penetration up to her chest like it was an Oscar. 'I want to thank the academy!'

She was cracking them up.

The Hitachi Magic Wand. 'These have been around for decades. They last decades. And lots of women love the head on this one. It's sort of like a tennis ball.' She waved it like a racket. 'Tennis, anyone?'

Tara was laughing louder than anyone.

'These edible massage creams . . .' Coco picked one up, unscrewed the top, passed it around. 'They have a great texture. Delicious. Vanilla cream, raspberry cream, and cool mint, which has a tingle . . . You each get a sample in your goody bag, by the way. . . .'

'Is it safe?' someone asked. 'Because then it gets inside you.'

'Sure, and it's kosher, too, so your rabbi won't have a problem.'

More laughter.

'I have a question.' It was the bride-to-be. 'If the clitoris is all about pleasure, why does it seem like men are the ones who want sex all the time?'

All heads turned to Coco. 'Men have an easier time *accessing* it. Women have too much bullshit getting in the way. We worry about making him happy. We worry about taking too long. Is he bored? Is it that time of the month? Will he be too disgusted at the sight of my period? Get over it! Guys love that stuff!'

My mother, the sex therapist. Since she'd been practically 'born' having orgasms (claimed she could remember masturbating when she was three) she had little sympathy or even comprehension for women who couldn't. For her, sex didn't seem to be connected to emotions. She was like a guy that way. 'Anyway,' she went on, 'that's why things like the creams are important, because it gets the mind to relax.' She segued into the task at hand, selling the products. 'So like, here. This is great. The weekender kit.' She held up a little carrying case that had all sorts of little samples nestled in it. 'I love this. You plan a little trip to get away from it all. Or a honeymoon?' She nodded at the bride. 'You take this with you. It's so cute and fun. I love samples, don't you? A little of everything. It's all edible too. Pleasure balm. Flavored condoms. Flavored lube. Massage oils . . .'

Snake oil, I thought. Because if the relationship was a mess, no amount of goop was gonna fix it. But she was a good saleswoman – that was for sure.

'So. Now. The vibrators!'

Ah yes. The main event. Everyone sat up a little straighter. She launched into her 'lecture' that I'd actually helped her put together. 'The first vibrators were manufactured at the turn of the century when . . . ta da . . . electricity was invented! So you all have Thomas Edison to thank. After the light bulb, they were one of the first appliances. Why? Because they were used by doctors to treat hysteria. In those days, women weren't supposed to enjoy sex or have orgasms, so it's no wonder they were all hysterical. They would go to their doctors for a weekly appointment, and she'd lie down and he'd give her a hand job. Not bad, huh? So all these doctors were really happy when vibrators were invented. It made their jobs a helluva lot easier!

'Try them out, ladies. Pass them around. Turn them on. Let them vibrate on your fingers. Some are more intense, some are less. This one has a remote. Twelve-foot range. You can sit on the couch watching TV with your boyfriend and let him turn it on and off . . .'

Everyone was talking at once as they picked up the vibrators, played with them, passed them around.

'I like the glove.'

'Maybe for my sister . . .'

'The lipstick one is so cute.'

'No one would even know . . .'

'Teacher,' someone said, 'we have a question. Can you explain this?'

The woman had picked up the Rabbit. The most intimidating one of all.

'Okay. Yes. That, ladies, is the king of the dual-action vibrators! It's known as the Rabbit because of that little guy on the side with the bunny ears. Those ears tickle your clit. They feel like two tiny little tongues darting around. Then you have the twirling shaft for penetration. And another special feature is that belt of pearls you see around the shaft. You see, when it rotates, they tumble around in there, and it adds stimulation to the lips of your vagina so you're getting it three ways! This is really the closest you're gonna get to the real thing. Actually, this is better than the real thing. But some people find it overwhelming, especially if you're just starting out. That's usually something people work up to.'

'Once you've mastered that,' someone said to the bride, 'you won't need your husband!'

Everyone cracked up.

That's when Tara raised her hand. 'Do you think you really need any of this if you're involved in a good relationship?'

Coco looked at her like she was speaking Swahili. 'Excuse me?'

'You know. If two people really love each other. It's just so . . . mechanical. What about, you know, love, and romance?'

'Romance,' Coco said, 'is what men use to get you to go to bed with them.'

'That's rather bitter,' Tara said. 'Don't you think?'

I listened with interest.

'Women use it too,' Coco said with disdain. 'Because they feel guilty about sex. If they're "in love," then it's okay.'

I'd never heard Coco say she was in love with a man.

'So you think love and commitment are totally separate from sex?'

'Hey, listen, if you need that to help you have sex with a guy, fine. But you can have sex without it. You can have sex without *him*! Men are really quite expendable, and look at all these choices you have!'

'But don't you think it's more meaningful to do it with an actual person? Rather than one of these appliances?'

I liked it that Tara was being provocative instead of eating everything up. But I also wanted Coco to chew her up and spit her out on the bride's parquet floor.

'Why does it have to be either/or?' Coco said. 'These are great to use *with* your guy. Let him stimulate you with it. Or use it in front of him. Or do it on him. They *love* watching you do yourself. And it takes the pressure off him if you've already gone a few rounds.'

Coco grinned. I smirked. Tara was silenced.

'I couldn't,' said one woman. 'In front of him? No way.'

'Okay, you know what?' Coco said. 'You have to get over that.'

I had to smile to myself – I knew Coco would get her for that.

'I can't,' she said, looking miffed. 'It would be too embarrassing!'

'Let me tell you girls, because I know how it is from being on the other side.'

Uh-oh. Please, I was thinking, please don't go there . . .

'I worked for years as a stripper. And let me tell you. Women are out of touch with what their men want!'

Damn. Okay. Now Tara was going to know everything. By tomorrow, this would be all over the school. The crowd got very quiet. Tara stared at my mother with her eyebrows raised. Oh yes, she was all ready to be disapproving. They all waited with bated breath for her to go on. And go on she did. 'You wanna know why men cheat?' This was one of her favorite rants. 'Because women are all obsessed with how they *feel*. They always want to analyze it, and talk about it. Men don't want to talk about *feelings*, okay?'

She said the word 'feelings' with this really snide voice.

'They're sick of hearing about how you *feel*. And they don't want to hear about what you got at the mall that day either.' There were some glances exchanged and giggles of recognition. 'Talk about your *feelings* and your shopping with your girlfriends, okay? Not him. He just wants your pussy. That's right. That's what he's interested in. Unless he's gay. And whether he's gay or not, all he wants is someone to suck on his dick. That . . . right there . . . is the secret to men, ladies. It's simple!'

Now Tara had an evil grin. She had a whole arsenal to use against me. *Guess what*, I could hear her in the locker room. *Ginger's mother is a stripper. What a mouth on that ho!*

I would be snubbed right along with my mother. Even though, god knows, I would've loved to raise my hand and go, *Okay, so then Mom, if it's so simple, if men just want someone to suck them, then why have all your relationships with men sucked?*

'Don't be afraid,' Coco commanded the class, 'of trying new things!' She picked up the Rabbit and turned it on. It rotated like a slightly lopsided sausage on a skewer. The crowd hung on her every word. 'Don't judge him if he wants to do something you think is gross or disgusting or kinky. Don't get all hung up about it! You need variety to keep it fresh, right, ladies?'

I was almost mauled by the throng as they gathered around me to buy. I couldn't take their credit cards fast enough! They were asking me for advice, asking Coco, buying buying buying. I dreaded the moment when Tara would approach me. She waited until almost everyone else was gone. Was she going to taunt me immediately? Or wait until school so she could do it in front of everyone there.

She was holding the Rabbit. 'Look at this. Makes you go all mushy inside, doesn't it?'

'Cash or credit?'

'How absolutely amazing that your mother used to be a stripper. And now she sells vibrators!' Tara could barely contain her glee. 'Who would ever have guessed it?'

'Look, Tara. I know this is amusing for you. But I would really appreciate it if you would be discreet.'

'I'll bet.'

'And I'll be discreet about the vibrator you've chosen.'

'Oh,' she said, turning it on and off. 'I don't need one of these. I've got the real thing. Tom just took a job working at my father's restaurant. One nice thing about guys in their twenties. They don't need batteries!' She laughed, or should I say cackled, and handed the Rabbit back to me.

emma actually got up from the couch when I came in the door, and then (gasp) turned off the TV. I decided to play it as if I came to see her. As it happened, I had stopped at the grocery store on my way over and bought more baking supplies.

'How did Eugene like the cupcake?' I asked, taking the groceries to the kitchen. She followed me in.

'He ate it in like one bite. And then he didn't even thank me.'

'Typical.'

'I have a picture of him. Would you like to see?'

'Yeah!'

'It's in here.' She headed into her room.

I paused, unsure if she wanted me to go in there with her.

She turned and looked at me. 'Are you coming?'

Her room was a disaster area. Clothes all over the floor. Makeup and jewelry and belts and purses and knickknacks everywhere. Walls plastered with Britney and Justin and Ashton. Buried in all the chaos was a matching pink flower power theme on the blanket and curtains and rugs. Leah had ordered it all from Pottery Barn. The 'perfect room' for the 'perfect daughter.' Leah had been so happy to pick out the ultrafeminine design. 'This is why it's so fun to have a daughter,' she'd said.

Emma got Eugene's photo from her journal. The boy was skinny, holding a skateboard, wearing a baseball cap. 'He's cute.'

'I think he looks like Ashton Kutcher. Don't you?'

'Sort of. The hair-in-the-face part.'

'I love his eyes.' She carefully put it back in the journal, which she placed back in her desk. I thought of Ian. We hadn't spoken since I'd kept him from eating my leg of lamb. Maybe he was missing me, regretting the breakup, waiting for me to call. Maybe he wasn't thinking about me at all.

We went into the kitchen and made shortbread cookies using a special

old recipe I'd gotten from my grandmother. I toasted some sliced al-
monds on a baking sheet. Pulsed them with confectioners' sugar in a
food processor. Added the flour and some orange zest. Then I let Emma
cut up the cold butter into little pieces and we pulsed that in. The orange
almond scent was mouthwatering.

When it was in the oven, I thought of all those shoes that were still in
Leah's closet. Should I start on them? No. I had a better idea.

'Would you like me to help you organize your room?'

'You don't want to do that.'

'Why not?'

'Ugh. Daddy doesn't even let the cleaning woman go in. He says
it's a waste of her time. He even makes me do my own laundry. Doesn't
that suck?'

I didn't think it sucked, really, but I wasn't about to side with him in
front of her. 'Let's do it,' I said.

'Really? 'Cuz, I don't know, it's such a mess. I can't deal with it.'

I could tell she was pleased with the idea. 'I can deal with it. Come on.'

I began with the clothes on the floor. Sorting the clean things from the
dirty ones. Folding. Putting them away in the drawers or throwing them
in the hamper in her closet. The hamper had been empty because so
many clothes had been piled in front of the closet, it was impossible to
get to. This girl had a lot of clothes.

When the timer went off, Emma ran to the kitchen to check the
shortbread.

'Make sure they're golden brown around the edges,' I called after her.

Meanwhile, I checked under the bed to see if there were any more
clothes down there. And pulled out a wad of underwear. The crotches
were all stained with blood. Menstrual blood.

'They're done!' Emma called out from the kitchen.

'Take 'em out!' I called back. Was she just sloppy? Or was she in dire
need of supplies? Fathers couldn't deal with those things, could they? I
couldn't imagine going to Ben for a supply of sanitary napkins. Or did the
housekeeper take care of this? If so, she wasn't doing a very good job. At
least Coco had made everything very accessible. I remembered finding a
box when I was about five years old and unwrapping a bunch of them because I thought they were mysterious little presents. Once they were un-

wrapped, they were still pretty mysterious. When Coco found the mess I'd made with the little white papers all over the bathroom rug she was annoyed at first, but then she explained everything. She'd gotten me using tampons before I even wanted to. The idea of sticking those things up inside me made me feel like I was deflowering myself. But she pushed me, saying I could not possibly want to walk around with a hunk of paper between my legs. At first I'd resisted, but once I got used to it I could never go back.

Now I had to decide. Confront Emma? Or ignore it? Would it embarrass her? Or be a relief?

Emma had transferred all the cookies to a plate and poured two glasses of milk. We settled in at the table. I decided I couldn't pretend. She'd know they'd gotten into her hamper somehow. And, most likely, she needed me to interfere here, even if she was resistant to the idea.

'Emma,' I said, picking up a cookie but not actually bringing it to my mouth, 'I noticed you had some underwear under the bed.'

Her cheeks blushed scarlet and she looked down at the tabletop. 'Oh. Right . . .'

'I put them in the hamper.'

'Thanks.'

'So you're getting your period?'

'Yeah.'

'For how long?' I still held my cookie in my hand. My hand was perspiring.

'A few months.'

'So it started when Leah was in the hospital?'

She nodded and picked up a cookie and broke off a piece.

'Does your dad know?'

She shook her head.

'Are you going to tell him?'

She made a face like she'd just smelled something bad.

'You should tell him,' I said, breaking my own cookie in half but still not eating it. 'Don't you think?'

She shuddered.

'Do you want me to tell him?'

She shrugged.

I have to say, the idea of telling him was not so attractive. It wasn't like I was so close to him. But the guy had to know.

'You need some sanitary napkins.'

Saying it out loud made it sound so stupid. Sanitary. Like our blood was dirty. Full of germs. Jesus.

She threw her remaining piece of shortbread back on the plate.

'I'll go to the drugstore and get you some.'

She looked up at me. 'You would?'

'Sure.'

God, she looked relieved. I thought she was gonna cry. Or was it me?

'I'll go right now if you want.'

She nodded. 'Sure.' She said it casually, but there was an undertone of desperation. Maybe she was having a period right then. With toilet paper stuffed into her panties.

'Okay. I'll go right now.' I took a bite of my shortbread. It was good, but could've used some dressing up with some fruit or jam or ice cream, I thought – and stood up. 'Maybe you can start on cleaning off the top of your dresser while I'm gone. Do you think?'

'Okay.'

'Okay. I'll be right back.'

'Okay.' She stood up. I could see it was really hard for her to look me in the face. Her gaze was fixed on the floor when she said, 'Thanks, Ginger.'

'No problem.' I made an extra special effort to be really casual about it. And why not? It didn't have to be a big deal. It certainly never had been at home. Coco left her tampons sitting around everywhere. You could often find one in the jar by the phone where we kept the pens. 'I'll be right back,' I said.

'Okay.'

'Don't eat all the cookies!'

'I won't!'

I went to the Duane Reade a few blocks away and picked out the smallest size tampons, some regular napkins for overnight, and some minipads. As I stood in line at the cash register, I couldn't help but think how Emma had no idea what she was in for, and no mother to help her through it. Years of cramping, leaking, ill-timed periods that would start on the wrong day or be mysteriously late and sure, it's a wonderful thing to be fertile and of course I wanted to give her as much positive reinforcement as possible. But. However. On the other hand. Getting your period was a pain in the butt. And it was for this kind of stuff that a daughter needed a mother. All Emma had, at the moment, it would seem, was me . . . poor thing. I thought affectionately of Coco. She could be annoying and problematic, but there was no doubt, she was there for me. I handed the boxes to the cashier and made a silent promise that I would do my best to be there for Emma. Even if I couldn't possibly fill Leah's shoes.

chapter eighteen

i couldn't do anything right: spilled a saucepan of roux all over the stove, burned a tray of tart shells, even chopped my parsley wrong. 'She cuts like a girl, this one,' yelled Jean Paul. 'Chop chop chop. It will take you all night to get through the box. *Vite! Vite!* Time is money!'

I could chop as fast as anyone if not faster. Why didn't he yell at the assorted bums standing around doing nothing?

I sucked it in, finished off my parsley, and went into the walk-in to organize the produce. My new philosophy: stay busy, stay out of his sight, stay out of his mind.

The only good news, I reflected, as I rotated the strawberries, was that to my knowledge, Tara had not told anyone about Coco. Maybe she was actually taking pity on me. Why not? With Jean Paul dumping on me as usual and Tom working for her father and probably having sex with her, maybe she simply didn't see me as a threat.

I snuck myself a raspberry, but it was disappointingly tart. How likely was it that she and Tom were having sex? I'd really thought he liked me. But we hadn't spoken much since we took our walk together. Matter of fact, he'd pretty much been ignoring me since he'd started working at L'Etoile. I removed some moldy lemons from a cardboard box. God knows, I didn't look as good in my chef's outfit as Miss Cover Girl Chef. Tara never got food stains on her radiant white jacket. Tied her apron taut as a corset. Wore pants so tight in the ass you could see her butt-crack. I preferred to be able to lean over and breathe while I worked. Was this why I was languishing on the shelf? Waiting to be discovered by the discerning shopper not deceived by fancy packaging?

I gathered the pile of moldy lemons in my apron and took them out to the garbage.

'I was about to send out a search party for you.'

I turned around. My would-be rescuer was Tom. 'Oh,' I said casually, 'hi.'

'I thought maybe you'd turned into one of Chef Seigfried's ice sculptures.'

'Just straightening up a little, and staying out of Jean Paul's way.'

The garbage bin was totally full, so I went to the storage room to get a new liner and refrained from asking him why he'd been a little aloof lately or was it just my imagination?

Tom followed. 'That guy loves you,' he said.

'He really does,' I agreed.

He followed me back to the garbage. 'Let me help you.'

'That's okay, I've got it.' Feeling a little defensive about my kitchen skills, even if it was just garbage management. 'So I hear you're working at L'Etoile now,' I said, as I lifted the old bag of garbage out of the bin.

'Yeah. It's great. I'm learning a lot.'

'That's fantastic.'

While I tied up the bag, he put a new one in. Since the garbage bin provided such a romantic setting, why not go for it? 'So you remember how we talked about going to the restaurant supply store?'

'You still want to go?'

'I know you're really busy now.'

'I'm free on the weekend. I don't have to be in till three.'

'That sounds good.'

'Great.'

'So.' I nodded at the bag of garbage. 'I'm gonna take this out back.'

He nodded. I tried to look as graceful as I could because I knew he was watching me as I carried the bag, which weighed about as much as I did, to the freight elevator.

In the kitchen, Tara was sharpening her ten-inch chef's knife, glaring at me. Tom was wiping down the stove. Had she seen our tête-à-tête over the trash? Too bad. I took out my chef's knife and sharpened it too.

The only material object I might love more than stainless steel is chrome. Both make me happy. So smooth. So shiny. They have a way of seducing my eye. A promise that I'll find something in the reflection, something comforting and safe.

So, while other women might get excited by strolling down Fifth Avenue past Harry Winston and Tiffany's, I get excited going down to the Bowery to the best restaurant supply stores.

I loved the gleaming sauté pans not yet marred by burnt grease. The stacks of individual-sized tart shells. The glistening glass sugar pourers with chrome caps.

Tom was already there by the time I arrived. 'Look at the pancake dispenser,' he said. 'Makes one-half to three-ounce portions – dollar to king size.'

'That's so cute. And the pie cutter!' It had four blades fixed to a large ring, like a star. Just push it through the pie and *voilà*: eight slices.

'Cool. How about this?' He went to a huge glass-encased popcorn popper cart, made to look like the kind street vendors used around the turn of the century. 'They sell the red and white striped boxes too.'

'How about the fudge warmer? And the hot dog grill? Oh, look at these signs.' They had classics like NO SHIRT, NO SHOES, NO SERVICE.

'How about this one? He nodded at THIS IS A CLASS JOINT. ACT RESPECTABLE.

'Yeah.'

'If you could open any restaurant that you wanted,' he asked, 'what would it be?'

'A bakery café,' I said. 'On Main Street.'

'Main Street where?'

'Doesn't matter.'

'City? Suburb? Town?'

'Big enough so everyone doesn't know you. Small enough so lots of people do.'

'Do you know what it looks like inside?'

'Wood tables. Wood floor. Lots of light. Comfortable to sit in. Nice big windows up front so you could see people going by on the street.'

'Main Street.'

'Right. And a huge glass case up front with all my desserts, of course. Maybe there would be a counter up there too, where people could have a quick cup of coffee and chat with the waitress before heading back to the hardware store, or the five-and-dime . . . They still exist somewhere, don't they?'

'Ours went out of business a long time ago.'

'And we would have free newspapers on a rack. So people could come in and have their cake and stay as long as they wanted. But there would also be a big take-out business to keep us going financially.'

'Would you serve hot foods?'

'Limited menu,' I said, but then I added, to let him know if he wanted, he could go in on it with me, 'Or bistro food. I could go more elegant, more upscale. White tablecloths. Good wine list. What kind of restaurant would you want?'

'I don't want my own place.'

'No?'

'The business end doesn't interest me. I just want to work in the best restaurants in the city. Plan the menus, do the cooking, create new dishes.'

'So, you'd be happy if you worked your way up at L'Etoile.'

'Yeah.'

'You're on your way, then.'

'I heard the sauté guy is leaving. Mr. Glass said something about letting me train to take his place. That would be incredible, to learn all the sauces. Meanwhile, I'm happy on the grill.'

'You'll move up there,' I said. 'I'm sure of it.' Especially since Tara wanted to get in his pants. Or already had. I still couldn't figure out if her boast had anything to do with reality. I hadn't yet seen them actually touching.

At least it still seemed she hadn't told him about the bachelorette party or Coco. Or maybe she had, but he was too embarrassed to mention it.

'You seem to be one of Jean Paul's favorites,' I said.

'I'm sure he'll come to see that anyone who empties garbage cans with your dexterity has a great future in the kitchen.'

'Thanks.'

'Look, it's possible he's picking on you because you're a woman.'

'He doesn't pick on Tara. I don't even know why he teaches. He seems to hate it.'

'I think he gets into it, actually. In his own sadistic way . . .'

'Mmmmmm,' I said, noncommittal. I didn't want to complain anymore. I picked up a napkin dispenser. Rectangular, with chrome sides, like you see in diners.

'You should buy it,' Tom said.

'It's impossible to find the napkins that fit into it.'

'You could buy them in bulk from here, I bet.'

'Maybe it's silly to have restaurant supplies at home. The point is you get to have them when you're at a restaurant. That's why going out is an event. If the line blurs, it'll lose its appeal.'

'You think?'

My gaze lingered on the shiny metal. I thought of Coco letting men buy the chance to look at her almost naked body. A blurred line if I ever saw it, but she still enjoyed sex, and she'd been the one who was bought. I forced myself to continue down the aisle. Tom caught up with me. 'You shouldn't get down on yourself about Jean Paul. It's obvious you're one of the hardest workers in the class.'

'Right. I have to try harder than anyone else just to keep up.'

I paused in front of the mixers. They had all the different sizes displayed – like a family. The huge daddy-sized industrial Hobarts for really big jobs, the familiar mama-sized one like we had in school. And an array of KitchenAids in different colors, for the decked-out home.

'That's not true,' Tom said.

I'd always wanted a red one. Or a blue one. Or maybe stark naked chrome. It didn't matter anyway, since I could never justify the three hundred dollars and my handheld worked just fine. 'Why do you say that?' Admittedly, I was fishing for compliments.

'I saw from the first week. You're one of the ones who knows your way around a kitchen.'

'You did?'

'Even the way you deal with Jean Paul. I've heard stories, from past classes, about how he's made tough guys break down into tears! Not you, though.'

'Thanks.' I decided to bask in his praise instead of mention that I'd escaped to the walk-in refrigerator on more than one occasion to shed a few hot tears.

'You should be proud of yourself, not down on yourself.'

I met Tom's gaze. It was very nice to get this praise, it really was. It felt bad enough doubting myself. I'd been afraid everyone else was doubting my talents too. I picked up a huge dough hook attachment that was for the industrial-sized Hobart. 'Are you just saying this to be nice?'

'It's the truth. You're thick-skinned . . . and you're tough. Matter of fact, I wish I was more like you.'

'Really?' I put down the hook as if I'd been caught fondling it. More like me? Thick-skinned and tough? Was this why he never seemed to want to touch me? Was this why he was presumably touching Tara?

He looked at his watch. 'Maybe we should push on.'

We wandered back to the door. I didn't want our time together to be over, but I knew he had to get to work.

As we passed the cash register, Tom slowed down. 'I'm just gonna buy one of these paring knives,' he said. There was a basket of them by the cash register. 'I think I lost mine.'

'Yeah. They always seem to disappear.' As he paid, I said, 'So maybe we could get something to eat, or go to a movie sometime, or something . . .' Something like a real date. I looked at him and blushed slightly. Was that a look of panic on his face?

'Yeah, maybe,' he said.

And then I added, because he didn't, 'That would be great.'

chapter nineteen

*e*lvis Montgomery, a party planner transvestite, had organized Coco's birthday party. The invitations had been printed with gold glitter glue on the crotch of black thongs. There were party games like Pin the Penis on the Life-sized Poster of Derek Jeter. And everyone was getting a doggy bag (decorated with a picture of two doggies 'doing it') to take home, with plastic handcuffs, a black felt blindfold, and fruit-flavored condom party favors.

Jack was sitting on the couch talking to anyone who would listen. His voice was really getting on my nerves. He was going on and on about some business deal he once did involving toggles.

'So when they ordered 'em the first time I gave 'em a special price . . .'

Every few sentences he laughed at something he said.

'So they come back six months later, and they want to order more. They give me some bullshit about honoring that first price.' He snickered, then paused to scratch the back of his ear, betraying, could it be, an iota of (did he notice I was glaring at him?) self-consciousness.

' "But that was a one-time deal," I said!'

No one else seemed annoyed at his booming voice droning on.

'So I charged them the regular price.'

They just listened politely. And it was a pretty wild crowd that included lots of my mom's old friends, who were most definitely not in his typical circle. Did he care? Did he not appreciate that most of the others had much more interesting stories than he did? Like Linda Spangles, one of the premier porn star/performance artists of the 80s, or Heidi Ho, an old pal of my mom's who'd worked in peep shows for years and now designed porn Web sites.

I'd invited Ralph. I wanted him to know 'the real me.' In high school I'd never cared what other people thought of my home life. All my friends knew what Coco did, and lots of my teachers too. Most people thought it was cool. Others disapproved. I tried not to let it affect me much either way, though that seemed to be getting harder, not easier. But I knew if Ralph was critical, he was only looking out for me.

We stood in the corner observing Heidi Ho and her girlfriend, Melissa, who did publicity for HBO. They made an unlikely-looking couple. Melissa was a real lipstick lesbian – peroxide blonde, pink heels, silky pink polka-dot dress. Heidi had a crew cut, muscles. Her entire arms were tattooed with dragons and she had one of those rings in her nostrils like you usually see in a bull's snout. I wanted to grab it and lead her to a trough.

'Is that your gorgeous mother?' Ralph asked.

Coco, in a silver minidress and clear plastic platforms, was talking animatedly with Pong, a performance artist. 'Yep.'

'She's a knockout.'

'Ummm.' Not what I wanted to hear.

'I feel bad for ya.'

I wanted him to feel bad for me. But now it was annoying to hear him say he felt bad for me. 'She's actually been a pretty good mom.'

'Uh-huh.'

'At least she's lively and affectionate and knows how to have a good time.'

'I'll bet she does.'

Elvis joined us and I introduced them. 'Elvis planned the party. Isn't it great?'

'It's marvelous! I can't wait to see what shape the cake is!'

'It would've been a breast.' Elvis nodded at me. 'But since we have a professional here . . .'

'I made a pie. Cherry. It's Coco's favorite. I should go check on it.'

I went to the kitchen. The pie was cooling on a rack. I planned on smothering it with fresh whipped cream, then using some sparkler birthday candles. It was still too warm, though, so I went back out into the living room and had the unpleasant surprise of seeing Ian walk in the door. What was he doing here? I looked around for Coco, but she was gone, so I checked in her bedroom.

She was on the bed with Linda, talking about a mammogram she'd had earlier that week. 'It's like inserting your breast into the refrigerator, and having someone very strong slowly *smash* the refrigerator door against your breast and then *lean* against the door as hard as she can . . .'

'Why is Ian here?' I said.

'Ian?'

'He just walked in. Did you invite him?'

'Why would I do that?'

'Then why is he here?'

'I don't know.' She turned back to Linda. 'So she told me I have to go back because of the implants.'

'Bummer,' Linda said.

'She didn't get a good view. I could tell she didn't know what the hell she was doing – '

I went back to Ralph, who was now by himself admiring the framed prints of the women with their underwear down around their ankles. 'These are hilarious.'

'Sidesplitting.'

'What's wrong, Your Cuteness?'

'My ex-boyfriend is here.'

'Point him out.'

'The guy at the potato chip bowl with the blond hair and the little goatee which he didn't used to have, by the way.'

'Love the goatee.'

'Hate the goatee.'

'Very adorable.'

'Very pretentious, just like he is, and why is he here?'

'He's madly in love with you and can't let go?'

'He's madly in love with my mom. He knows it's her birthday. She must've invited him and didn't tell me. I mean, how shitty is that?'

'You really think she invited him?'

'How else would he know there was a party? He should at least have the decency to stay away – '

'She shouldn't have invited him, though.'

'He's coming over here.'

'That sucks.'

'Doesn't it?' I turned my frown into a smile. 'Hello, Ian.'

'Hi, Ginger. Good to see you.'

'Good to see you too.' Maybe the goatee was kinda cute . . .

'Nice to meet you. I'm Ralph. I go to school with Ginger.'

'Great. How's that going?'

'She's the star of the class,' Ralph said. I gave him a dirty look. He feigned innocence. 'What?'

I saw Coco heading into the kitchen with an empty platter. 'Excuse me, I have to check the pie.' I followed her in.

'That pie,' she said, 'smells so good.'

'So, Mom. Are you saying that he somehow knew you were having a party and just showed up?'

'Look,' she said, putting on some coffee, 'I sent out a group e-mail. And it was the same group e-mail I put together for my New Year's party, so Ian was probably still on there.'

'Mom!'

'I really should update that thing, but who has the time? It doesn't matter. Just ignore him.'

I tried. I really did. I got out my carton of whipping cream and poured it into a bowl and inserted the whisk attachments into the slots on my handheld mixer and then added some sugar to the cream and started blending. Everything was fine. But then Ian had to come into the kitchen.

'Happy birthday, Coco!'

'Thank you!'

He gave her a hug. 'How are you?'

'Great! How are you? Is your CD ready to go yet?'

'Yeah! As a matter of fact, I met this guy who's interested in doing a distribution deal, and he introduced me to a producer in LA, and they're interested in picking up my stuff. . . .'

It was really nice, I thought, as the cream began to stiffen, to hear that his life had gotten so much better since I broke up with him.

'Congratulations!' Coco said. 'That's fantastic!'

'I'm thinking I might even move out to LA. Why not? My own place on the beach sounds great, so I'm pretty happy. . . .'

It was so nice to hear how happy he was, I wasn't really paying attention to my whipping cream as it got thicker and thicker and thicker, and I swirled the whisks around and around and around and around, and they were laughing and laughing and laughing, and getting along so well so well so well together, and shouldn't she be telling him that she didn't mean to invite him and what the hell was he doing here and maybe he should just get the hell out of here?

'I was meant to live in LA,' Coco was saying. 'I don't know why I never have. When I was doing the circuit, I loved Florida. Loved Houston. Loved it, loved it. Let's face it, I'm a sun person. It's crazy I live here.'

'The sun is cool,' Ian said.

'The sun is *warm*,' I said. They ignored me.

'My body,' Coco said, 'craves the sun.'

'We all need that Vitamin C,' Ian agreed.

'Vitamin D,' I corrected him. Not that anyone cared that I'd wasted the past two years of my life telling myself I meant something to him even if he did want to date other women and he was probably going home to surf porn Web sites while fantasizing about my mother's big tits and my thoughts were so unrelentingly toxic right then, I almost ended up whipping that cream into a brick.

I unplugged the mixer and put it away. Ian ignored me. Because I was ignoring him? Or because he had no interest in me, and didn't have to *pretend* he had an interest in me anymore?

Coco went out into the living room. I heard her say to everyone, 'My pie is almost ready! Come to the table! I've already had three orgasms smelling that thing!'

I wasn't sure if I was glad Ian stayed back with me or not. Was I still actually wishing he would appreciate me? Ridiculous.

'So,' he said, 'you seem a little tense.'

'Me? Not really.' I piled the (rather firm) whipped cream onto the top of the pie.

'I've missed you,' he said.

'Really.' I started to smooth it out.

'But it doesn't take long to remember why we had our problems.'

I resmoothed out what I'd already smoothed. 'I have no idea what you're talking about.'

'Come on. Yes, you do. You can't compete with her. It makes you crazy.'

I stuck the sparklers into the cream. 'Did anyone invite you to this party?'

'Your mother.'

'She forgot to weed you off her e-mail list.'

'You are so jealous,' he said. 'Are you ever going to get over that?'

Coco poked her head in. 'We're ready!'

I smiled at Coco. 'Coming!'

'I know that sounded harsh,' Ian said as soon as she was gone. 'But you have to admit there's truth to what I'm saying.'

I knew it was true, but did I have to hear it from him? I went to the drawer to find my pie server. 'Maybe I'd be a little less jealous,' I said as I searched in the drawer, 'if you could keep your eyes off her tits.' Whenever I looked for this pie server, it seemed to be hiding behind every other utensil.

'Maybe I wouldn't have been looking at hers if you'd let me see yours!'

I considered grabbing a potato peeler and gouging his eyes out with the tip. Luckily for him, I found the server. 'This is my mother's birthday,' I said, gripping the handle. 'If you can't be pleasant, then just do me a favor and leave.'

He shrugged. 'I'm just saying, if you did compete, you would do just fine.'

'Ian. I don't want your advice. Okay?'

As he went out to the living room, Linda came in. 'Are we ready? Do you need some help?'

'I just have to light the sparklers.'

I was so distracted by Ian's words, I kept letting the match burn my fingertips. Why did he say that? Because he was still interested in me? Doubtful. He was leaving for LA soon. Residue guilt was more like it. Or was it just a simple piece of truth? 'Ouch,' I said, as I failed once again to light a sparkler. Linda helped me finish them off, and then held open the door for me.

'Here we go,' she said.

I slowly made my way out of the kitchen with a smile pasted on my face. Everyone began singing the Happy Birthday song. I held my beautiful pie (homemade, not store-bought crust, I might note) out in front of me. It was filled with plump, succulent cherries (a special brand I'd ordered from Williams-Sonoma that didn't have corn syrup) topped with the luscious white cream and illuminated by the sparkling sparklers. I saw Ian standing in the back and Jack to my left, but nothing mattered right at that moment except for the happy look on Coco's face as I set the pie down. 'It's gorgeous!' she said before blowing out the sparklers, and everyone laughed as the candles relit themselves, and she blew them out again. I sliced the first piece and lowered it onto a red plastic plate. Ralph put a fork on it, and handed it to Coco.

'Thank you!' she exclaimed.

'Tart for the tart!' Jack said.

'It's not a tart,' I said, 'it's a pie.'

'Pie,' Jack said, 'tart. What's the difference?'

'There is a difference, actually.' And I was just about to explain it to him when he made his announcement. 'I think this is a good time to tell everyone! Don't you, Coco? Shall we tell everyone?'

'Yes,' Coco said, looking at me for a split second with, what was it, apprehension? 'We have an announcement, everyone!'

I continued to transport a slice of pie to a plate that Ralph was holding out for me.

'Coco and I would like everyone to know . . .'

I was in the middle of digging out another wedge.

'. . . that we're getting married!'

My pie server slipped into the front rim of the tin and brought the entire pie down into my lap.

Ralph screamed, 'Oh, my god!'

The tin fell to the floor, but most of the pie remained on my thighs. Ralph seemed to be the only one who noticed. I stood there with the whipped cream and the cherries slopped all over my legs while everyone applauded and yelled out congratulations to the happy couple. Gradually, though, everyone started to realize they might not be getting dessert.

Coco was the first to notice. 'My pie!'

'It's ruined.'

'Nuts!' Coco put down her own slice and came to help scrape the mess off of me and back into the tin.

'I'm sorry, I don't know how that happened!'

'We're just going to have to *lap* it up!' she said, and everyone laughed as she scraped some cherry goop off my lap and licked it off her fingers.

I sat down on the chair, more to escape her finger than anything else, but that only encouraged her next move. She swished her ass on my lap, and then offered some to Jack by wiggling her butt at him.

'Come and get it . . .'

'Mom, would you please . . .'

Everyone was hooting it up, and that just encouraged her to parade around the room with my cherry pie all over her butt asking, 'Who wants to lick my ass? Lick my ass for a dollar!'

'It's not funny,' I said.

'Oh, lighten up.' Coco said. 'It's not that big a deal.'

'Maybe you don't have any idea what is and what isn't a big deal to me – '

'Would you calm down?' Coco tried to squeeze my shoulder. I shook her off.

'Calm down?' I screamed. 'I worked hard on that pie!' As if it was the pie . . . 'And then you go around and stick your ass in everyone's face – '

'What are you talking like that to your mother for?' Jack yelled. 'And on her birthday!'

'Stay out of this, Jack.' Coco turned to me. 'You know what? You really need to loosen up. I was just having fun.'

'It wasn't fun. It was embarrassing. Do you know the difference?'

'How did I ever get such an uptight daughter?'

There was a really awful silence. Everyone was staring at me, and Ian was smirking. How could I behave this way on her birthday? I had to be a lousy kid. I *was* uptight. Even Ralph was stunned into silence. There was nothing to do but get myself out of this room and remove these clothes. 'Happy birthday, Mom,' I said. 'I'm sorry you gave birth to such a dud.'

'You're not a dud,' she said, as I walked out. 'You're just uptight!'

'Apologize to your mother,' Jack was still yelling as I shut my bedroom door. 'I want you to apologize to your mother!'

Safely in my room, I took off my cherry-soaked clothes and got into bed and under the covers. A few moments later there was a knock on the door.

'Ginger?' It was Ralph. 'Can I come in? Are you okay?'

'One second.'

I got back out of bed and put on some sweats and a T-shirt and let him in. 'I'm really sorry you had to witness my idiocy.'

'Don't apologize.'

'I am such an idiot!'

He sat down next to me on the bed. 'Would you stop calling yourself an idiot? I mean, my god. Your mother is a trip! And I don't mean like as in a guided tour kind of trip. She's out there. She's like a "go to Africa and take your chances with the wildlife on a safari" kind of trip. And a little problem with boundaries, don't ya think? So don't be so hard on yourself.'

'I was just so mad to see Ian.'

'And?'

'I know I probably sound like some stupid teenage brat. And of course she should do whatever makes her happy. And it's not like I even have to live with them or anything. But I don't want her to marry Jack!'

'You know what? Neither do I.'

'Really?'

'And I've only known both of them less than an hour.'

I gave him a little hug. 'You're so sweet to me.'

'Don't get too cuddly, or I'm gonna convert.'

'No, you aren't.'

'You never know.'

I didn't think he was serious, but you never knew. He must've seen the look on my face, because then he said, 'Don't worry. I'm not gonna convert unless hell freezes over, so chill out.'

I looked down at my lap and then at Ralph again. 'Do you think . . .'

'What?'

'Do you think Tom could potentially find me attractive?'

'Huh?'

'You know. Unlike me, Tara knows how to do all that stuff men like. That's why Tom is falling for her, and I'll end up being just his friend.'

'If that's true, then we'll have to convert him.'

'Or convert me.'

'Into a sex object?' He laughed. 'Right.'

The odd thing was, when he laughed, I felt insulted. 'You don't think I can be a sex object?'

'Do you want to be a sex object?'

'No. But theoretically. If I wanted to. I could. Don't you think?'

'Fine,' he said, avoiding, I noticed, my question. 'Put on some makeup. See if it wins you Mr. Carpenter.'

I stood up. 'No. The idea disgusts me.'

'Of course it does.' He stood up too. 'Let's blow this joint. Let me take you out to dinner. I'll make you listen to all *my* trials and tribulations.'

'Such as?'

'How to get Robert Kingsley to notice me.'

I had to laugh. 'If you saw the way he looked at my mother, you'd know it was a losing battle.'

'Not to mention the way he looks at you.'

'Me? Right. He probably just sees me as potential cheap labor.'

'That's true.'

'You didn't have to agree so quickly!'

'You're just the sort of person he'd want working in his kitchen.'

'Hey. I'd sell myself cheap to him any day.'

As we sneaked out, part of me wanted to say good-bye to Coco, but I didn't want to have to speak to her. Luckily Heidi was in the hall and saw me heading towards the door, so I asked her to tell Coco I was leaving.

'Your mom means well, Ginger.'

'I know. Will you just tell her I took a walk?'

'Sure.'

When we were out on the sidewalk, Ralph reminded me of one good thing. 'Hey. When your mom marries the Button King, you get the apartment to yourself!'

'That's something to look forward to.' Tom could come over and I wouldn't have to worry about Coco parading by in her underwear. That was worth something. That was worth quite a lot. Maybe worth having Jack as a relative.

Of course, I'd still have to worry about walking around in my *own* underwear. Could Tom find a woman wearing hipsters attractive? There was only one way to find out. And I had to try to make it happen before Tara got the chance to undress in front of him first.

*i*t was my lucky day. Jean Paul assigned me to make cheesecake. And my partner was Tom. It was going to be so easy. The graham cracker crusts had already been prepared, so all we had to do was the filling.

We gathered our ingredients. I made sure to do this in a very calm, businesslike way, not wanting to let him perceive that I was delighted just to be working with him. We stood next to each other over the mixer beating a huge clump of cream cheese into smooth softness. Maybe he thought I was 'tough and thick-skinned,' but while standing next to him, his tallness sure made me feel small, and delicate, and fragile. His broad shoulders seemed to provide a protective shield that would ward off all the evils of the world.

I didn't say much, and neither did he. We hadn't actually spoken much since the restaurant supply store. Had I scared him away by suggesting a movie? Maybe Tara had finally told him about Coco, and he was mortified. Maybe he was in love with Tara and too guilty to look me in the eye. Maybe all of the above. I was afraid to ask. I didn't want to know. Why was I even alarming myself with all these thoughts?

We set the pans into a water bath, which would surround the cake with a gentle, moist heat. Then we put them in the oven to bake.

'We make a good team,' he said.

'Yeah,' I agreed, though I would've preferred the word 'partner' or 'pair' or, let's see, how about 'couple?'

And then it hit me.

I had fallen in love with Tom Carpenter.

In the locker room, Tara was crowing to Priscilla. 'It's so great being with Tom almost every night at the restaurant.'

I concentrated very hard on tying the lace of my sneaker.

'How are his *knife* skills?' Priscilla asked with a grin.

'Quite advanced, thanks for asking.'

'Is he being trained to do sauces?'

'I'll try his sauce any day.'

'But will you swallow his sauce?'

They both cracked up. 'You guys,' I said, 'are worse than a couple horny jocks.'

Tara pulled off her chef's jacket, revealing a purple lacy little bra. 'Oh! Are you the new spokeswoman for male sexual harassment?'

'If I knew some guy was talking that way about me, I'd be offended.'

'But there isn't any guy talking that way about you,' Tara said. 'Why would he?'

At home, Coco and I avoided each other. We crossed paths in the hall, got food from the fridge, took turns with the TV. We made sure not to eat in the same room at the same time. Maintained a stony silence. I was aware that I owed her an apology. She'd decided to marry Jack, for whatever reason, and I was just thinking about myself. She was the one getting married; she was the one (shudder) who was going to live with him.

But why had she changed her mind? For the money? And why didn't she tell me before announcing it to everyone else? She could've at least run it by me first and pretended like my opinion mattered, even if it didn't. I wanted an apology too.

My father asked where I'd like to go to dinner. I told him L'Etoile. After all, the place had such a great reputation and the menu was brilliant, and . . .

Okay, I wanted to spy.

Okay, not just spy. I wanted to be in the same room as Tom. Just knowing that he was in the vicinity was becoming a goal in itself. I had it bad.

The restaurant was really lively. And large. Located in Times Square just five blocks from my apartment, it was a destination for Broadway 'stars' to come before or after a show, and then the audiences followed, sort of like a modern-day Sardi's. But whereas Sardi's menu was typically ancient, with the old standbys like steak tartare, filet mignon, and baked Alaska, L'Etoile was all about trendy, with entrees like farfalle with mascarpone, asparagus with hazelnut purée, and flourless chocolate-orange ricotta cake. The place was packed. Considering the dining room seated around three hundred people, that was impressive.

Despite the white tablecloths and chandeliers, the place was relatively informal. I liked it that I didn't have to feel intimidated to come in. It was noisy and lively and people were wearing everything from black tie to blue jeans. On one side, there was a very long and populated bar with people eating as well as drinking. The walls were decorated with framed, autographed photos of stars, and the wallpaper was a running list of celebrities who'd performed on Broadway. Bernadette Peters Hugh Jackman Liza Minnelli Madonna Rosie O'Donnell so on and so forth.

I counted no less than ten cooks working their stations in the narrow strip of kitchen that was open to the dining room. Tom was one of them. My heart fluttered when I saw him standing back there like an angel in his whites. His look of semibored competence made him all the more alluring.

Tara was nowhere to be seen.

While we were eating our appetizers, I managed to talk with my father about Emma.

'I've been getting to know her more,' I said, chewing on my braised baby artichokes, 'which is nice.'

'She told me. I'm glad.'

'At first she was resistant. But gradually, she's started to get more relaxed around me.'

'She really seems to like you.'

'I like her.'

'I'm glad,' he said, in his usual stiff way. Like he knew he was supposed to be glad, so he said he was glad, but was he really able to feel gladness? 'I had one of those cupcakes you made. It was good.'

I thought he sounded somewhat surprised. 'You didn't think it would be?'

'I did. It was very good. Really.'

'Thanks. Yeah. So.' I took a deep breath. I figured I would take care of this during the appetizer. 'I was helping Emma in her room . . . to clean up a little . . .'

'I can actually see her floor for the first time in years.'

'Yeah.' It flashed through my mind that maybe he didn't even need to know this. It could be my secret with Emma. I'd be in charge of her napkin supply. He didn't need to be involved. But, on the other hand, she did say I could tell him. And I wanted him to get a dose of reality. His little girl wasn't so little anymore. 'I'm sure you haven't noticed, but Emma's got her period.'

'What?'

I had to repeat myself? 'Her period. She's menstruating.'

'Really?' He swallowed his last bite of prosciutto and fennel, looked over towards the bar, then back at me. 'I didn't know.' Then back towards the bar. Then back at me. 'She told you?'

'Yes.'

'She didn't tell me.'

'Probably, you know, because you're a guy.'

'Of course.'

Or perhaps because he was cold and distant. 'So I told her I would tell you. And I got her some supplies, you know, so you don't have to worry about that. At least, not for a few months.'

'Thanks.'

'I could check in with her about it again. But I think you should say something to her. Give her something positive. Some kind of encouragement, you know, something supportive? So she can feel good about it.'

The waiter came and took our plates. It felt odd to be giving my father advice for a change. After the waiter was gone, he said, 'Of course. I'll say something.'

I exhaled. Good. I was glad to get that done with. Why did it have to be so painful to talk about anything personal with him? And I wasn't even done.

I brought up Coco during the main course. We'd both ordered the same thing. Salmon with sesame and orange-ginger relish. I wondered if Tom had made it.

'This is really good.' I waited until after we'd both had second bites. 'Can I ask you something about Mom?'

'Sure.'

'When you first knew her in high school. Before you were married. Do you think she was in love with you?'

'In love?' He shook his head. 'I have no idea.'

'Really?' I leaned forward against the table, my biceps pressing against the edge.

'I suppose . . . maybe she was.' He shrugged.

'Were you in love with her?'

'Ginger. Words like that . . .'

'You aren't on trial here. I just want to know. What was it like? I mean, were you two *ever* happy together?'

'Look. We were young. I was ambitious. The timing was bad. And your mother . . .' He took a stab at his fish. 'She liked to do what she liked to do. And I was not about to . . .'

'What I don't fully understand . . .' I put my fork down. 'I never understood . . .' My voice was wavering. The muscle under my right eye twitched. I couldn't say it. I couldn't ask why he never did more about me. Sharing custody of me. 'I can understand,' I said. 'Coco can be pretty wild. No boundaries.' But at least she'd raised me, with Grandma's help. He'd done nothing. 'Sometimes she drives me crazy.'

'Uh-huh.' He nodded sympathetically, and I could see it in his eyes, he wanted to hear more.

'I feel like I can't bring any friends around to see her. Because they never look at me the same again.' I savored my salmon. All the flavors really did complement each other.

'That must be tough.'

'And everything always has to be about sex. I get sick of it!' I glanced over at Tom. He looked flushed from being over the stove. I wished I could wipe his forehead with a cool cloth. 'Sometimes I just wish . . . she did something normal, you know?'

'Sure. Of course you do.'

Oh, god, I was betraying my mother. 'And now she wants to marry this guy Jack.'

'Really.'

I sensed my father's interest. Had I gone too far?

'You don't like him?'

Was my father jealous? Of Coco? 'He has a lot of money. An apartment on Central Park South.'

'Uh-huh. Well. It's her life.' My father patted his mouth with his napkin. 'You can't tell her what to do with it. She wouldn't listen to you anyway.' He looked away then, and I knew our semi-intimate conversation was over.

My father paid the check and offered to get me a cab. I preferred to walk home. My mind was spinning. I needed to think. I wanted to be proud of the woman who'd raised me. In some ways, Coco really was strong. I'd grown up hearing countless stories about her dancer friends who needed alcohol and/or drugs to get through a shift, and then they'd start sleeping with customers for extra cash, and there'd be a whole downward spiral.

Not Coco. She didn't smoke or drink or take drugs. She had never, so far as I knew, slept with a customer. And the fact was, she really had enjoyed her work for many years and was sad when she got too old for the clubs. That was the hard part for her – when she had to stop.

And wasn't it, really, when you got down to it, a very positive thing, the way she was so comfortable with her body, so free of inhibitions, so without guilt for doing something society condemned but was really, in the end, about experiencing pleasure, and what was wrong with that? I knew from one of my cultural anthropology classes that dances centering around rolling hips and bellies were originally performed by women for other women and were all about fertility and the land. It was only after it was for the men that it came to be considered dirty.

At the bottom of the park, I passed a lineup of horses and carriages waiting to be hired. I breathed in the manure and remembered how it had made Tom think fondly of home. I sat down on a bench and took another whiff. It made me think fondly of Tom.

chapter twenty-one

Kingsley stood up at the front of the demo kitchen with an impressive lineup of expensive wines and a tall stack of trays from the dishwasher filled with glasses. 'Your wine list is going to tell your customer about your level of sophistication, so educate yourselves. Learn how to choose wines, buy them, and store them. I hold wine-tasting seminars every few weeks so my staff has firsthand knowledge about what we're serving.'

Yet one more enticement to work for Kingsley.

As he lined up a dozen glasses along the side of the table, he went over some of the basics, like filling the glass only one third of the way so the 'imbiber' can swirl the liquid around, release the aroma, let it breathe . . . Then he got into the difference between reds and whites.

'Shall we do reds first?' he asked no one in particular as he uncorked a few bottles of Cabernet and poured a taste into each of the glasses. This promised to be the best class ever. 'White wines are made from green grapes or red grapes that have been skinned. Red wines use the whole grape, skin and seeds. This has a big impact on the taste. Leaving the skin on produces tannins. The more tannin, the more bitter the drink.'

He passed out the glasses of wine. 'How many of you prefer red wines to whites?'

I raised my hand. So did Tom. Tara didn't. 'I myself have a bias towards reds. They're fuller, richer, earthier . . . Once you take that layer of skin off that grape, it tends to be lighter, less complex.' I took a sip of my Cabernet and craved a piece of cheese to go with it. 'Some people think whites are more approachable for that reason,' Kingsley continued, 'and that's not necessarily a bad thing. But I find the complexity of a full-bodied red to be much more satisfying.' Kingsley swirled his wine around in his glass. I could've sworn, when he raised it to toast the class, he looked straight at me.

Did that mean something? Was I totally reading in? I took another sip. It couldn't be. I wanted to think he was interested in me. Not that I would do anything about it. Not that he would. But it would be so amazing. And scary. I would have to convince him I was . . . refined. He would never think enough of the real me. It was too unsettling to think about. Anyway, Tom was the one I was thinking about. Wasn't he?

By lunchtime, we were all enjoying the lesson quite a bit, and some particularly diligent students were more than a little soused. Ralph was wagging his tongue at Kingsley, and I was toying with the idea of sauntering up to Tom and planting a big wet kiss on his lips. He couldn't fall for a rotten tomato like Tara, could he? Maybe the problem was, I'd been too passive. And I was being a fool, just letting her steal him away. I had my chance to make a move when Kingsley asked Tara to help take the used wineglasses back to the dishwasher. Tom mentioned to me that he was going to get some air on the roof. I figured that was more or less an invitation to join him. 'I'll come too.'

I followed him up the stairwell and he pushed open the heavy door that led onto the gravelly rooftop. There was a rumor floating around that a distraught student had once jumped over the edge after burning a tray of crème brûlée.

'The air is sweet!' I said.

'I'm not used to drinking so much in the middle of the day.'

'That was fun, though. And informative, of course.'

'I'm still not sure I can identify the difference between a fat wine, a round wine, and a plump wine . . .'

'How can words ever really adequately describe a taste?'

'So,' he said, sitting down on a bench that looked like it had been stolen from the park. 'I saw you at L'Etoile the other night. Why didn't you come say hi?'

I felt like I'd been caught with my underwear down. 'You looked busy. I didn't want to interrupt.'

'You should've! What did you think of the food?'

'I loved it.'

'What did you have?'

'The salmon with the orange-ginger relish.'

'Good choice,' he said. 'Orange and ginger. Those flavors "marry" quite well.'

'Oh, yes. It's inspiring when you can find two flavors that are willing to commit to each other like that.'

'So often, ingredients get mixed up with any old seasoning that happens to be around.'

'Or they get involved with some totally unreliable exotic spice.' I giggled tipsily. 'You looked pretty good back there cooking away.'

'Thanks. It's been kind of scary, to tell you the truth. Tara's dad is a real perfectionist. I keep worrying I'm going to fuck up.'

'Oh, come on.'

'No, really. It's a lot of pressure. And you can't hide. The orders come in. You're doing ten things at once. Do something wrong, you get yelled at by the sous chef, yelled at by the waiters. You wouldn't believe how tired I am at the end of the shift. It's really exhausting.'

'Yeah. I got a lot of that when I was at Chantal.'

'And then it's torture waking up in the morning to come here.'

'Maybe you're doing too much.'

'But I have to. It's such a great opportunity.'

'You have too much on your plate. I hate that phrase. Too much on your plate.'

'But it's all good.'

'It's just . . .' I paused. He looked at me. I edged closer to him. 'It's too bad you've gotten so busy.' I gazed into his blue eyes in the most inviting way I could conjure up. 'I had a good time with you that day, at the restaurant supply store.'

'Restaurant supply store' didn't come out sounding quite as seductive as I might've liked. I wasn't quite drunk enough to actually kiss him, but I did lift my chin and pout my lips very slightly in his direction.

He slid ever so slightly away from me. 'I know,' he said. 'That was fun.'

'Yeah,' I said, telling myself that the fact that he slid ever so slightly away from me was only because he wanted me to slide ever so slightly closer to him. 'And I was looking forward to . . . um . . . showing you around . . . the city . . . some more.'

'That would be nice,' he said.

I smiled. He smiled. It was the perfect moment for him to kiss me.

He stood up. 'The thing is . . .' He seemed engrossed with the view. 'The thing is, I can't quit that job. It would be smarter to quit school. I'm getting paid to learn. It's great. I really have to feel lucky. And Tara. She's been great. She really made it happen. The way she introduced me to her dad. I'm sure she convinced him to hire me. So I really have her to thank.'

'Mr. Glass wouldn't have hired you if he didn't think you had talent.'

'Are you kidding? He can hire anyone he wants. But he hired me.'

'Uh-huh.'

He sat back down next to me. 'Look, Ginger, I'm sorry, but . . .'

Suddenly I didn't feel tipsy anymore.

'Tara and I . . .'

His voice trailed off. He didn't need to say any more. I didn't need to ask either, but who can resist a little masochism? 'What, she's your girlfriend?'

'We're kind of . . . involved right now. It turns out.'

'Oh. Well. That's nice.'

'I . . .' He hunched over, elbows on knees, and stared down at the gravel.

He actually looked ashamed, like I'd walked in on him stealing twenties from the till. 'It's not surprising. She's a very beautiful girl.'

'I really like you, Ginger. I hope . . .' He turned to me. 'I really want us to be friends.'

'Of course.'

'You aren't mad?'

'Why should I be?'

There was a cement barrier that ran around the edge of the roof. I treated my brain to a symbolic jump over it. A quick drop, one bounce on that blue awning way down there, then splat.

'I never expected . . . I didn't expect it . . . to happen . . . so fast.'

'I guess she just swept you off your feet.'

'I guess.'

'So.' I stood up. 'I wonder what interesting assignment Jean Paul has for me this afternoon. Maybe he'll ask me to scour the fat drippings off the bottom of the stove. Oh, no wait, I saw a shipment of calamari. Perhaps he'll ask me to degut all six million . . .'

'Don't give up on him, Ginger. Jean Paul must see what a hard worker you are. That's what's so great about you. You're just like one of the guys.'

'Thanks,' I said. Okay. Now, not only was I tough and thick-skinned, I was *one of the guys*! I knew he meant it as a compliment. And god knows, on another day, from anyone else, I would've taken it as one. But right then? From him? It burned. 'I'm gonna go back inside.'

m y mother was right. No man would ever find me attractive if I didn't inflate my boobs, hide my pores, streak my hair, cripple my feet. I cut my way through Rockefeller Plaza hoping to find her at home. I owed Coco an apology. I'd been fooling myself all these years, was deficient as a human being, a downright failure as a woman. I went past Dean and Deluca, and resisted going in there to buy a large carrot muffin with cream cheese frosting that would most certainly help dull the pain. I had work to do.

Coco was doing crunches on the floor of the living room. She had on black stretch yoga pants and a black tank with two intertwined red dragons on her chest. Judy Garland belted out 'The Man That Got Away.'

'Mom? Can you turn the music down for a sec?'

'When I'm done . . .'

'I need to talk.'

'Can you wait until I do a hundred?'

I sat down on the sofa, took off my sneakers, and waited. Even in my distressed mental state, I almost had to laugh, considering the absurd juxtaposition of Judy's angst and flat abs. But it gave me a chance to give myself another pep talk. Yes. It was necessary to do all these things girls do to attract men, and I'd been wasting my youthful beauty, or potential beauty, all these years in some self-defeating act of rebellion. But all was not lost. Who better to have in my corner? Tara's advantage would not last long, because I had the expert at my disposal, and the expert was chomping at the bit to coach me.

Finally she crunched her last crunch. 'Whoo! So what's up?'

I turned off the sound as she stood. 'I want to apologize.'

She took a long sip from a water bottle. 'Good. Go ahead. I'm just gonna do some poses.'

'I'm sorry I made a scene at your birthday party.'

'Okay,' she said, sitting with her butt on her heels, spine straightened, hands on knees.

'And I'm sorry I made a fuss about the plastic surgery concept. If you want to get some work done, go ahead. It's your decision even if you do ruin your looks and die on the operating table.'

'Thanks,' she said, raising her butt, reaching her hands back, arching her back, dropping her head back and grabbing her ankles. It made my back hurt just to watch.

'And . . . if you want to marry Jack . . . I suppose . . . that's your decision . . . and I'll try not to be so negative about the whole thing, even if – '

'Great!' she interrupted. 'I think that's a good place to stop.' She released forward again, legs folded under her, butt on her heels. 'Apology accepted.'

'But can I just say one thing?'

Now she leaned forward over her thighs. 'Can I stop you?' Her forehead rested on the floor, arms along her sides.

'You should've told me about Jack before you announced it to everyone.'

'You're right. I'm sorry.' She aimed her eyeballs up at me. 'It's just, he popped the question right before the party, and he was all excited . . .'

'And then you completely embarrassed me with that stupid lap dance.'

'Oh, come on,' she said, looking down again, 'I was just having fun!'

'It was humiliating! Really! I mean, sometimes you just don't have boundaries. And it's screwed up.'

She gave up on the hope of achieving her Zen state and sat up. 'I have boundaries. They're just farther out than you want 'em to be.'

'I think a lot of people would find 'em pretty far out.'

'A lot of people think women should wear veils in public.'

'Your point?'

'I don't care what people think.'

I swear, I could feel my blood pressure rise. 'But do you care how I feel?'

She closed her eyes, brought her thumb to her right nostril and pressed in. Took a few deep breaths out of her left nostril. I'd seen her do this before; it was supposed to be soothing, but to watch it when you're waiting for an apology is downright infuriating. Finally she opened her eyes, looked at me, and said, in a controlled way, 'I'm sorry if I embarrassed you.'

Well, I had my apology. Not too exciting after all that. Rather anticlimactic, really. Worse yet, now I had to eat my crow. I hesitated. She lay back flat on the floor and looked up at the ceiling. 'Ohhhhh,' she groaned. 'My back. My lower back. It feels so tight. I think I might be getting arthritis.'

'Arthritis? Come on.' The idea of Coco getting arthritis! She was in better shape than I was. 'That's for old people.'

'I'm not kidding. I went to a physical therapist yesterday and he said it's possible.'

'Are you sure it's not just stress?'

'Stress over what?'

'Well, like, the idea of spending the rest of your life with Jack?'

'Didn't you just promise . . . ?'

'Sorry. Forget I said that.' She closed her eyes. I wanted to ask her why she'd changed her mind about him, but wasn't sure I wanted to know. Maybe she was simply doing it for the money. Why make her admit that? Or maybe she really did love the guy. Was that possible? If she was finally going to fall in love, why Jack? I stared down at a food stain on the carpet. That stain had been there for years. It was somewhat comforting. 'So, Mom?' I hesitated. This really felt like major defeat. 'I've been thinking . . . maybe I should start doing something about how I look.'

She opened her eyes. 'What?'

'You know, like, makeup?' It was excruciating, telling her the words she'd always wanted to hear. 'New clothes?' Relinquishing the small bit of power I'd always had. 'Something more feminine than I've tended to wear in the past.' Surrendering to the enemy. 'Something more . . . you know . . . sexy.'

She practically leaped up off the floor. 'Let's go!'

'Where?'

'H & M! We'll buy you a whole new wardrobe!'

'I didn't mean right now – '

'If not now, when? Come on! Quick! Before you change your mind! Do you know how long I've been waiting for these words to spring from those lips, young lady? Let's get the hell out of here!'

The music was booming. I mean, what is it with the booming music? Are people so plagued by their thoughts that when they shop, they need to have them blasted out of their heads? Yes, okay, the beat could make you feel sexy. Get you in touch with your jungle side. But it was all so silly, wasn't it?

No. I had to try to take this seriously. So I would be taken seriously as a woman. I could be sexy too. I could get down with that jungle beat!

Or could I? Huge posters of skinny/sad/angry/seductive models looked down on me from the walls. They were totally imposing, totally condescending, totally pompous, impossible to replicate.

Okay. Calm down, already.

They were just pictures. Fantasy images. No one really expected you to actually *look* like that. Just an approximation of that. An attempt. To show men that you *wanted* to look like that, even if you both knew you couldn't *actually* look like that. To let the guy know you were on the same wavelength. The 'I submit to being a sex object' wavelength. Don't fight it. Use it. Like everyone else. Because really. It didn't have to be such a big deal.

The store was three stories high, and crowded with customers caught up in their own individual dreamlike dazes. An elevator wound its way up the center, delivering endless streams of dazed women to aisles crowded with endless racks of clothing. The dazed women unselfconsciously paused to touch the fabrics, imagining the cloth against their skin and draped on their bodies.

I tried to turn myself into one of the dazed women and dutifully strolled past aisles of racks crammed with clothing. I repeated the phrase that had gotten me here. *One of the guys.* At least the clothing was cheap. A pair of black slacks was only nineteen bucks. A party dress was only twenty-four dollars. You could wear it once and throw it out before it fell apart.

Coco was pulling things off the rack. She loved this store, and it was easy to see why. Almost everything was hooker chic. Hooker chic for the masses.

'How about this?'

Coco held up a slinky red dress. It was made out of some kind of flimsy spandex-y material, and it was obvious it would be totally form-fitting, and it was too low-cut, and too short, and my body wasn't good enough. 'It's nice.'

'Very sexy.'

'You don't think it's too tight for me?'

'Work with your curves, girl, not against them!'

'Okay. I'll try it.' Apart from my hesitations, I was curious to see what it would look like. How it would look encasing my body.

Coco forged on. I followed after her, and even started getting into the music. It was that old disco song, 'Boogie Oogie Oogie.' I moved my hips to the beat. This was fun!

Our arms full, we headed to the dressing room. My shopping high turned to anxiety and irritation. There were about ten people ahead of us in line. As we stood there in the hot, stuffy area that seemed to be de-signed specifically to induce sensory deprivation (except for the earsplit-ting, unrelenting techno music that was now playing) a woman behind us jabbered on her cell phone about trying to quit cigarettes and a girl be-hind us argued with her mom about her curfew. Finally, we were first. A tall, hulking guy counted our stuff and led us to a booth. 'For you,' he said, 'I have the executive suite.'

We both laughed. It took a lot of ambition (or was it a lack of it?) to do a godawful job like dressing room attendant and maintain a sense of humor. How did he do this every day? There was something oxy-moronic about a guy doing that job. Was he there guarding our virtue? Or violating it? Maybe he got off on handling women's clothing. Espe-cially when customers handed him slinky nighties and bras after trying them on.

Maybe my imagination was a bit too fertile for my own good.

Coco followed me into the cubicle, but I didn't want her in there with me. 'Can you wait outside?'

'Why?'

'I'd just like some privacy.'

'How can you be so modest around me of all people?'

How, indeed? Yet I was. Even though I'd seen her naked a million times, I still didn't like the idea of her seeing me. 'I'll call you in when I'm ready.'

I tried a cotton halter top on first. I'd liked it when I saw it on the rack because it had a vintage fifties look and the material was this pretty lilac plaid. But the top was so low cut, if I leaned over, you could almost but not quite but just possibly, depending on how the fabric wanted to behave, see my nipples. I pulled open the curtain.

'It's so cute!' Coco said.

'I don't like it.' The pumping beat from the loudspeaker right overhead was making a mockery of my modesty.

'It's adorable. You should get it.'

'My boobs are hanging out!'

'Ginger. The world will not stop spinning just because you have cleavage.'

'It's the opposite I'm afraid of.'

'What the hell are you talking about?'

'I don't want anyone to notice me.' I knew she couldn't conceive of such a thing.

'I thought you wanted to sex up your image.'

'I do.' But maybe it wasn't worth it. Better to just disappear. Who needed attention from perverted, slimy men?

Except, of course, it was Tom's attention I wanted to get. Tom, the known quantity. The nice, sensitive guy. There was no way to look sexy for him, yet hide my appearance from every random, skanky man on the street. And if he saw my boobs, especially my nipples, maybe he would dump Tara. Except maybe I was too flat. But I wasn't any flatter than Tara, so maybe I had a chance? Oh, god. How could I be thinking these thoughts? How desperate had I become? If this was love, give me cold in-difference, please!

'Stop fighting nature,' Coco said. 'Nature is not out to get you. Now I'm not leaving until we buy you at least three things. How about this skirt?'

She looked at me with such hope; I didn't want to let her down. Plus, it really was cute. It had cherries on it. I loved clothing with fruit on it, especially cherries.

I made her leave the dressing room, took off the halter, put on my bra and T-shirt, took off my jeans, noticed the wayward pubic hairs extending down below the edge of my hipster cotton panties, and stepped into the skirt. At least it went on easily because of an elastic waistband. But it barely extended past my upper thighs!

I called Coco back in. 'It's too short.'

'It's adorable.'

'My legs aren't good enough.'

'You've got great legs. You've got *my* legs.'

'No, I don't.' Did I? Maybe if I lost five pounds, so my thighs were a little thinner . . .

'It's a crime you've kept them hidden all these years. And you can wear your white sneakers with it, if you want.'

'Really?' If I could wear my sneakers . . .

'White sneakers with red laces. Cute. After you shave your legs. And I have some tanning lotion you can use. Or maybe we should just get them sprayed. But you need to exfoliate first. You can use my loofah. Oh, and by the way, you could *really* use some new underwear. They have a great selection – we'll go pick out some thongs before we leave.'

'I'm not getting any thongs.'

She put her hands on her hips. 'What is the deal with you?'

'I don't want anything in my butt-crack.'

'Jesus, you're stubborn. Here,' she said, throwing the slinky red dress at me as she went to wait outside. 'Try this.'

I looked at it like there was mold growing on the seams. I would never wear it in public. And there really was no air in the room and the music was extra loud from that speaker right above our executive suite and I was getting the worst headache but then Tom's words came back to me.

I really want to be friends.

After wrestling on the stretchy but tight material, I discovered you could see the top rim of my bra peeking up above the low neckline. And, since the red straps were so thin, you could see my white bra straps. So I had to take the dress back off, take off my bra, and put it back on again. By then I had nipple-itis. Why was this so impossible?

'How is it?' Coco asked through the curtain.

'Way too tight – forget it.' I started to take it off.

'Don't take it off! Let me see!'

'Mom . . .'.

She came in. Looked at me. My nipples, I swear, were big as thimbles. Mom didn't seem to notice. She was looking at my feet.

'How can you tell what it looks like with those damn gym socks on?'

I pulled the socks off. We both looked at me in the mirror. The dress completely outlined and clung to my body.

'Now that,' Coco said, 'is fucking sexy.'

Her words made me want to put on a muumuu. 'I hate it.'

'You look hot!'

'I could not go out into public with this. I might as well be naked!'

'They had it in black, but I think you should stick with the red. Just stand up straight. And you need a thong – I can see your panty line.'

'What is it that you *can't* see? My appendix?'

'Why do you insist on hiding your assets? Is it so important for you to not be like me? Well, get over it. You look fantastic.'

'But I have all those bulges . . . bulging out all over . . .'

'Those aren't bulges! Those are *curves*, my dear. Women have them. Men love them. Curves,' she proclaimed, 'are nature's way of making you powerful.'

Yes. It did look . . . womanly. No doubt about it. I was a woman. I could have that power. It was within my power to have that power. Me. A powerful woman!

No. Better if men could take me or leave me. Instead of taking me and taking me until there was nothing left . . .

'Buy it,' Coco said, 'and think about it. We can always return it.'

'Okay,' I said. 'It's a deal.' I'd had enough. 'Let's go.' I picked my jeans up off the floor and put them on under the dress.

'After we get you new underwear.' She stepped out and closed the curtain, but from the other side she was still going at it. 'And a bikini wax. You just need a bikini wax and thongs and bras and . . .'

'Mom. I'm done.' I wrangled the dress off. The thing was so tight, it seemed to be fighting me to stay on.

'Most important of all, you need shoes. You can't wear the dress without a pair of red heels. Let's go to Nine West, there's one right around the corner.'

I found my bra on the floor. 'Not now. I don't even know if I'm keeping it.'

'You have to wear heels with that dress.'

'Mom.' I kept my voice calm. 'You aren't listening. I can't shop anymore.'

'You must be hungry. We'll get you a slice of pizza and then we'll hit the shoes.'

'Pizza yes. Shoes no!' I was aware of the fact that if I did ever wear this dress, I would need some kind of heels to go with it. Even my one pair of black flats wouldn't fly here. But in my mind, heels were the most offensive of all the sex object wardrobe dictates. By giving in, I'd be surrendering to the enemy, a fashion war Benedict Arnoldette.

'If you just try a pair on . . . you'll get used to it . . . It's just a matter of – '

I pulled open the curtain. 'Mom. If I decide to keep the dress, I promise I will buy shoes to go with it, but for now, I am not getting heels.' By the look on her face, you'd think I was telling her I'd decided not to give her grandchildren.

'You know what?' She pulled herself together. 'There's probably a line at the cash register. I'll go pay for these.'

'Good idea.'

She was gone. Thank god. I put my T-shirt back on. Phew. Finally felt like me again. I sat down, exhausted, on the little corner bench and got out a roll of Life Savers. There was a pineapple on top. My favorite. As I sucked on it, I tried to reclaim my equilibrium. There was a conversation going on in the cubicle next to mine. I realized they'd probably heard our exchange. I couldn't help but listen to theirs.

'Mom, please? I really want it.'

'Over my dead body.'

'Why do you always do this? I'm never going shopping with you again.'

'You don't need any more clothes anyway, young lady. You already have too many.'

'Are you insane? Mom! I have nothing to wear!'

They were having a normal argument. The kind daughters were supposed to have with their mothers.

'I don't even know why we came here.'

'Ummm. Because I love this store?'

'Well, I hate this store.'

I pulled on my socks. Yes, the mother sounded like a mother. The daughter sounded like a daughter. I knew they probably wanted to kill each other at that moment, but on the other hand, it must've just felt so right. I crunched on my Life Saver, swallowed it down, and tied my nice, comfortable, gorgeous, good-for-my-arches sneakers that helped me get where I wanted to go and do what I wanted to do. My neighbors were still at it behind the curtain.

'No way you're wearing that dress.'

'Mom, I love it. Pleeease?'

'It makes you look like a hooker!'

Even though I'd had the same thought about half the stuff I'd seen on the racks, hearing this woman say it made me flinch. As I left my booth and passed theirs, they were outright screaming at each other.

'Are you kidding? All my friends dress like this!'

'That doesn't mean you need to! Where's your self-respect?'

Self-respect. Well, hey. Coco had self-respect. Matter of fact, she had more self-respect than this woman, because she truly loved and appreciated her own body. I left the fitting rooms thinking maybe it was a good thing not to fit in. Especially if fitting in meant being narrow-minded.

Four long lines of people waited by the cash registers. The music was this extremely hyper rap. I thought I would faint from lack of oxygen. Man, these stores took advantage of people. Undoubtedly they couldn't get employees to stay because they paid them next to nothing. There was Coco, second from the front, yakking with the woman in front of her. In some ways, yeah, I was lucky to have her as a mom. She meant well. Was only trying to help me in the way she knew how. And if Coco hated this store, then I'd probably have to love it just to show her, and then I'd have to be a slave to cheap clothing mania, so maybe I was spared from living out this insanity.

As I joined Coco in line, I felt a wave of tenderness. 'Thanks for doing this, Mom. I know it's a challenge.'

'Are you kidding?' she said. 'This is fun! I can't wait to get you in a pair of six-inch heels.'

I smiled. Kept my mouth shut. And let it go.

chapter twenty-three

'**W**hy did you let Mom become a stripper?'

It was a Saturday night. Grandma and I were in the kitchen eating spaghetti. I was in my first year of high school. That day, a guy in one of my classes had told me he'd snuck into a topless bar on his older brother's ID and it was really cool.

Grandma chuckled as she twisted strands of pasta around her fork. 'You think I could stop her?'

Grandma was born and raised on Long Island and escaped to Manhattan as soon as she could. Her white hair was always pulled up into a bun. She had beautiful dark, olive skin that neither Coco nor I were lucky enough to get. It seemed less naked than my pale skin. An extra layer of protection. I never saw her wear a dress. She favored white jeans, blue work shirts, and Birkenstocks.

'But didn't you disapprove?' Coco was working at the Classy Lady, right around the corner. I passed her club on my way to school every morning. I'd never been inside. Never seen her at work since that one time I went when I was seven. Coco had invited me to come – figured I might as well know firsthand what everyone else was going to condemn her for, and anyway, she wasn't ashamed. I'd refused. I preferred to cloak her activities in my 'glamorous' childhood memory of the Platinum Club. But now it bothered me that this guy in my class knew more about what went on than I did. *Was* it really cool? Or did he have to act like it was to prove *he* was cool. I was going to have to see it for myself. But still, the idea of going in there made me queasy.

'You think she cared what I thought? Your mother did what she wanted, and to tell you the truth, even though I was never for it – secretly, I was always a little bit in awe of her.'

'Really?' I sprinkled more Parmesan on my pasta.

'I always wondered how she could dance around naked like that.'

'You were a nude model, though, when you met Grandpa.' He was an art student at Cooper Union. She did poses in his life drawing class. He asked her out after what must've been a pretty inspiring session. They got married and were pretty happy together as far as I knew. He worked in an ad agency for awhile as a graphic designer. She got pregnant. He got drafted. Wasn't in Vietnam for a month even, before she got the news he'd been killed in a helicopter accident.

'You know why I modeled? Because I was very self-conscious, and I wanted to get over it.'

'Come on. If you were able to do it, you couldn't have been all that modest.' *I* was modest. *I* wouldn't have been caught dead.

'I was! It was a personal challenge for me. Coco? She never even liked wearing diapers. Pulled them down every chance she got . . .'

I smiled. That seemed so just like her.

'And,' Grandma added, 'she always loved to dance.'

I knew Coco had taken ballet as a kid. Tap. Ballroom. 'So why didn't she try to do musicals, like on Broadway? Why strip clubs?'

'Let me tell you. At nineteen, she was already making twice as much as I did, maybe more. She was socking it away. Sometimes I wonder about my own career choice more than hers.'

Grandma was a public school teacher. How could they allow a teacher to make less than a stripper? Disgusting. But I was impressed. Coco made more than Grandma.

When I was about ten, Coco had been laid off by the Platinum Club. They liked their girls to be in their early twenties. She worked for awhile at a place on the East Side, then ended up around the corner at the Classy Lady. It was a step down, but at her age, jobs were harder to get. And at fourteen, it was harder for me to 'get' her job.

'So what do you want to make tonight?' Grandma asked as she cleared away our plates.

'I feel like dirt. How do you feel?'

'I feel like dirt too.'

That was our routine for making dirt cake. It was something you could throw together quickly. While she finished cleaning up dinner, I ran down to the grocery on the corner to get the ingredients we were missing – Oreos, whipping cream, chocolate pudding.

After we'd put it in the oven, the phone rang. One of my friends from school.

'Everyone's meeting up at Columbus Circle. You wanna come?'

That was the year we all started spending our nights basically cruising the sidewalks. I loved growing up in the city. It was a huge, amazing playground to hang out, go to movies, eat at restaurants, walk around aimlessly, and be endlessly entertained. But Saturday nights had always been reserved for Grandma. I'd started wishing I had it free, but I couldn't get myself to bring it up with her.

'I don't think I can make it.'

After I hung up, Grandma asked who it was.

'You know. The crowd. They're just hanging out.'

'You should go if you want to.'

A powerful chocolate smell emanated from the oven. 'But we haven't had dessert yet.'

'Why should you wait around for that? It'll be here when you get back. Go!'

'Are you sure?' It broke my heart. The idea of her sitting on the couch. Watching *The Golden Girls*. Eating dirt cake. Alone.

'I'll be fine. Go!' She paused from wiping down the table and looked at me. 'I think you're right. You should see what your mother does first-hand. Ask her to take you one of these nights.'

'But I'm not really sure I want to.'

Grandma shrugged. 'The worst thing that will happen? You'll know the truth.'

A few days later, Coco and I were at the grocery store doing the weekly shopping. I told her I wanted to come to the Classy Lady.

'I was wondering when you'd finally take an interest in my work,' she teased with a fake offended tone.

'Don't get your hopes up. I'm not gonna follow in your footsteps.'

'A mother can always dream.'

The Classy Lady occupied a basement on Broadway and Forty-seventh Street. I'd passed by many times, avoiding the guy handing out flyers advertising a discount for 'gentlemen' arriving before nine. We walked the two blocks to the club, past the corner with the Korean grocery's display of flowers, fruits, and vegetables. I tried to reassure myself that this didn't have to be a big deal. I'd seen Coco dance often enough at home, at parties. I'd seen her give lap dances to friends who refused to set foot in a club but wanted to know what one was. I'd seen her in every gradation of undressed. So why was I shaking as I went down those red-carpeted stairs behind her? Why was my stomach churning as if a woman's hips were gyrating inside my rib cage?

I tried to appear nonchalant as I stood next to her at the bottom of the stairs and we faced Jer, the manager. Theoretically, the age minimum for the club was twenty-one. Coco had been sure that getting me in wasn't going to be a problem, especially on a weeknight when things were much quieter. 'Hell, some of the dancers are younger than you are,' she'd told me when I expressed my reservations.

She explained to Jer that I just wanted to hang out back in the dressing room. 'You don't mind, do you?'

The burly middle-aged guy looked me over from behind his podium. I had tried to dress up (for me) and look older (for me) and so was wearing black sneakers, a pair of red cotton capris, and a black denim jacket that belonged to my mom. In my imagination, the real reason he shouldn't have let me in was because I'd be so disapproving of the goings-on – not because of my tender age. So I angelically projected goodwill to him. I'm open. I do not judge. I accept.

'Just make sure,' he said in his thick Queens accent, 'she's not out on the floor.'

'Of course, Jer, what d'ya think? She's gonna write a report on it for school?'

I actually did have a gigantic report on religion in Japan due in two days. Should've been home working on that. And some algebra. And a lab. Oh, well. Jer grunted us in. And so I was allowed to cross the threshold into the world I was not supposed to enter. The world that was all set up for *them* – the men. I was now penetrating the zone. I felt like a spy who was in danger of being assassinated if the enemy found out my true mission. Because I *would've* liked to write a report on it for school (smile innocently for the bouncer who stood by the inner door), a scathing report, in which I criticized every aspect of this pitiful business and portrayed you, Jer, and all the men who make money off the 'girls' to be scumbags (convey complete acceptance while Coco says 'Hiya' to the friendly bartender) and nod (with good cheer) to the 'girls' who sat in stretchy evening gowns (reminding me of when I was little and went to the Platinum Club). A Bee Gees song played over the sound system. We made a sharp left into the bathroom.

Yes. The women's bathroom. That was the 'dressing room.' The Classy Lady couldn't even provide a real dressing room for its dancers! I'd once told Coco to complain, but she said it didn't matter. The point was to be on the floor, making money, not gossiping with the girls. She'd heard all the gossip before. This was all getting old. Her real concern was figuring out what she was going to do after she retired.

Coco applied her makeup, and I settled in, perfectly happy to observe the scene, even though it was pretty dingy. It was a fluorescent-lit, gray-tiled bathroom with two beige metal stalls (but only one had a door that latched) and a crapload of makeup on the counter. There was the constant commotion of women in various states of undress running in and out to redo their lipstick, complain about their boyfriends, and catch up on each other's news. This all felt familiar. She had friends from work over all the time. It was fun and cozy back here with the 'girls.' 'Out there' was what made me nervous.

And what I needed to see.

I wanted to hate those men out there.

But. I also wanted those men to show me I didn't need to hate them. They were simply enjoying the bodies. Feeling turned on. That didn't have to be a bad thing. After all, the old argument went, who was really doing the exploiting? The men used the women by paying for them with cash. The women used the men by pretending to be interested so they could get the cash. Sex for cash. Cash for sex. That was fair. As long as everyone was on the same page. As long as no one got confused that this had anything to do with *feeling* something.

But was that possible? Could people really be sexual with each other and not feel? People were always saying that men needed more sex than women. They have to 'spread' their seed and all that. But didn't the men feel something for the women? Didn't the women feel something for the men? I couldn't spend half a second *not* feeling *something* about every damn person I came across. Cabdrivers, cashiers, waitresses.

So how could these people manage to avoid feeling something for each other?

'I am so horny!' a blond girl with exceptionally pale skin exclaimed as she sailed into the stall with the broken latch and plonked herself on the toilet to pee. 'I really need a good fuck.' She wiped her totally shaved crotch with a complete lack of inhibition. I wondered if she was horny because of what she was doing, or despite what she was doing. These women did like being looked at. And the men liked looking. So in that sense, the Classy Lady was providing a service. This was harmonious, like any design of nature. And it was, generally, a jovial scene back in the dressing room, full of cheerful complaining. And it was particularly entertaining when the occasional female patron came in to go to the bathroom and realized she was also 'backstage.' I couldn't help but wonder, if the men had to use this bathroom too, would it get in the way of their fantasies about these women, or just enhance them?

'So did you hear about Trista over at Scores?' a short blonde asked as she applied pink lipstick.

'No, what?'

'She was out there doing her thing when one of her bags popped.'

'You're kidding! Right there onstage?'

'In front of everyone! And you know what? She was on the floor in a heap. They carried her off. Everything went on as usual. No one had any idea.'

'Fuck.'

'She'll be okay, though. Happens sometimes.'

The blonde checked out her own boobs for a second. Nope. They were fine.

After awhile, the air in the bathroom was making my head feel thick and the constant chatter was ringing in my ears. I edged out the door and stationed myself in front of the bathroom ready to duck inside if anyone noticed me. It was crowded out there now and business was humming. The décor. It reminded me of a roller rink in Jersey. Formica fake-wood tables. Brass banisters that hadn't been polished in years. Colored spinning lights. Pumping music, most of which seemed to be from the seventies. A DJ constantly urged men to visit the VIP room with one of the 'foxy ladies.' A stupid disco ball even hung from the ceiling.

Of course, the central focus of attention was the platform extending out into the middle of the room, where the dancers showed their stuff. Wooden chairs lined the edge. Small tables and chairs filled up the rest of the floor. And then in the back, in the shadows . . . well . . . I didn't really want to look back there. But I did. But I didn't. My eyes turned to the relative safety of the stage.

I'd thought each of the strippers would have a chance to go up and perform on her own. A five-minute showcase featuring each woman's individual talents. But that's not how it worked here. There were a bunch of them up on the long runway-like stage all at the same time. Right then, my mother was one of them. She was better than the others. I could see that immediately, and it had nothing to do with daughterly pride. She was so obviously a real dancer, with real striptease moves, and you wanted to watch her. In the dim lights, all the clues that would reveal her age were washed out, and she looked beautiful as ever.

Lucky thing the lights *were* down low, or the customers would see what I was seeing, because I wasn't being taken in by all this. How cheap the furniture was, how old and faded the carpet was, how thin this façade of 'pleasure palace' really was. So heartbreaking, really, to see that *this* was what grown men thought up to give themselves; *this* made their lives seem more thrilling. It reminded me of how a kid at a country fair sees only the pink cotton candy and stuffed animal prizes, not the alcoholic barker one step away from being homeless.

The other dancers just seemed to want to expend as little energy as possible, barely moving their hips as they stood in one place and, every once in a while, shedding a piece of clothing until they were left only in G-strings and high heels. But Coco was doing a real striptease. And she had her following. Men sat at the edge of the stage with eyes only for her, sticking bills into her garter, laughing, having a good time. Who was I to disapprove? Did I not want them to have a good time? She peeled off a long white glove and threw it to the side. The men cheered her on.

No, I didn't.

She peeled off another glove. The men cheered some more. She smiled down at them. Basked in their gaze. Jealous feelings crowded out my goodwill. Their good time was at my expense. Her smile was for them, not for me.

Get over it, I told myself, as I pulled my eyes away. Get over it! I wasn't a little kid. I didn't need her attention. Let the men enjoy her. Let her enjoy the men. She was still Coco. She was still my mom. She still loved me. It could all coexist. *Get over it.*

I tried to distract myself. At one of the tables, I saw a girl I recognized from the bathroom; her name was Amber. She was one of those pretty blond cheerleading types, and she was sitting with a very fat man with very fat lips – a man no woman would be predisposed to have sex with. Amber was in a gold spandex strapless gown, and he had his arm possessively draped over her bare shoulder, and I saw, the way he looked at her, it was like he wanted to devour her. Out in the 'real world,' Amber would never spend two seconds on him, but he could just walk in here and buy her company. No wonder this was a booming business. Just walk in off the street and, just like you bought that hot dog from the guy with a cart on the corner, buy a woman. I'd always known this in the abstract. But to see it playing out before my eyes, it just seemed really profound.

I turned my eyes back to the stage. Coco was stepping out of her dress. She was down to her G-string and heels. I told myself I could be brave enough to see this. It would not have to upset me. I could overcome all these mixed emotions, get a handle on it, contain it, not take it as some kind of personal affront.

Now that she was almost naked, it was time for her to hustle lap dances.

Lap dances. Coco said lap dances were what ruined the stripping profession. They caught on in the early eighties, around the same time strippers all started to get breast implants. Connection?

Before lap dancing, strippers were untouchable beings who looked down on the audience from a stage. The men were like privileged guests in the presence of an unattainable woman. Now the dancers had to go down to the floor and not only mingle with the guys, but hustle dances. It made the work much more stressful. Lots of people don't even realize dancers have to pay a fee for the privilege of doing a shift, then share their cut with the owners. If they don't keep hustling the lap dances, they don't make the good money.

The Platinum Club had very strict rules. Even during the lap dances, the men weren't supposed to touch the dancers; they were only allowed to look at that butt wagging three inches from their face. If those hands tried to cop a feel, they could get bounced immediately. The Classy Lady had lower standards. Admittedly, that's one of the reasons they were willing to hire my mom when she was on the wrong side of thirty-five. They allowed the men to touch the women when they danced.

I never understood how she could stand it. Coco claimed that the constant rejection was even worse than the touching. I couldn't imagine being turned down a hundred times a night. It sounded like being at a friggin' school dance every night of the week.

I saw her approach a man. He could've been any man, with gray thinning hair and a nice, kind-looking face – the kind of guy you'd want to be your grandfather. He wore white slacks and a plaid shirt and a white jacket. Nothing fancy. Maybe he was someone's husband. Maybe not. He seemed lonely. Until she came up to him. His face woke up with a smile. Did he know her? Was he a regular? I saw her hands run down his back as she whispered into his ear. He stood up and followed her to that dim area in the back, where a banquette was up against the wall in the shadows. I saw him sit. I saw my mother position herself between his legs. And she began.

I watched with a mixture of horror and amazement, worried that Jer would find me standing there and send me back to the bathroom, half wanting him to, half not. The man was like a lizard in the sun having his belly stroked. Transfixed by the sight before him. I was mesmerized too. Even though I knew I should look away. I couldn't. I ate the scene up with my eyes. She rubbed against his inner thighs. Leaned against his crotch. Let her breasts hang in front of his face, always keeping a bit of a smile on her face, as if this was bringing her pleasure too, only letting the boredom show when her back was to him and her ass was in his face. Then she could look around the room. Yawn. Stare at the ceiling.

I flinched when he put his hands on her, caressing her writhing hips, the indent of her waist. *Take your hands off her!* I wanted to yell. *That curve is not yours. She's not yours. She's mine!* Okay, this was silly. She wasn't mine, but she most certainly was not his. I crossed my arms over my chest. Felt the violation that she did not seem to feel. Felt it for her. Felt it for her, magnified eight million times. It was obvious he wanted to possess her, be inside of her. Didn't that make her nervous? He was a stranger. Strangers were dangerous. You never knew what a stranger would do. How could she be so trusting? My whole body seemed to contract, collapse inside, to make up for the fear she didn't have. Take your hands off my mother. Stop looking at her. Stop devouring her with your eyes!

I wanted to avert my own eyes, but I couldn't. No one could tell me there were no feelings involved there. Those were feelings I was seeing; he was *feeling* something! You think she wants you to touch her? You think this is real? You think she cares anything about you? You should hear what she says about you people when she comes home from work. She laughs. She thinks you're all fools. Don't you know that?

She didn't, actually, laugh at them, though, not so often. She was more likely to feel affection for the men, especially her regulars. But still. She would never want to see them outside the club. She didn't want to know them. None of this had anything to do with who they were, much as they wanted to think it did. Maybe I'd do him a favor and explain that. Tap on his shoulder. Wake him from his stupor. *Excuse me, mister. My mom? She couldn't care less about you.*

Oh, wait. Right. I didn't need to tell him that. He didn't care about her either. They didn't want to care about each other. This whole thing was set up so caring didn't enter in.

But, man. He sure was looking at her like he cared. Did caring have to be such a fleeting thing? The length of a lap dance? Three minutes? Then gone?

She smiled, and accepted his caress. Why didn't it make her cringe like it was making me cringe? She was used to it. Probably didn't feel it. Or did she like it? Had it ever made her cringe?

The DJ faded out 'I Feel Love' by Donna Summer and segued into 'Every Breath You Take' by the Police. I finally realized why most of the songs were so old. Most of the customers were middle-aged.

I felt overcome with a horrible feeling of sadness. A sadness that landed in my gut, as if those gyrating hips in my rib cage had landed, in a heap, on the floor of my stomach. People. So vulnerable with their needs! Maybe they were right, trying not to feel. Feeling could make you feel so goddamned lousy. I went back to the dressing room. I'd seen enough.

That night, as we walked the short walk home, I asked Coco, 'What do the men do with it?'

'Do with what?'

'They get all aroused, right? So what do they do with it?'

'Oh. They jerk off in the bathroom. Or go home to their wives. Or it ends up in their underwear, I guess. It's only about a teaspoon, ya know. It's not a big deal.'

'But doesn't it make them all frustrated?'

'They come in frustrated, sweetie. They don't leave that way.'

I didn't believe that then. I believed it even less as I grew older. He would hand over the money, which had to lead to some anger, because he would know she was just doing it for the money. And she would feel angry because he could have her for the money. So they *both* would be left with anger for being used. And all this anger spread like waves and polluted the world.

We reached the apartment and I followed Coco up the stairs. That's when I remembered I was now behind on all my homework. Math? Yuck. Religion in Japan? Who cared? This had been totally fascinating, even if it did rile me up. A strip joint sure did take your mind off the hassles of everyday life.

No wonder people went there.

i 'd finally, with Emma's help, gotten all of Leah's clothes packed up. Emma had decided to keep some sweaters, a beautiful full-length wool coat, and some dress-up dresses. I was glad she'd been able to face the 'things' finally, and that she'd set some of them aside for herself.

Now it was time to start on the desk. Emma was in the living room doing homework. Some chocolate chip cookies were baking in the oven. I sat down in Leah's swivel chair thinking this would be easier than the clothes, less personal.

The front top drawer was straightforward enough. Crammed with pens and papers and stamps and odd keys and packets of sugar and old receipts . . . I threw out everything that was obviously garbage and organized the rest into neat piles. Next to the desk, there was an oak wood filing cabinet with two drawers. The top drawer was full of work documents. I didn't know what to do with them, so I left them alone. The bottom drawer was locked. Probably more work papers. Oh, well.

I turned to her desktop. There was a pile of books: *Strangers on a Train*, a biography of Zelda Fitzgerald, *Moby Dick*, some old issues of the *New Yorker*, a Coach catalog. A huge stack of correspondence. I didn't feel right looking through it; there were some personal letters there, sympathy cards from when her father had died, letters from friends. I neatened it up, but didn't throw anything out.

Then I started in on the three side drawers of her desk. It was really getting overwhelming, and I was thinking I should just tell my father to do this himself. Tax forms, old Visa bills. In the bottom drawer was a spiral notebook. It had a yellow-and-orange plaid cover. I flipped it open. It was a journal. The first date went back about six months. The last date was from a few days before she died.

'Ginger!'

Emma was screaming from the kitchen. Still, I closed the notebook. 'What?'

'I think the cookies are ready!'

'Will you take them out?'

'Okay!'

I opened the journal back up and looked at the end of the last entry.

I don't believe there is a separation between the mind and the body. They are inextricably joined. What happens to one happens to the other. I wish I'd lived my life realizing that more.

I read it again. And again. As if it would keep her alive a little bit longer. Even though I'd purposely looked there first, I hated how it took on an extra power of profundity just because it was positioned at the end. Did she even know it would be her last entry? It took my breath away, realizing all over again that she was gone forever. How could it be?

Emma called from the living room. 'Are you coming? The cookies are out.'

'I'll be right there!'

I put the notebook back in the drawer. If there was one journal, shouldn't there be more? Or had she just begun this one when she saw that she didn't have much time left?

My gaze went to the file cabinet. The locked drawer. Maybe one of those keys in the desk fit that drawer.

I found the keys. There were three. The smallest one seemed like it would fit.

But I really shouldn't. It was none of my business. If she locked up her journals, it was because she didn't want anyone to see them. I should respect that.

I tried the small key. The drawer opened.

It was packed with spiral notebooks. Thirty or even forty of them. All plaid like the one in the nightstand, but in different colors. I flipped through the blue one on top. Yes, another journal. A lilac one. A green one. All journals. My father wouldn't want me to find them, so why ask me to go through her things? Maybe he didn't realize she kept journals. Yeah. Typical.

I took one out from almost the bottom of the pile. It was dated 1985. Wow. I put that one back and took another from near the top. January 2003. What a wonderful gift. Emma would love to read these one day. I turned to the first entry.

I hate my husband.

Or maybe not.
I read on.

I never thought I could feel these feelings, least of all towards him, but I do. I could kill him.

I looked up at the doorway. My heart was pounding. I couldn't resist.

He has made me so unhappy. And he doesn't seem to care! I thought he loved me. But when I told him I knew about that woman, he didn't even seem to feel any regret! And it's so, God, so disgustingly typical. She's young, she's got a perfect body. I never thought he would actually succumb to that. I thought he was above it. Hah! Maybe no man is above it. That's why they all . . . No. It doesn't do any good to generalize. This is him. My husband. My own husband. I hate him. I hate him!

I skimmed down the page, hungry to know exactly what it was he'd done. Had an affair, that was obvious, but with who? For how long? Where? How?

I couldn't find the answers. It would take more digging. I'd probably have to go back in time to piece it together.

I put the journal back in the drawer, locked it up, put the key in my back pocket, and went out to Emma in the living room.

'How's it going?' she asked, not looking up from her history book.

'Okay.'

'Want a cookie?'

'Yeah.'

I was trembling. What if Emma happened upon these? I couldn't just leave them there, even if there was a key. What if she found the key, like

I did? I could keep the key, but what if my father asked me about it? I felt very protective of the journals. Would Leah want him to see them? I went to the refrigerator to pour myself some milk.

'Are you okay?' Emma asked.

'Yes!' I took a bite of cookie.

'They turned out well, don't you think?'

'They turned out very well.'

Before leaving, I found a large Duane Reade shopping bag in the back pantry and piled in all the journals. Then I covered the journals with some of Leah's scarves. I set the bag out in the hall by the elevator so Emma wouldn't see me taking it. I wasn't planning on keeping them; I just really, really didn't want her to find them by accident. I'd figure out later where to put them back, so I'd know they'd be safe.

As soon as I got home, I laid them all out on my bed and put them in chronological order. Then I went back to the one I'd looked at before and started to skim forward until I found the entry where he admitted that this woman wasn't even the first one he'd been unfaithful with. Evidently he liked having little flings with younger women.

At first, Leah was relieved that it wasn't a real affair, an emotional affair, with a woman he cared about. She thought he would stop as soon as she confronted him and beg her forgiveness. But he didn't.

I am truly floored. He seems to think the only problem here is that I found out. I thought he would offer to stop, but he says he doesn't want to. He doesn't even seem to feel guilty! And now I feel like there's something wrong with me, because I can't compete with these girls. I feel so horrible. It hurts so much. Can I forgive him? Does he even want my forgiveness?

I closed the journal, lay my head back on my pillow, and stared up at the ceiling. The idea that he didn't care whether she forgave him or not made me so mad. He was the one failing her, but he made her feel deficient!

A conversation I once had with Leah came to mind. It would've been soon after she found out about my father's cheating. We were strolling through Central Park. I was complaining about Coco, who'd just self-published her 'how to strip' book and was busy trying to publicize it and get people to take her classes.

'I just wish,' I had said, 'I could have a normal mother.' I'd totally expected Leah to chime in and run Coco down.

'But you know what?' Leah responded. 'In her own way, Coco is a very strong woman. Do you realize she's never been dependent on any man? That woman knows how to take care of herself. Sometimes I wish I could be more like her.'

It had really annoyed me at the time. Now I knew what she'd been driving at.

chapter twenty-five

Chef Jean Paul waited to speak until we were all standing around the butcher-block tables. 'There will be a banquet in two weeks. We will prepare a buffet. Investors and potential investors are invited. I will assign each of you a dish. Please do not ask me if you can make a salad or a soup or a vegetable or a fish or a chicken or a cow. That is my decision. However, if you are planning on continuing in pastry next year, let me know, and I will assign you a dessert.'

Tara raised her hand. 'Will this count heavily towards whether we're admitted into the Master Class?'

'Everything you do,' he yelled, 'counts heavily towards whether you are admitted into the Master Class!'

It gave me a certain amount of satisfaction to see him bellow at her like that.

'Needless to say,' Jean Paul continued, 'this banquet is very important to Mr. Knickerbocker.' Mr. Knickerbocker was the president of the school. I'd only seen him twice: once when I toured the school, and once when I was giving the school secretary my tuition check. Both times, he was sitting behind a huge mahogany desk. He was about eighty years old, and he'd never once come down to our floor, but rumor had it he ate upstairs in the school restaurant all the time with his thirty-year-old peroxide blond girlfriend.

'So!' Jean Paul continued. 'Please raise your hand now if you are hoping to continue in pastry!'

This was it. The moment for me to come out to Jean Paul as a pastry chef. Ralph raised his hand, and a couple of the second careerers. Then I did. And then Tara. What a drag.

'At the end of the day,' he said, 'I will post a list. It will say what you will make. Please do not come to me and complain because I will not change my mind. Now separate into the following groups. Half of you will be making tomato *concassé*. Half of you will be making pastry cream.'

Of course, I wanted pastry cream. I'd made *concassé* up the wazoo at Chantal. But no, I was doing *concassé*. The only good thing was that Tom was doing it too. Tara had been assigned pastry cream. I noticed her pout to Tom. Aw, too bad. Ralph, who was also assigned pastry cream, winked at me as I put my cutting board next to Tom's.

'So how's it going at the job?' I used a tone that I hoped would convey that I was adjusting to the concept of us being friends, of course we were friends, there'd never been any reason to think we were ever going to be anything but friends, so please don't imagine that you've decimated my soul.

'Pretty good.'

After I was done sharpening my knife, he asked if he could borrow my steel.

'Sure. Nothing worse than slicing a tomato with a dull edge.'

It was no use thinking I could seduce him away from Tara. Especially since I wasn't going to wear that red dress. Especially since I had no shoes to go with it. So he might as well see what a good sport I was.

Once the tomatoes had been doused in boiling water, we all set to peeling. I picked out a nice plump one, slit an X at the bottom and pulled back the skin. 'So. Is Mr. Glass treating you well?'

'I have to say . . .' Tom looked up just to make sure Tara was not nearby. She was heading towards the walk-in. 'Jonathan Glass is a very arrogant man. He's constantly letting us know in one way or another that we all can easily be replaced.'

'Is he that nasty?' I wasn't really surprised, but I wanted to encourage Tom to run him down some more.

'Yeah. I mean, I know I have to be grateful for the job. I'm learning a lot. But it's not easy.'

'Especially after being here all day.'

'I counted thirteen burns on my hands and arms last night.'

'Get out!' I halved my naked tomato.

'Look at this!' He pulled up his sleeve and showed me an assortment of red welts.

'Ouch.'

'Last night, I got my palm. Could barely hold anything, but he made me finish the service.'

'What a jerk.' Maybe Tom noticed I was enjoying the crit too much, because then he started defending the guy.

'Of course, I can understand that. He needed me. And it was my own clumsiness. I got through it okay.'

'But still . . .' I squeezed a tomato over my cutting board to get the excess seeds out, then diced it up and threw it into a huge bowl our group was rapidly filling.

'The guy is a genius,' Tom insisted. 'Sometimes I think it's absurd that I'm paying so much money to stand around and do this.' He nodded towards the bowl.

'Right,' I said. 'I know.' As I pulled off a nice swath of skin, I couldn't resist saying, in a subtly catty tone, 'At least you have Tara there to make it easier.'

He was silent a moment as he chose a tomato to work with. 'Yeah.' He slit it with an X. 'Tara idolizes her dad. I don't think I could ever be as good as he is.'

'You mean as good as he is to the world? Or to her?'

He hesitated. Cut his tomato in half. 'Both.'

'I have no doubt that you will surpass Jonathan Glass one day.'

'Why do you say that?'

'Because I've seen what you can do. I know you're ambitious. And you have what it takes. There's no reason why it won't all happen for you.'

Maybe I was trying to butter him up. But I did truly think he had a perfectly good chance to succeed out there. He was a competent, attractive white male with ambition. Why shouldn't he?

'Thanks,' he said, wiping his hand on his side towel, then pressing my arm. 'It means a lot to hear that from you.'

'You're welcome,' I said, glancing at where he'd touched me. Actually touched me! Maybe I wasn't completely out of the running.

At the end of the day, a bunch of us were waiting in the lobby for Jean Paul to post the list of assignments for the banquet. Kingsley got off the elevator.

'Ginger! Just the person I wanted to see.'

'Hi.'

'How are you?'

'Fine.'

'And how is your sister?'

'She's good.'

Ralph looked at me, like, *What sister?*

'I was wondering . . .' Kingsley was speaking in a hushed voice and sneaking a look sideways to make sure no one else could hear. 'I'd like to invite you and Coco to dinner . . .'

'I . . .' . . . didn't know what to say. Was he just asking me along so he could get Coco there? Or was he asking her along so I wouldn't feel like it was 'a date.' Would I have wanted to have dinner alone with Robert Kingsley?

'Nigel Sitwell is in town,' he went on, 'and I thought I'd have a little get-together. Try some new recipes on him. . . .'

'Nigel Sitwell?' Ralph asked. '*The* Nigel Sitwell?'

Nigel Sitwell was royalty in the cooking world. Somewhere in his seventies, fat, British, effeminate, he had the reputation for being the know-it-all of know-it-alls.

'You can come too, Ralph,' Kingsley said. He turned to me. 'I think Nigel would love Coco. And I'm developing some ideas for a new menu, and would love to have some guinea pigs, so . . .'

'Sure,' I said. Ralph was nodding his head vehemently. 'We'd love to come.'

'Great. I'll get back to you about a date. Nigel wasn't sure about his schedule. And if you could keep quiet about this . . . I don't want anyone to feel snubbed.'

Kingsley headed to the kitchen. I turned to Ralph. 'Do you think he's lusting after Coco?'

'Your "sister"?'

'She likes to pass herself off that way. Just play along, okay?'

'How can you let her do these things to you?'

'She's not doing it to me. She's insecure about her age.'

'Honey, you cut her way too much slack. You should definitely out her that night at the dinner table.'

'No way. Sometimes I worry about her, ya know. She's been so dependent on her looks for so long. What happens when they go? If it makes her feel better . . .'

'But how does it make you feel?'

'I can handle it. Look, I don't have to invite her. I can just say she won't come.'

'But you will invite her, won't you.'

'I'm with Kingsley. I bet it will be easier to deal with Nigel Sitwell with Coco in the room.'

Jean Paul emerged from the kitchen and posted the list. Immediately, like actors competing for the lead, we all flocked around to see. No one wanted to get stuck with a 'supporting role' like fruit salad or butter cookies.

Priscilla was assigned an endive with bacon and goat cheese appetizer. Tom got roast beef au jus. Ralph was down for apple tartlets. I looked for my name, and saw that he'd assigned me choux swans.

My first reaction was disappointment. I hated choux swans. True, they were a crowd-pleaser. But they were prissy. Traditional. Outdated. Lots of steps to make a pastry that ended up looking like a cream puff waterfowl.

Then I heard Tara complaining. 'Biscotti? He wants me to make biscotti? They're so dull! Who cares about biscotti?'

No one. It was true. But the swans would be a good showcase for my skills.

I rode down the elevator with Ralph feeling a bit, dare I say, cheerful. As soon as we were out on the street – and away from any potential eavesdroppers – I asked his opinion. 'Do you think he thinks the swans are beyond my ability so he's setting me up to fail in front of everyone?'

'Ginger, darling. I can believe he might enjoy watching you fail. But in front of the investors? That would be self-destructive.'

'So . . .' We stopped at a red light. I turned to him. 'Do you think he's actually showing some faith in me?'

'It's hard to believe. But yes.'

The light turned green, and we crossed.

chapter twenty-six

When I heard Coco come home, I was in the kitchen drinking some hot chocolate and eating peanut butter out of the jar.

'So I went to get my mammogram today. The follow-up, because the first one wasn't good enough, remember?'

My first thought was they found something. 'And?'

She got some Muenster and a hunk of duck pâté from the fridge. 'Everything's fine.'

'Oh. Thank god.' I took a sip of hot chocolate. It was made from powder and hot water, but I'd added a bit of half-and-half, and it wasn't bad. 'Have you ever considered taking those things out? I mean really, Mom. You don't need 'em anymore.'

'Have you seen pictures of women who had their implants removed?' She put some cheese in her mouth. 'Their breasts look like cow dung.'

'Cow dung?'

'Cow dung that's been stepped in. I am really getting sick of this diet.'

'You want some wine?' Wine was one acceptable indulgence she allowed herself on Atkins.

'Desperately.'

I retrieved an opened bottle of Cabernet from the fridge. While there (ulterior motive) I took out a jar of grape jelly. I love eating peanut butter and jelly straight, no bread. I'd been resisting the jelly, though, because it made me want more peanut butter, which then made me want more jelly, a vicious cycle.

'I know you're just looking out for me but really, Ginger, you worry too much.'

'Maybe you're right.' I poured her wine.

'So Jack and I are making plans. We're thinking of going to Vegas and doing the marriage thing there. But I wanted to make sure that's okay with you. I mean, I'm guessing you won't mind missing the actual ceremony. We'll have a party here when we get back.'

'That's fine. So are you excited?' I tried to keep the doubt out of my voice.

'I'm a little freaked out, to tell you the truth.'

'It's a big commitment.' I dipped my spoon into the jelly jar, and savored a half spoonful of the purple corn syrup, pectin, and what had to be a trace amount of actual fruit.

'Yep.' She took a gulp of wine.

I chased down the jelly with some peanut butter. 'You must be pretty fond of the guy.'

'I know you find that hard to believe. But we do have a good time together.'

'And the financial security will be nice too.'

'He's not making me sign a prenup, if that's what you're wondering.'

'That's nice.' A little more jelly.

She laughed. 'It's the most romantic thing anyone's ever done for me.'

I put down my spoon. 'I actually have some good news of my own.'

'Do tell! You know I love good news.'

I told her all about the banquet and the choux swans.

'You see,' she said, 'I knew he'd learn to appreciate you.'

Then I told her about Robert Kingsley. 'He invited us to his place for dinner. And guess who's going to be there. Nigel Sitwell!'

'He wrote that famous book, didn't he?'

'*The Art of American Cookery.* He's like a hundred years old and really cantankerous and really rich and really gay.'

'This is so exciting! You know what? You and I are going to Sephora. We'll have someone do your makeup. Stock up on everything you need. Then get your eyebrows waxed. A facial . . .'

'Why?'

'Obviously Robert Kingsley has a thing for you.'

'Mom, he's my teacher! You're the one he's after.'

'I am otherwise engaged. Come on! The guy is attractive, successful . . . you gotta exploit the situation, girl! We'll make an appointment with Christopher. Let him give you a trim, highlights, and a conditioning treatment, because your hair' – she lifted a few locks, then dropped them – 'is so dry. And, by the way, you need new bras. Your boobs are sagging.'

'Mom . . .'

'What?'

'I'm not being auctioned off like a slave.'

'You've just got to use your equipment! Would you stop trying to fight biology?'

I took a sip of hot chocolate. It was tempting. But if I got all done up like that, I'd be buying into the same crap that made men like my father cheat.

Plus, what if it worked? How frightening was that? Could I deal with a handsome, successful man like Robert Kingsley desiring me? 'Anyway, you're getting carried away. Robert Kingsley is way out of my league.'

Coco looked at me. 'What's the matter? Does he remind you of your father or something?'

'No!' Where'd she get that idea? That was ridiculous. Kingsley was nothing like my father. 'Kingsley is nice. And Kingsley is much more interested in me than Ben ever was. I mean, in a professional way, of course.'

Coco belly-laughed. 'You're funny. I'm gonna take a shower.'

I was about to tell her about Leah's diary. But it was so likely she'd say something that would upset me. Kingsley like my father? No way. I took one more half spoonful of peanut butter, and kept my mouth busy with that.

*t*he lingerie section on the fourth floor of Bloomingdale's had *too* big a selection. But Emma was like a kid in a candy store. I followed her as she waltzed past the carousels of racks displaying one designer brand after another. 'Ooh, look at these! They're so beautiful. And these! Aren't they cute? Is this too expensive? Can I get one of these?' She held up thongs with three slot machine cherries and JACKPOT! on the crotch.

I said, as neutrally as possible, 'Funny.' I was clinging to her concept of me as someone cool and not uptight.

'Please?'

'Let's look around some more.'

'Which is your favorite?' she asked.

'Maybe the Hello Kitty.' It was sort of cute, with a picture of Kitty on the miniscule crotch and rainbow elastic on the waist and the leg holes. 'But you're too young for these.' At least I could try to dissuade her by playing the age card.

'Too young for Hello Kitty? I'm too old! Anyway, all my friends have 'em, so what's the big deal?'

A saleswoman approached. 'May I help you?' She was in her seventies with a low V-neck that showed off her cleavage and a very short pixie cut dyed blond.

'Just browsing.'

'May I interest you in today's special?' She held up a bra. 'A gorgeous lace demi with support wires that won't dig into your rib cage.'

I wanted to say, *So you admit those wires dig into your rib cage?* 'No, thank you.' But then I couldn't resist asking, as I held up a thong that said NO DICE! with two dice on the crotch, 'Do girls her age wear these things?'

'They love 'em. Aren't they cute?' She pulled a few more thongs off the rack. 'Isn't this funny?' There was a picture of an astronaut, and the words INVADE MY SPACE. 'So playful.'

Playful. Yet screwed up. 'Thanks for your help.'

'My name is Fiona if you need anything else.'

I steered Emma towards the regular bikini underwear and a display of boy-cut briefs. At least they were adorned with icons like Miss Piggy and Kermit the Frog. 'These look good.'

'I want thongs!' Emma said.

'Why don't we check out the bras?'

'I want padded,' Emma said.

'Why?'

'Why do you think?' She looked at me with distrust. My cool image was fogging up.

'You don't have to pretend to have more than you've got. It's absurd. You are what you are. And you aren't exactly flat.' She had as much going on top as I did.

'But I want to look as good as possible! And I need at least one pretty one for a strapless dress I'm wearing to my friend's bar mitzvah. Oh, look at this.' She pulled out a black lace Wonderbra.

'Can I just ask why, at your age, you need such fancy underwear? Who's gonna see it?'

'No one. It's just so I feel good while I'm wearing it, duh.'

Duh. Or . . . was thirteen-year-old Emma already playing around with boys? This young, innocent thing who'd shoved menstrual-stained underwear under her bed? Come to think of it, those underpants had all been much more conservative than the ones she was ogling now. 'Did Leah let you buy sexy stuff like this?'

'No, but she was *so* much stricter than all my friends' moms, I swear to god. She just didn't get it. But you're not like her. I mean, my god, you grew up with Coco!'

'Why don't you pick out an assortment and see what feels comfortable.'

'Look at this!' she said, beelining it towards the teddies. 'Isn't this funny?' It was totally sheer pink and then had two pink hearts – one to cover each nipple. Another larger heart was on the crotch of the matching thong. Who said romance was dead?

'Cute,' I said.

She fingered an ice blue sheer number that tied between the breasts and then draped open to expose the belly and had matching bikini underpants. 'This one is so beautiful. Do they have a medium?' She started to look through.

I was about to express horror that she would seriously consider wearing a teddy. The thing was completely see-through, except for an extra layer of lace around the bosom area. But she pulled one out and draped it in front of me. 'You should *really* try this on.'

'I don't think so.'

'It's perfect for your coloring. And so pretty!'

I wondered how Emma could envision me in something so feminine and delicate when she'd only ever seen me in jeans and T-shirts. She just seemed to assume I was capable of this too.

Maybe I was.

Maybe this was an opportunity. Just to see myself in it. No one else would have to. It would be in the name of research.

'It would drive your boyfriend crazy,' she said. 'What's his name? Ian?'

'Ian and I broke up.'

'Oh. Sorry. Then you need it for the next guy.'

Tom? Worse yet, Kingsley? Oh, man. Could I parade around in front of him like a sex kitten? Would he find this cheesy? I certainly hoped so. But. This stuff was hardwired into men's brains to bring about erections. It had nothing to do with common sense. One thing was for sure. No one would look at me in this and think I was one of the guys. I took it from her.

'Yay,' she said.

We searched out the entrance to the dressing room. The attendant paused from her Sisyphean task – putting a huge pile of bras back on their hangers – and led us to some curtained booths right next to each other. Fiona must've had her eye on us, because she swanned in just as I was about to close my curtain. 'Let me know if you need any other sizes, ladies.'

'Thanks.'

'Good luck,' I said to Emma across the way.

'Have fun,' Emma said back.

I took off my sneakers and my baseball cap, then my jeans and underwear, and stepped into the bikini bottoms. Then I pulled off my T-shirt, undid my bra, and slipped my arms through the thin straps. I adjusted the bow so it landed between my breasts, and took a good look in the mirror.

It was obscene. My god. Even though the bra part had an extra layer of lace, you could totally see my breasts. I felt like I was spilling out. Flooding the dressing room. Flesh everywhere.

This went beyond the red dress. This was downright . . . hot.

I undid my ponytail and fluffed up my hair. Leaned on my right leg, letting my hip jut out. Put my hands on my hips. Lifted my ribs so my breasts pointed up and out. Oh, yeah, I was a sexy babe. Dangerous curves. Legs not bad. Pink, young flesh. I raised my eyebrows. *Come 'ere . . . Kingsley. I mean, Robert. Bob. Hi there, Bob. Surprised? Well, don't be. It's been there all the time . . . waiting for you to notice . . .*

'How's it going?' Emma asked from the next booth.

I panicked, and tugged the curtain, which was already closed, over some more. 'Forget it!'

'Wrong size?'

It fit perfectly. 'Too expensive. Fifty-eight dollars.'

'We'll put it on my dad's credit card!'

Her dad. Like he wasn't my dad? Well, I'd never had a credit card with his name on it – that was for sure. I slid the underwear off and stepped back into my own pair. 'Have you found anything?'

'I guess.'

'Good!'

'Ginger? Can I please, please, please get a couple thongs? Just a couple?'

I pressed my lips together, zipped up my jeans, and censored the urge to ask her if wearing a thong wasn't like voluntarily walking around with a piece of gristle stuck between your two front teeth. 'I guess.'

'Thank you!'

Once I got all my clothes back on, it sure felt reassuring. As if the world had been tilted too far over, and now it was back where it had always been. Though the same old view did seem a little tired.

We took the escalator down. I was dying for a cup of coffee and something sweet. The restaurants in the store were usually crowded, and I felt the need to get some air. 'Are you into getting a snack somewhere? Something sweet?'

'Sure! Where should we go?'

It was four o'clock. Teatime. I loved afternoon tea. There weren't all that many places in the city that served it, with the whole watercress-sand-wich-and-scone routine, but we did happen to be within walking distance of one of the best. 'Have you ever had tea at the Plaza?'

'I don't like tea.'

'You can have hot chocolate.'

'I like that.'

Tea at the Plaza was usually reserved for special occasions like birth-days or whatever. Coco and I had gone there about five times total in my life. But today did seem like a special occasion. Emma's first thong with a padlock on the crotch. And my first time in a teddy.

'Do you like scones?'

'Do I breathe air?'

'And baby sandwiches?'

'Can we go? Please?'

The Palm Court was right off the lobby of the Plaza Hotel. It had the feel of an enclosed garden, with its four potted palms in giant marble urns, cane-backed chairs, and the magnificently tall arched faux windows. There was a spectacular display of beautiful (though conventional) desserts on a round table in the center of the room. A woman in an evening gown played the harp, and an elderly man in a tuxedo with bow tie strolled around playing the violin. The subject of my father came up right after the surly waiter delivered our scones and clotted cream.

'So how,' I asked with extreme caution, 'has it been? Living, you know, with just Dad?' I was not fishing for dirt. I wanted to give her a chance to vent.

'Oh, you know. He's so busy all the time.'

'Yeah . . .'

'And he's not really very good at talking.'

'Right.'

'But he does try.'

'Uh-huh.'

'Last weekend he took me to Ralph Lauren and bought me a Polo shirt.'

'What color?'

'Purple. With a green horse.'

I'd packed away a Polo of Leah's that was magenta with a yellow horse. 'That's nice.'

'In a way, it doesn't seem fair. He buys me lots of stuff, but not you. I mean, you're his daughter just as much as I am.'

'Yeah, well, it's not the things I miss so much. He's just so emotionally distant. He's always been like that with me. Always has to maintain a distance.'

'Yeah, well' – she was spreading some clotted cream on her scone – 'he's like that. You know. With everyone. To some extent.' She put the knife down. 'I guess.' And took a bite.

'But he's like that more with me. And Coco.'

I knew I should keep my mouth shut. She didn't need to hear this.

'Well, god,' Emma said, chewing with her mouth open, 'he couldn't risk having Coco in his life. Just imagine.'

'Why not? She's in my life.'

'Yeah, but, you know.'

'No. I don't know. Tell me.' I took a sip of hot tea.

'You know . . .' Emma leaned forward, whispered with relish. 'Coco is like . . . you know . . . basically a whore!'

I put another scone on my plate, but I knew I wasn't going to be able to eat it. 'How can you call her that?'

'I'm not saying she was a whore *really*. But you know . . . come on . . .' She turned red, realizing she'd said something wrong. 'You know what I mean.'

The strolling violinist came by right then and started playing 'The Sound of Music' in our ears. I was tempted to tell Emma that her 'high and mighty' father was not above sleeping around, lying, and cheating. The harpist, who looked like a sixty-year-old virgin, was plucking at those strings like there was no tomorrow. Why did harpists always come off like old maids? Even for people like me who were offended by the concept of old maids. 'You shouldn't judge someone when you don't know the whole story,' I said, silently apologizing to the harpist.

'I'm not judging her.'

'No?'

'No! I mean, she was a stripper, right? So everyone knows what strippers do.'

'Yeah, they dance around in G-strings. Which are almost exactly like the thongs you bought today.'

'Yeah, but I'm not gonna dance around in public . . . Look. This is stupid. Why are you getting so weird?'

I wanted to do a smear job on our father so badly. Tell her all about his slimy little affairs. 'I'm just saying that life is complicated and we don't always understand why people do what they do.'

Emma glared. 'You're just jealous, that's all. And you always were.'

We both sat back in our chairs, back from the table, back from the food. It took some self-control not to suggest that perhaps *she* was jealous of *me*. I had the 'fun' mom. The 'cool' mom. The mom who was alive. She was stuck with the Sheriff. So what if Coco had been a 'whore.' At least she could show her feelings. Even if she said the wrong things to me, at least she *said* things to me!

'Look,' I said, 'let's just forget about it. I don't want to fight.'

Emma stared down into her lap.

The waiter came by and asked if I needed more tea. 'No, thanks. Just the check.' He bowed, and returned promptly with the bill. Each of our 'teas' had been $29.90. I'd known the price going into it, but right then it sure seemed like a major rip-off.

I took Emma home in a cab. The meter ticked away. We were silent. Do cabdrivers notice when people don't speak? Probably all their customers ran together in a big blur. As we pulled up to the front of her brownstone, I considered saying something to smooth things over. After all, she was a teenager. Best not to take any insensitive comments or waves of emotion too seriously. She got out without a word and slammed the door shut before I figured out what to say. It made me feel lousy. After all, she was the one who'd insulted my mother and then accused me of being jealous. All I'd said was her father wasn't perfect. Big deal. I didn't deserve the cold shoulder for that.

Maybe I should keep my distance. I was a fool for thinking I could get close to her and the Sheriff. They were the enemy, weren't they? Always looking down on us. Coco had always known that and tried to warn me.

The cabdriver asked me, 'Where to?'

I told him to take me to Lexington and Sixtieth Street. I went inside Bloomingdale's, took the escalator back up to the lingerie section, and went straight to the rack with the ice blue teddy and pulled out a medium. Then, as I was passing the display of thongs, I grabbed a Hello Kitty in a large. Fiona was on top of me immediately.

'So you couldn't stop thinking about it,' she said, giving me an (ugh) wink.

'Do you take a check?'

'With the proper ID.'

I followed her to the cash register. This was shaping up to be a very expensive day.

chapter twenty-eight

'Restaurant management.' Kingsley stood up at the front of the demo kitchen and looked us all over. 'How many of you really know what that means? For example. Who can tell me exactly what a manager does?'

At Chantal, they bossed people around, hired and fired the waiters, and made sure there was toilet paper.

'Order the food,' Tara said, 'and plan the menus.'

'And how,' he asked, 'do they decide what to order? What to plan?'

Silence.

'Restaurants,' he said, 'are not in the business of serving food just to make a room full of strangers happy every night. This is not charity. And it's not vanity either, though for some it starts out that way, and if it does, you won't last a year. This is a business. You have to make a profit. You have to, at the very least, break even! So. Whether you end up owning your own restaurant or just working in one, it's vital that you understand how it all works.'

He launched into a speech about weekly numbers and cost of sales and gross sales and deducting fixed costs and gave us a formula for how to cover overhead to make a profit. I stared at the way his nice broad shoulders emerged up out of his slim hips and wondered for the zillionth time why he was honoring us with his presence, how his own restaurant was doing, and was he really planning on opening a new one in New York City.

'The manager makes a budget every week,' he continued. 'He bases it on how many meals he thinks he'll serve that week. Then he takes the average check into account. And that will let the chef know how much money he can spend. Now. When does that become a problem?'

Tara raised her hand. 'When the chef spends too much. Because the chef wants to look good. So he'll order all these expensive ingredients to impress everyone, so you could have a totally packed restaurant but lose money because the food costs are so high.'

'My point exactly.'

She smirked.

'That is why,' he said, 'it can be a problem if the chef is the owner. How do you stop yourself from spending too much? Especially if you want to make a name for yourself?'

Did he have that problem? Was Zin failing?

'It's a very unstable business. Unexpected problems are going to happen. The refrigerator breaks down. There's a snowstorm on a Saturday night. Everyone cancels. The bartender is drinking up your wine and the waiters are stealing your silverware. Truthfully? Owning a restaurant is one big pain in the neck.'

I raised my hand. Kingsley nodded at me. 'So do you think it's smarter, from a chef's point of view, not to own your own place? Because of all the headaches involved?'

'Certainly, while you're just getting started, work in different places. Absorb what you can and move on.'

He smiled at me. My heart pitter-patted. I smiled back.

'Oh,' he said, still looking at me. 'One other thing I wanted to mention.' It felt like he was talking only to me. 'Private parties.' Was he referring to our dinner party? No, that was our secret. 'Hiring your restaurant out for private parties is the key to financial stability.' Of course that's what he meant. I nodded. He broke eye contact. 'Many people don't realize that. But it's ideal. The customer gives you a deposit. You know exactly how many people you're going to cook for. Nothing is left to chance. So they're very important for the manager to actively pursue. Remember that. Private parties.'

After Kingsley dismissed us, I walked with Ralph to the lobby. Did Ralph notice how Kingsley's eyes had lingered on me? Or had I just been imagining that? Tara and Tom were ahead of us. They had their arms around each other.

'Looks like they're having their own private party,' Ralph said.

'Not so private, if you ask me.'

Ralph and I held back as Tom and Tara parted ways at the doors to the locker room. Then I followed her in.

'I'm helping plan a private party for next week,' Tara was telling Priscilla. 'It's hosted by the Association of Women Chefs.'

'That's cool,' Priscilla said. 'Can I come? Maybe I can schmooze around and get some job leads.'

'Sure. It should be fun. Those women chefs know how to party.' And then she added, 'I hope Tom stays over with me tonight after work, so he doesn't have to go all the way back to Astoria.'

'Poor guy,' Priscilla said, 'going to school all day, working all night and then having to take the subway home.'

'But I'm happy to provide a bed for him.' She slammed her locker shut. 'Hey, you feel like hitting Victoria's Secret? I'm sorely in need of bras.'

As I pulled on my jeans, I thought of the teddy. It was in my bottom drawer, hidden under a stack of old bathing suits I hated. One night, when Coco was over at Jack's, I could invite Tom over for dinner. We could have some pasta and wine. Just as friends. Watch TV. As friends. After sitting all close and snuggly next to each other on the couch, as friends, I'd demurely retreat to my bedroom, and reappear in the teddy looking absolutely ravishing. Before we knew it, we'd be more than just friends . . .

I had one foot up on the bench, and was balancing on my other foot as I tied my Pumas. As Tara passed behind me, she bumped into my rear end and almost knocked me over.

'Oh, sorry,' she said. And then, as if she was trying to be friendly, 'You know, I have to say. You have a very impressive collection of sneakers.'

'Thanks,' I said, wary.

'So did I,' she said, as she walked out the door, 'when I was ten.'

I finished tying my shoe and slumped down on the bench. Yes. The shoes. The importance of shoes could not be denied. It was time to do something about the shoes.

chapter twenty-nine

'What exactly are you looking for?' Ralph asked, as we strolled around the maze of footwear on display at Shoe Biz. I couldn't help but go to the sneakers. There was a really cute pair of purple-and-black Kangaroos with a little baby-sized change purse Velcroed to the lip.

'Don't even think about it!' Ralph commanded, pulling me away.

'But they're adorable.'

'You must focus.' He steered me to some lethal-looking, almost vertical high heels. 'Dangerous for anyone who doesn't know how to dance *en pointe*,' I said, giving the French my best Jean Paul flourish.

'It takes practice. Wear them at home first. Build up the ankle muscles, the calves. It's not like you could walk into a gym and suddenly do a hundred bench presses.'

'I think I could do that more easily than get down the street in those.'

'Bad attitude, missy. Come on. You want Mr. Carpenter to realize you're a female, right?' He picked up a slightly less scary-looking pair. 'Try these on.'

'You know what? This is incredibly stupid.'

'You're right. And you know what else? People are stupid. Your problem is that you think you're better than people. But I've got news for you, honey. You're one of us.'

'Okay, you pick a pair. Surprise me. I wear a size ten, and no cracks about Bigfoot.'

I sat down by the wall and let Ralph consult with the shoe guy.

'He's bringing you a selection.'

'Thanks.'

He handed me two Peds. 'Put these on.'

I tried. I did. But when I got one end of the Ped around my toes, it would pop off the heel, and when I got it to hook on my heel, it would pop off my toes. 'Were these designed by an angry midget? Why can't they make them just a little bit larger?'

'Can't you stretch it? Jesus, why is everything so hard for you?'

The shoe guy put a stack of boxes on the floor. Ralph opened the first box. The Ped was gripping the perimeter of my foot like Wile E. Coyote on the edge of a cliff. 'Basic black heels.'

'Hurry, before the Ped pops off.'

I crammed my foot in as quickly as I could, but wouldn't you know it, the Ped slipped off as soon as I had it on. Now there were lumpy folds of nylon under my arch. 'My feet are just too big,' I muttered, as I leaned over, blood going to my head, cheeks flushed. I hooked the Ped back over my heel again and jammed my foot in. Felt the hard leather imprison my foot. Poor little scrunched toes pleading for mercy. Was I really going to relent? Join the enemy? Give in to the insanity? My foot was unrecognizable. The top of it was almost bursting out, and the toe cleavage only seemed to broadcast that I was an animal, a Homo sapien, related to apes and monkeys – not some svelte babe. 'Ralph. You know the bathing suit competition in the Miss America pageant?'

'Put on the other one.'

I crammed it in. 'They wear high heels with the bathing suits. Who does that? You go to the beach, you wear flip-flops.'

'You want Miss America to wear flip-flops?'

Like a bride in an arranged marriage about to be deflowered, I made one more futile protest. 'I don't want to be an object!'

'Ginger. Darling. You *are* an object. Whether you wear the shoes or not.'

'I am?'

'People are objects. We just are. We take up space. We appear in photographs. We fit inside coffins. There's no way to avoid it. You are an object.'

'I am a subject.'

'Yes, you are – a wacko subject. But you are also an object. You are both. Get it? Both. It's weird, I know. Perhaps an object should not be able to conceive of her own objectness. That's why it's so weird being a human. But we can, so stop fighting it and try to enjoy it a little. Now would you please stand up and model them for me?'

Enjoy it. Yes. He was right. If you're going to wear something that causes you physical pain, you might as well enjoy it for all it's worth.

I forced myself to slowly rise. Felt all the weight go to the balls of my feet. Gripped the bottom of the shoe with my toes. Felt my pelvis stiffen and my lower back arch and my breasts thrust out as I made myself erect or risk falling on my face.

Hmmm. I did like the way my body seemed to become very long. Tall. Towering, in fact. My feet – they seemed very far away. All the way down there, all the way at the other end. Could there be some power in surrendering to this? I leaned on my right foot, jutted out my hip, and crossed my arms. The words *Here I am, don't fuck with me* came to mind. Where did that come from?

'You okay?' Ralph asked.

'As long as I don't move.'

'Try walking.'

'Okay. I'm going to casually stroll to that mirror over there.' I took a few steps. My calves were clenched, my knees were locked, and I really felt like at any moment one of my ankles would buckle and twist and I'd be on crutches for two months.

'You look like you're wading through cement.'

'Okay, this is harder than learning how to ice skate backwards.'

'Come back,' he said, 'try this pair. The heel is a little lower.'

I got back to the chair and slid them off with relief. Except now I was intrigued. There had been something . . . interesting . . . about that. He opened the next box. It was a pair of red heels. They had an open toe and a bow on top. Cute – in a way I didn't usually associate with myself. Maybe they would go with the red dress. It was hard to tell if the colors would match or clash. Since the Ped popped off as soon as I took the black pumps off, I decided to skip it and slipped my bare foot in. Again, the leather encased my foot.

I rose. Because of the open toe, they weren't quite as painful. And at least the heel was only three inches as opposed to five. I pulled up my jeans and saw there was indeed something attractive about what it did to the shape of my calves. How it flexed my foot and extended it. Didn't my foot tense up like this when I was having sex? No wonder men liked this.

The whole posture it forced you into – it was like parading around in a sex position while you walked!

I strolled to the mirror. Couldn't help but feel like I was presenting my body to the world. Here I am! Up here on my pedestal! Glorious me . . . most definitely *not* one of the guys.

Before handing over the cash, I made sure I could return them in case they didn't go with the dress, or in case I decided to return the dress, or in case my normal state of mind returned to me. They said I had thirty days. I figured that was enough.

chapter thirty

'Stripping is a slow form of torture.' Coco was doing a special work-shop for a support group of divorcees. 'That's right, ladies. I'm go-ing to teach you how to torment that very special man in your life!' The women laughed. After all, many of them were here to figure out how to attract men even though they now hated men. 'It's all about revealing yourself, but in a very controlling way, okay? You're the one who decides *what* he sees, *when* he sees it, and for *how long* he sees it.'

Hmmm. Maybe I'd been performing the longest striptease in history. Well, it was time to throw in the thong, so to speak. I was gonna get over my inhibitions and practice what my mother preached.

'And you know why it works? Because all men are afraid. And what are they afraid of?'

She looked around the room. There was silence. I knew I knew the an-swer, but for some reason I was having a mental block. What was the damn answer? Finally one short skinny woman in the back said in a small voice, 'Getting it up?'

Coco pointed at her. 'Bingo!'

Of course. How could I forget?

'They all live in fear that *they won't be able to get it up*. This motivates everything they do. And chances are, the more successful he is, the more he has to prove. And why is striptease so effective?'

Again, she waited for someone to answer. A woman with black hair and blond streaks gave it a shot. 'Because he just gets to sit there and watch?'

'Not only does he sit there and watch. He is denied. Deprived. No privileges. No rights. No mercy. Striptease is the ultimate hard-to-get. That's why it works. The more he's denied, the more he wants it. So what's the most important thing for you to do?'

No one dared speak. I too waited for her to continue. It was as if I was hearing everything for the first time. Never before had I listened with the intent to actually try out what she said.

'Go slowly! Draw it out. Don't just tease him. *Torture* him. It's like a mystery novel. Let the suspense kill him. Get him so he's dying to get to the last page. To know who the killer is. To see you naked. Any of you ever been to a strip joint?'

Only two of the women raised their hands.

'So what happens,' Coco asked, 'when the stripper gets naked?'

The two club veterans started to speak, then shrugged.

'Once she's naked,' Coco said, 'she's done! Oh, sure, she may dance around a little longer, but basically, the story is over.'

She didn't go into the lap dance phase of the event.

'The audience wants to start with someone new. Because once the mystery is solved, it's not interesting anymore. They're all ready to solve the *next* mystery. And each of you, no matter what you look like under those clothes, is a story waiting to be told.'

Was this profound? Or was I losing my mind.

Coco had all the women stand in rows. I put on that song from the seventies, 'Midnight at the Oasis.' It was so languid, it usually got people going. Even I started to sway with it.

She had everyone mimic her. The bump. The grind. I did my own mini bumps and grinds. She tried to get them to thaw out their pelvises. 'Move those hips, ladies! Imagine you're trying to touch every wall! Make your bodies take up as much room as possible!' She happened to notice me moving to the music, raised her eyebrows, and grinned. 'That's right, go for it!'

My first impulse was to stop moving. After all, I didn't want her to have the pleasure of thinking she was 'getting through to me.'

But then I decided, what the hell. Let her be pleased. I kept on dancing. Allowed my bumps and grinds to get less mini. She gave me a happy nod. It was almost embarrassing to get her approval. I blushed and felt dizzy, like the room was swaying, but it was only my hips.

chapter thirty-one

i caught the end of their fight when I was coming out of the locker room.

'But you're always working! I thought we could at least do something together on your night off.'

'I'm really exhausted. I just want to relax.'

'Fine. Let's go to my place.'

'I really think I should go home.'

'All the way to Astoria? Why?'

'Tara . . . I'm just really tired.'

That's when she saw the little grin on my lips, which had some of my mother's Hard Candy 'Daringly Diva' lipstick on. Which the salesgirl at Sephora had said went perfectly with the Hard Candy blush, mascara, and eye shadow.

We three got on the elevator.

Silence all the way down.

Tom seemed puzzled by my altered appearance. I tried not to wipe my mouth with the back of my hand.

As we got off the elevator, Tom said to me, 'So how is it going?'

'Not bad . . .'

Tara turned to Tom. 'I'll walk you to the subway, then.'

'That's okay.'

'Oh. I see.' Tara gave me a dirty look. 'Fine.'

She left, and Tom turned to me. 'You were saying?'

'Was I saying something?'

'Things aren't bad?'

'Oh, yeah, not bad.' I tried not to rub my fingers in my eyes.

'You want to get a bite to eat? I heard there's this really great place in the Village. I've never been down there. You wanna go?'

The Village was in the opposite direction of Astoria. I tried not to jump up and down with excitement. 'Sure.'

We headed for the '1' train.

The waiter gave us the wine list and a menu. Tom ordered us each a fourteen-dollar glass of Cabernet and the cheese sampler plate. 'My treat,' he said, after the waiter left.

'Are you sure?'

'Have to have some fun with my slave wages.'

Tell me this wasn't because of the damn cosmetics.

I began our conversation on safe ground: my anxiety over the upcoming banquet. 'I've been practicing my choux paste at home. I really want them to turn out perfectly. It's tricky, because if you add too many eggs, the dough won't hold its shape.'

'I'm sure you'll do fine.'

'He'll find something wrong with them no matter what.'

'His culture says women shouldn't be chefs, but he can see you have talent. It probably scrambles his brains. Plus, you're attractive.'

'Maybe,' I said, my heart skipping about three hundred thousand beats. I suddenly wanted to check my makeup. Receiving the compliment made me insecure about my looks all over again. That was the trap, wasn't it?

'So how's it going at L'Etoile?'

'The job is okay.' He took a sip of wine. 'But it's getting kind of awkward.'

'Oh?'

He looked down at his empty place setting. 'I think Tara got me the job because she's attracted to me. And . . . well . . . you know . . . she is pretty, and smart . . .'

'You can skip this part.'

'Sorry.' He looked back up at me. 'I guess she's not your favorite person in the world.'

'I didn't want to be her archenemy. It just seems to have evolved.'

The waiter brought our plate of cheese: Brie de Meaux, 'grassy flavored with a hint of nuttiness'; an aged goat's-milk Gouda, 'tangy and smooth';

and a Bleu d'Auvergne, 'herbaceous and pungent.' I took a bite of the Bleu. It was so good. I took another bite and spread it on a slice of baguette. Very tasty. Took a sip of wine. It was particularly sweet for a Cabernet. Oh, yes. A person could live off this. I was happy.

'You look different,' he said.

I spread some Brie onto a slice of baguette. 'Do I?'

'Did you do something to your face?'

'I might've put a little makeup on this morning. I've been so careless about that since starting school . . .'

'Oh.' He wrinkled his eyes, scrutinizing me. I waited for the compliment. It didn't come. 'So anyway,' he said, taking a piece of Brie, 'things with Tara. It's getting to be more than I can handle.'

'Really,' I said, going for a sliver of the Gouda.

'Working for her father and everything . . . She seems to be into me more than I'm into her. And I'm not sure what to do about it.'

A warning light was flashing in my head. Was he using me as a pal to discuss his love life? Or was he confessing this because he was attracted to me? And were they or were they not having sex together? And did he or did he not want to have sex with me?

'Which one is your favorite cheese?' I asked.

'I don't know. They're all good in their own ways, don't you think?'

After we'd each had another glass of wine and finished off the sampler and every scrap of bread in the basket, I was feeling quite dizzy. 'Let me take you home,' Tom said.

We strolled down Bedford Street through a really old, pretty part of the city where there were still lots of turn-of-the-century redbrick brownstones adorned with eyebrow-like shutters and festive flower boxes that made me think of dollhouses. What would it be like to live in one of these houses? Could life possibly measure up to the appearance of serenity? It sure was tempting to think so. You could imagine going down the winding lane one beautiful evening a hundred years ago in a horse-drawn carriage with gas lanterns lighting the way.

For once I felt thankful that the train was crowded, because we were forced to sit squished up against each other. We didn't even try to carry on a conversation, just sat there swaying against each other every time the train accelerated and slowed down. I luxuriated in our private bubble, oblivious to the crowd around us. I wished Tom would put his arm around me so I could lean my head against his shoulder, but he didn't, which made me want him to do it even more.

As we pulled out of Penn Station, my dizzy high was deflated by the realization that Coco was most likely going to be home. And so I really couldn't let him up. No way I was taking that risk, especially at this critical juncture. Much as I would've liked for him to come over, it was not going to happen, so there was no reason for him to bother to get off with me, and I had to let him know that before we got to Times Square.

'You know what,' I said, 'you should just stay on the train.'

'But I want to walk you home.'

'I don't want to inconvenience you. And this will take you straight back.'

'I'm not in any hurry to get home. To tell you the truth, it's sort of dull out there. I thought maybe you'd show me your place.'

'Oh. Well. You know . . .' Damn! What to say? 'It's a mess. And I have to study my notes. And I'm really kind of tired.'

'Oh, okay.' He shrugged. 'Sure.'

The train pulled into the Forty-second Street station. 'So . . . good night.'

'Good night.' I hesitated, thinking maybe I should just invite myself to his place.

'You'd better move,' he said, 'or you're going to miss your stop.'

I popped up out of my seat, dashed to the door, ducked under someone's arm, stepped on about three people's feet, and barely remembered to yell, 'Thanks for the wine!' as I hopped onto the platform of the grubby station. Hordes of people headed towards me on the narrow platform. I snaked through them to the dirty cement stairs and emerged up on Forty-second and Seventh Avenue, which had to be one of the most crowded streets in the world, except maybe somewhere in Bangkok. As I made my way through the chaos of cars, buses, cabs, sirens, street vendors, tourists, and commuters, I felt utterly anonymous. Such a contrast to the quiet closeness I'd just had down in that underground tunnel with Tom. Up here, people were lining up for ultimately disappointing movies, wandering out of ultimately disappointing plays, searching out strip clubs and peep shows for ultimately disappointing encounters, spilling out of bars and restaurants celebrating their short, sorry little lives.

What a world.

chapter thirty-two

Coco, Ralph, and I stood in front of the two tall white double doors of Kingsley's town house in the Village. Ralph lifted and dropped the brass knocker in the shape of a hand. Kingsley, wearing brown corduroy pants and a white button-down shirt, opened the door. 'Welcome!'

'What a lovely home,' Coco said, as we stepped into the elegant foyer that was all wood beams, wainscoting, and Oriental carpet.

'Isn't it? I can't take any credit, though, it's a sublet from a friend.'

'Lucky you.'

'I'm glad you could make it. Good to see you again.'

Coco looked out of place – but hot – in gold stilettos, black leather pants, and a gold Lycra bandeau top. I was wearing white Pumas with white bell-bottom jeans, and the lilac plaid halter top I'd gotten at H & M. As much as I'd resisted Coco's advice that day, I felt grateful to her now. Though I was relieved there was a chill in the air so I had an excuse to wear a sweater over it. 'Ralph, Ginger. I'm not used to seeing you in street clothes.' Did I imagine a look of approval as he looked me up and down? Did I dare take off my sweater? Not yet.

He led us to the living room. 'Come in!' It was Nigel Sitwell. 'Don't be afraid!' His voice boomed with a regal but swishy British accent. About two hundred pounds overweight, bald, mustached. He ruled the room from his spot in a huge easy chair. 'Did you find your way here without getting lost? I always get lost in the damn Village, and my driver was talking on his cell phone in some godforsaken Creole patois not paying attention to where the hell he was going and there was about five goddamn inches of legroom. With my gout, let me tell you, I was suffering. Had to keep my foot turned sideways the whole time!'

'The food is almost ready,' Kingsley said, 'so please relax and help yourself to some wine, and the marvelous duck liver pâté with pistachios that Akiko made.'

Akiko?

When Kingsley went through the swinging door to the kitchen, Ralph and I both caught a glimpse of an Asian girl. She looked like she was still in her late teens. I wondered if Kingsley had hired her just for this, or if she lived here with him.

'So nice to meet you,' Coco said, as she poured us each some wine.

Ralph and I sat on an antique love seat facing Sitwell. It was creaky and stiff, like it wasn't really meant to be sat on, with carved, curvy wooden arms. Tweedledee and Tweedledum.

'So you are Robert's students!' Sitwell exclaimed. If only I could be back in the kitchen helping Kingsley cook, not out here.

'They're Robert's *favorite* students,' Coco said.

'And you are?'

'Coco, Ginger's sister.'

Ralph nudged me in the ribs.

'And I suppose you have another sister named Cream of Tartar?' Sitwell exploded with laughter. I couldn't help but crack a twisted smile.

'I read in *Food & Wine*,' Ralph said, 'you're coming out with a new cookbook.'

'Am I? Who keeps track anymore? They want me to write another, but I have nothing left to say. Even my ghostwriters have run out of ideas!'

'Somehow I doubt that,' Coco said, perching on the arm of an empty easy chair kitty-corner to him. 'You look like a man who has something to say about everything.'

'And you look like a whore. Where did you get those fantastic tits?'

Coco burst out laughing. 'Where the hell do you think? Mother Nature?'

'Not unless Mother Nature is a very horny man.'

It was apparent why Kingsley had asked Coco. They were a perfect match – tactless and crass.

'I just had to go back for a mammogram. Let me tell you, it's like having a garage door close on your dick.'

'I have a male cousin,' Sitwell said, 'who had breast cancer.'

'Really.' Coco sampled Akiko's pâté. 'That must've been embarrassing.'

'He died, actually.' Sitwell laughed. 'Imagine being a man and dying of breast cancer!'

'How gauche,' Ralph said, then mouthed the words 'He's insane!' to me.

'Have they ever figured out why men have breasts?' Coco asked.

'Actually' – I dared enter the conversation – 'it is possible for men to breastfeed. Biologically, they have everything you need to do it.' Cultural anthropology, freshman year. 'It's just a convention of society that they don't.'

'That's disgusting,' Ralph said.

'I don't fucking believe you,' Sitwell said.

'Why would a man want to do that?' Coco said. 'He'd choke the kid with his breast hairs.'

'Sisters, you say,' Sitwell said, pointing his cane at both of us. 'Lots of rivalry between the two of you, I imagine?'

'No, not really,' I said. 'She's prettier. I accept that.'

'Bullshit, darling. You hate her and wish she'd get hit by a car and die an agonizing death.'

He laughed again. I felt lousy that no one tried to contradict me and say that I was in fact the prettier one. I was, after all, making an attempt. Did anyone else notice how hot it was in that room? I took off my sweater.

'Is anyone else going to eat this stuff?' Coco spread some pâté on a cracker. 'It's fantastic.' She looked at Nigel. 'Would you like?'

'Poison!' Nigel said. 'Cholesterol, it's bad for my gout. But what the hell!' He laughed.

Kingsley came into the room and announced that dinner was ready. I'd never seen him so nervous. I didn't like seeing him kissing up to someone more prominent.

We all moved to the dining room, where there was a beautifully set table. The room had bay windows, a huge chandelier, a tall, very grand-looking fireplace, more wood paneling all around. Akiko made an appearance, and Kingsley introduced her. She was petite and quite adorable and bowed at everyone. Then Kingsley sat down with us and let her serve the food. It was incredible. Something he called *gnudi*, like gnocchi, but made with sheep's-milk ricotta dusted in semolina, pan-fried in butter and topped with sage and Parmesan. Tuna tartare with wasabi roe. Roasted asparagus with a saffron-mustard sauce.

'So,' Coco said to Kingsley, 'how is your restaurant out there doing? Not too well, I imagine, or you wouldn't be teaching, right?'

Nigel Sitwell harrumphed, but was concentrating on fitting an asparagus into his mouth. I wished Kingsley would say something to her like *It's none of your fucking business*, but he didn't seem annoyed. And my ears did perk up, since I was still wondering why exactly he had decided to come to our school.

'Zin is doing quite well. My staff keeps it going. We have a new menu this year. You do always have to try new things, or people get bored, but luckily my reputation seems to keep people coming around.'

I couldn't tell if business was bad and he was trying to cover it up. Or maybe he was being gracious towards Coco because she had no idea how famous he was.

'But the restaurant business is tough,' he said. 'Very competitive.'

'Lots of egos involved!' Nigel said as he chewed. 'Lots of people hoping you'll fail. You have enemies out there, Robert, never forget you have enemies.'

Kingsley looked really uncomfortable and took quite a big sip of wine. Ralph and I exchanged glances.

'I didn't realize,' Coco said, 'it's so cutthroat.'

'It's a nasty business,' Nigel said. 'Always got to watch your back. Isn't that right, Ginger.'

I nodded and swallowed a *gnudi*. 'Yes.'

'So,' Kingsley said, 'I'm planning on Paris this summer.'

'Paris!' Nigel practically yelled. 'Paris is the answer, darling!'

'I find that I need to go back there periodically,' Kingsley said, 'just to get my bearings.'

'I've never been,' Ralph said, 'but I'm dying to go.'

'Ooh la la,' Coco chimed in. 'Gay Paree. Now that's a place I could get into. Those people know how to make marriage work!' She was already done with her first glass of wine. Akiko appeared out of the kitchen to pour her another and kept a poker face as Coco shouted, 'Bored with your sex life? Just fuck your married friends!'

Kingsley smiled at me (with sympathy?) and shook his head.

Nigel laughed. 'I love this woman!'

'Not that I'm some big advocate of marriage,' Coco went on. 'God knows, the best way to ruin your sex life is to get married.'

'Amen!' Nigel said. 'I can't figure out why gays think they want to get married.'

'Maybe,' Ralph said, 'so they can also get divorces.'

No one laughed at his pitiful attempt at a joke. He shrugged.

'This food,' Coco said, 'is fabulous!'

After dinner, I helped Akiko clear the dishes while the others went back to the living room. I was thinking I might be able to figure out her age and if she was his girlfriend. But I'd only had a chance to thank her for the meal when Kingsley came in. 'Ginger, you don't have to do this.'

'I want to.' I was leaning over, scraping bits of food into the garbage, wondering how much my breasts were showing.

'You're such a hard worker. Someone is going to be very lucky one day.'

'To have me as a wife?' I couldn't believe he was saying that.

He laughed, and then – did he just pat Akiko's butt? – 'To have you as an employee.'

'Oh, right.' Of course. Akiko was smiling to herself as she rinsed dishes.

'Would you like to see the garden?' Kingsley asked. 'It's incredibly beautiful, and totally unexpected right here in the middle of the city.'

'I'd love to.'

Whoa. He was taking me away. From the others. To be alone! How would I keep up a conversation with him, like an adult, just the two of us? Okay, not *like* an adult. I *was* an adult. I could do this. I could rise to the occasion. I could pretend to be his equal. Maybe I was his equal. If he thought I was, who was to say I wasn't? Maybe he didn't know me very well, but I could pretend that I was confident and self-assured, and then maybe eventually I actually would be. Except. Oh, god. Were my nipples showing? I glanced down. No. Calm down. Relax!

I followed him to the back of the kitchen through a small eating area and out some glass double doors. There was a slate patio with some bushes and small trees along the side and a little fountain with perpetually trickling water. We sat on a cement bench under a tall ginko tree.

'Your sister,' he said, 'was not entirely wrong about my restaurant. Zin has been losing money, losing customers. And, sadly, I have to admit the food has been compromised.'

'Oh. I didn't realize.' So he was going through a rough period. But why was he telling me? 'But it is a very cyclical business. I'm sure you can find a way to revive it.'

'People expect to see me there, but how can I cook and promote my book and do my shows at the same time? So when Nigel offered to invest, I jumped at the opportunity. I know he's a bit flamboyant, but I am fond of him, and he is pretty amusing – '

'It makes total sense.' Why was he telling me this?

'We're also planning on opening a café in Calistoga. A bakery café. Something more casual than Zin, of course, but with the same commitment to high quality ingredients drawing on local flavor . . .'

My ears perked up. 'Calistoga is right near Napa?'

'A lovely town famous for its hot springs. It has these lovely Arts and Crafts bungalows from the twenties and thirties. People are starting to buy them up and renovate; it's very exciting. The main street is a little rundown, but charming.'

'Main Street?'

'There are not one, but two bookstores, an old-fashioned candy store, some funky old motels from the forties that have mud baths and hot stone massages and that sort of thing.'

'Sounds wonderful.' Did he want me to come work for him? Because my answer was yes. Yes. Yes! I wouldn't have to care about Jean Paul anymore, or the stupid Master Class, or Tom, or Tara, or Coco or anybody, I could just fly across the United States and end up on *Main Street* with *Robert Kingsley* doing what I wanted to do most!

'You're a lovely young woman,' he said. 'And I think you're very talented.'

'Thank you.'

'I think you'll have a wonderful career.'

'It's nice to hear that.'

'I have to say, I haven't made very many friends here in New York.'

'No?'

'So I wanted to ask . . .' Kingsley leaned ever so slightly closer to me. Oh, my god. This was it. He was going to ask me to go to dinner, just the two of us, and then we would become lovers, and then I would move out to California with him, and then we would get married, and eventually I would take over the the Main Street Bakery, and our children would work behind the counter when they were old enough and I would live happily ever after for the rest of my life!

'Your sister.' He cleared his throat. 'She's not seeing anyone, is she? Because . . . I think she's a lot of fun, and I was thinking of asking her to dinner . . .'

My eye focused on a cigarette butt lodged between two slats of slate.

'But I wanted to check with you first,' he went on. 'You don't mind, do you? Since you are a student, I wouldn't want to make you uncomfortable.'

My skin felt raw. 'My sister . . .' Exposed. 'Is not my sister.' Freezing. 'She's my mother.'

'What did you say?'

'Coco is my mother. She likes to tell people she's my sister. But she's actually forty-three years old, and she's engaged to a man who used to manufacture buttons, and he isn't even making her sign a prenup.' I got up.

'I see. Well.' He stayed sitting. Rubbed his chin and chuckled. 'I guess it's a good thing I asked you first. Save myself the rejection.'

I nodded. 'Yeah. It's always good to avoid rejection.'

I went inside to get my sweater.

jack sat in the living room sewing a button on Coco's only white dress, a vintage full-length gown we'd found in a secondhand store in the East Village. Coco read a book on how to play craps. They were leaving for Vegas the next day. He licked a piece of thread before poking it through the eye of a needle. As I watched this cozy scene, I actually felt a thimbleful of warmth towards Jack. He would give my mother security for the first time in her life.

'If I don't see you before you leave,' I said, before going to bed, 'have a great time.'

'Thanks!' Jack said. 'We will!'

Coco seemed to be unusually quiet. Serene? I imagined she was in shock that she'd never have to worry about money again. I kissed her on the cheek. 'Good night.'

' 'Night, sweetie. Love you.'

'Love you.'

She gave me a wink as I went off to bed.

The weekend dragged. For once I had the place to myself, and should've enjoyed every second of it, but instead, I found it depressing. I missed Coco, who didn't call. I felt bad about Emma, but didn't call her. I thought about Tom, and even walked by L'Etoile Saturday night just to be in the vicinity of him, but didn't dare go in. Sunday was really depressing. I hated midtown when all the office workers were home and the streets were relatively empty and even the theater crowds were gone. Ralph came by Sunday night, thank god, and we watched *Mildred Pierce*, an old Joan Crawford movie we both loved about a woman whose husband leaves her and she starts her own restaurant and it becomes a big success – partially because of her pies – and she has an evil daughter who ends up sleeping with her new, rich husband who gets murdered . . . I'd seen it four or five times before. I went to bed feeling glad the weekend was over.

Monday morning, I woke up before my alarm went off and walked to school with purpose. Ralph and I had discussed it the night before. I had to seize my opportunity and seize it now. As soon as I got there, I went straight up to Tom.

'So . . . I was thinking . . . seeing as you want to experience the city, and I'd like to experience it the way tourists do, I thought maybe you'd like to go see a play on Broadway with me.' I continued in a rush, not wanting to give him a chance to turn me down. 'It's something I haven't done in years, but you can get cheap tickets when you stand in line at this booth in Times Square, and I thought maybe it would be fun in a cheesy sort of way. . . .'

'That sounds like fun.'

'Great. So. What's a good night for you?'

'I have tomorrow night off.'

'So should we go tomorrow night?'

'Let's do it.'

That night, I hardly slept. I was up obsessing about what I was going to wear. Did he even know it was a date? Because I was intending on dressing up. Would I feel like a fool? I didn't want to be dressed up if he wasn't dressed up too. My eyes felt sore in the morning, as if I'd been squeezing them shut all night against their will.

That day at school, Jean Paul was in a particularly bad mood. The banquet, two days away, was a logistical nightmare, and he was in a snit trying to organize everyone. There was going to be lots of competition for the ovens, so I had to get to work on my choux paste and bake it off in advance. I found myself resenting my task. I didn't want to think about making the swans. I wanted to think about whether I was going to wear the red dress. Already, being an object was getting in the way of being a subject.

I went to get my recipe and, even though I knew it well, stood there and read it over three times trying to focus. There were two shapes that had to be baked to assemble the swans: the main body, which would be cut open on top and filled with cream – that top piece would be cut in half and placed upside down on the cream to make wings – and the long delicate pieces that would make the swan necks.

I set up my *mise en place*. Measured everything out. Set it up on a spot I staked out on the counter next to the stove. Milk, water, butter, sugar, salt. Flour to be added later. Then eggs.

I mixed everything but the flour and eggs to a full boil. By the time I was adding the flour, I'd completely forgotten about my wardrobe crisis. I stirred fast without stopping until it was thoroughly incorporated. Then I continued to cook it, never letting up on my stirring.

Other than Tom, who was at that moment sautéing mushrooms at the next stove down, I was oblivious to everyone else in the kitchen. Baking really did make me happiest. It was all about combining things. Once you assembled your ingredients, it was a matter of letting it all fuse. By the time it was in the oven, your work was done.

'So we're on for tonight?' Tom asked, as he passed behind me on the way to the sink.

'Yep.'

Were we ever! My *mise en place*? Ready. The underwear. The dress. The shoes. The makeup. Sexy Ginger was ready to assemble. Teddy optional.

I focused back on my saucepan. My choux paste had formed into a big lump of a ball. I took it off the flame, transferred it into a bowl, and then immediately added my eggs. With each egg, it got smoother and softer and glossier. I checked with my spoon to see if it would peak. It still seemed a little thick. I added another egg. Tried again. It seemed good. I didn't dare add another.

And so, for better or worse, my choux paste was ready. I was counting on these swans to show Jean Paul that I was perfectly capable, no, *more* than capable to make it in this profession.

I filled a bag with the paste and piped out the delicate S-shaped necks. Did my best to make each one flair with confidence. Curvy and dramatic. Yes. They looked good. Then I pinched the end of each one to make a little beak.

With the rest of the dough, I made the bodies of the swans that would be filled with whipped cream, and put them in the oven.

Ralph was at the same time putting his tartlet shells in the oven. 'So you're coming over later, right?' I asked. He'd already promised to help me with my 'makeover.'

'Are you kidding? I can't wait! This is so exciting!' He looked at me, his blue eyes as wide as his smile. Sometimes he was just so cute.

I baked my swans to a light golden brown, checking the tray of necks often, because they didn't need as much time. When I took the mounds out, I made a small slit in the side to release the steam so they wouldn't soften while cooling. Jean Paul had not bothered to warn me to do this, but I'd read it in a recipe I had at home, so I felt clever about it. After letting them cool, I carefully covered them and slid my trays into the reach-in refrigerator. The morning of the banquet, I would make the raspberry coulis and the cream filling. Then I'd assemble everything, and *voilà*. My little flock of swans would be ready to be admired and consumed!

Ralph and I went straight to my place after school. Tom was coming by later, at seven, to pick me up.

The first thing I did (while I made Ralph wait out in the living room) was try on the Hello Kitty thongs.

Whoops. Hello, pubic hair. I could just see Coco melting her wax with glee.

I pulled off my T-shirt and forced myself to evaluate further. This was not for the faint of heart. The elastic from my hipsters left a jagged outline around the thongs that would totally destroy any sexy image the item was meant to promote.

Okay, the outline would go away, but who would've predicted such a thing? Why was achieving sexiness so complicated?

The worst thing was the back of the thong. It kept digging into my butt-crack. I kept pulling it out. My god. How did someone spend a day in this? I called through the door to Ralph, 'I'm taking a shower!'

'Don't forget to shave your legs!'

'Thanks!'

God forbid . . . I mean, GOD FORBID a woman wear a dress exposing hairy legs.

The spray of the shower cascaded on my back as I steadied my left foot on the edge of the bathtub and hoped I didn't slip, fall, crack my head, and bleed to death. Running my pink plastic razor through a cloud of apricot-scented shaving cream, I pondered the tyranny of hair. The folly of follicles.

Hair.

Always growing.

On the top of your head? Feminine power. On your legs? Too masculine. Armpits? Get rid of it. The space between your eyebrows? Bad news. Over your lip? The unspeakable shame!

I rinsed the razor under the spray and did my ankle. Somehow, over the years, women had become slaves to the management and maintenance of hair. Condemned to spend a great deal of time monitoring the constant, unrelenting growth. Why? The human race survived for a pretty long time before the invention of Nair.

One leg down, another to go.

Did men even appreciate how much effort women put into this? I planted my left foot on the rubber floor mat, balanced my right foot on the edge of the tub, steadied my hips, and slathered on a thick layer of cream. No, they didn't, because it was all done in secret. As if that sleek, silky skin came about naturally. Sure, it was okay to watch a guy shave his face. That showed what a manly hunk he was. But watch a woman pluck one stray little hair off her chin? Ew.

Yet, I had to admit, as I rinsed off, there was something nice about a freshly shaven leg. Sort of like a cucumber with the skin peeled off, revealing the slippery soft perfection underneath.

Next, my pits. I raised my left arm and slathered on more cream. At least the apricot scent was nice. Kudos to some chemist. Better than any real apricot I could remember whiffing. Hard to smooth that concave surface in there, but I persisted. Tom would not spy one stray hair on my body. I was even going to go for the pubes. Deceive him with my pristine hairlessness. Flawless. Defying age. Denying death.

Now for that remaining triangular patch – the most offensive growth of all. I wasn't going to get rid of it completely. Couldn't bring myself to. But I trimmed the hedges, knowing I would pay for this later with a rash. Good-bye, little hairs. Nothing personal. Off you go.

I gave myself one final rinse under the spray. Even if we did get down to the thong or beyond, was I about to parade myself around? Was he really going to notice my landscaping?

Stop thinking! Thinking, in this context, was blasphemy. This was about *not* thinking. I stepped out of the shower and dried off.

Ralph was knocking on my bedroom door. 'Can I look? Let me in!'

'Hold on!' I slipped on the dress and put on the red heels and avoided looking at myself. 'Be honest.' I put my hand on the doorknob. 'But be nice.' I opened the door.

His chin dropped.

'What?' I asked.

'I'm stunned.'

'Is it bad?'

'No.'

'Weird?' I looked down at myself. Why did dresses make me feel dorky?

He rubbed his chin. 'No . . .'

He stood back and looked me up and down some more. 'Ralph, would you say something? You're freaking me out!'

'You've got . . .'

He paused, and I filled in the blank. *Ugly calves. Boobs! Balls!* (to go out in public like that). *A lot of nerve . . .*

'. . . a nice figure! Look at those legs. You've been holding out on us!'

'You're just being nice.'

'Shut up and let me put on your makeup.'

I sat down at my desk. Submissive. Coco would've killed to have the chance to do this. She and Jack were due back from Vegas the next day in time for a strip class in the evening. I still hadn't heard from her. Oh, well. They were probably too busy celebrating. She'd be back soon enough. All ready to pack up. She was talking about doing a major purge of her stuff at the same time. But tonight, Tom and I could spend the evening together without any fear of Coco Interruptus.

I didn't watch in a mirror, just completely handed myself over to Ralph. He dibbled and dabbled, every so often stepping back and peering at me. 'I feel like a fairy godmother,' he said. 'Not really the part I always wanted, but . . .'

'Cinderella?'

'Of course.'

'Why? The prince had all the power.'

'You're hopeless.'

I sat quietly while he painted my lips. Maybe I was hopeless. Kingsley had failed to notice my 'charms.' Tom would too. He'd see me all done up and laugh hysterically. Finally, Ralph announced that I was done and had me walk, with my eyes closed, to the full-length mirror.

I opened my eyes.

I couldn't believe it.

'I look like a transvestite!'

'You look like a woman.'

I groaned. 'I'm so uncomfortable. I can't wait to take it all off.'

'When you do, hopefully you'll be with him.'

I guess I should've warned Tom that I was spending the evening as a woman. Because when I opened the door to the apartment he stood there in the hall and gaped at me like I was an alien from outer space. Come to think of it, from a Martian's point of view, I was an alien from outer space. I certainly felt like one.

'Hi,' I said. 'Are you okay?'

'Wow. Is that you?'

'Theoretically.'

'You look different.'

I couldn't help but respond with a tone of dread. 'I know.'

He didn't look thrilled, or not thrilled, just confused. He was wearing olive green khakis, a tan shirt, and a black jacket that did not look expensive, but did look ironed. Not as dressed up as I was, but more dressed up than usual. He didn't seem as tall as I remembered him – that was my heels, I realized – but his broad shoulders and slim hips were wonderfully reassuring as usual and I craved his embrace.

'You look great,' he said. 'I just have to adjust.'

'Don't bother. I'm not about to do this every day.'

I was somewhat aware that this was not the sort of thing one was supposed to say when one was presenting oneself in a new, supposedly better light.

'I feel honored.'

He was still standing in the hall. Scared to proceed? Or was I barring his way. I stepped back. 'Come on in.'

He entered with caution. Looked around. Took in the gold velvet furniture with the tiger-skin throw pillows. I didn't explain that I lived with my mother. My strategy – well, not strategy – my mindless approach was to completely avoid that subject. Let him think this was my place. Let him think I would buy framed prints of a woman with her underwear falling down.

'Cool. It's not how I would've imagined your apartment.'

'I guess you don't know me as well as you think you do.' True – just not in the way he thought. 'Would you like something to drink? Or shall we go?'

'I'm fine. Let's get in that line.'

I took my mother's short, boxy fake-fur black jacket (relieved to cover myself up, if only temporarily) and we departed.

The ticket booth was on a traffic island smack in the heart of Times Square, so there was lots of atmosphere for Tom to take in. Having grown up a few blocks away, I tried to avoid this dense concentration of humanity whenever I could, but I knew it was interesting for him to be there watching the swarms of people, the huge advertising signs, the inevitable preacher guy talking about the impending end of the world. At least the line wasn't too bad. They said it would just be a half-hour wait, more or less what I expected. I wouldn't have had any problem with that in sneakers. But heels? After five minutes, it was murder. And the damn thong was really bothering me.

By the time we made it to the front of the line, there weren't many choices. We quickly settled on 42nd Street, the musical. It seemed like a good touristy thing to do, and I wasn't in the mood for a serious play. We forked over fifty bucks each and got our tickets. They weren't too great. Towards the back of the orchestra. That's what you get for paying half price. I didn't care at that point; I was just looking forward to sitting down.

The inside of the theater was really pretty. They'd remodeled a few years back in that Times Square makeover. The street used to be a hotbed of porn theaters and peep shows that were more sleazy than even the Classy Lady. Ironically, once they closed everything down and rebuilt, I sort of missed the old seediness. Nostalgia seems to work that way. You feel sad for what's gone because now, you only have the memory of it, and that memory is a reminder that you're not going to be around forever either.

In the lobby, we looked at an old photograph from the 1920s of the corner the theater was on. It used to be called the Lyric Theatre. A place where they did vaudeville and burlesque. There was a sign on a storefront: DONUT AND COFFEE FIVE CENTS. At least people could always draw comfort from their sugar, white flour, and caffeine.

The lobby lights flashed. I hobbled into the theater and we found our row. Man, it felt good to sit. I slipped my feet out of the shoes immediately, but I didn't take off the coat. Not because I was cold. I felt more protected inside of it. Didn't want my boobs exposed to the world.

'You okay?' Tom asked.

'These shoes are killing me,' I admitted, aware that I was eroding the effect of wearing them by complaining. I really wished I could reach down and pull that damn thong out of my butt.

The lights went down.

The most entertaining thing in the play was the bevy of legs to look at during the tap-dancing scenes. There were some good songs too. I hadn't realized how many classics were in it. The plot was way too predictable, though. Still, it was fun to sit there next to him and watch all the big production numbers. I really wanted him to hold my hand, but he didn't.

At intermission, I slipped the shoes back on and hobbled to the lobby with Tom. He got in line for a drink. I decided I should pee and 'check my face.' The bathroom was down some stairs.

I had a moment's relief as I pulled down the thong and emptied my bladder. How do women function dressed like this? I was tempted to pull the thong all the way off, but wasn't prepared to go around without underwear on. In any case, the point of all this was supposed to be that incredible moment when I disrobed in front of him and he could see me wearing it. I pulled it back up.

I hobbled to the mirror. An attendant dressed in something like a maid's uniform passed out paper towels. I took one. Felt bad for her. Wondered if she could tell I was a female imposter. The makeup was pretty much intact, so I got my lipstick out and redid that. It was such a feminine action, applying lipstick. I smeared my lips together to even it out. Time to hobble back up. Before leaving, I placed a dollar on the tip plate.

'Thank you, ma'am,' she said.

Ma'am?

Tom was standing in the lobby sipping on a large cup of Coke. He'd bought a thing of candy too. Twizzlers. I took one happily. The plasticky cherry candy was so good, I almost drooled.

'The dancing is amazing, isn't it?' Tom said.

'Their feet must hurt like hell at the end of the evening.'

The lights flashed. I hobbled next to Tom back to our seats.

The second half was worse than the first. Mainly because the tap dancing became repetitive and I wanted the leading lady to sit down and relax, but whoever had choreographed this seemed to want to *really impress* us with how many times the dancer could twirl around while making machine-gun noises on those high heels. I guess she did impress the audience, which was mostly made up of catatonic-looking overweight people. There was something odd about paying admission to sit there to watch someone else move so much. The actress was smiling, but of course the most important talent for a dancer is the ability to smile through the pain. At least she did get a lot of applause, and she didn't have to go into the audience and give lap dances when she was done.

Despite all that, I was sorry when it was over. It had been pleasant sitting there next to Tom passively taking everything in. Now I was anxious. Unsure how the rest of the evening would play out.

'So,' he said, as we exited the theater along with everyone else, 'do you want to get a bite to eat?'

'Sure.'

'You lead,' he said. 'I have no idea where to go.'

So I took him over to Forty-sixth Street, Restaurant Row. If you're feeling extremely dreamy and sentimental, it's possible to imagine there's something romantic about the street, which has some nicely maintained brownstones with awnings bearing names like LE BEAUJOLAIS and LES SANS CULOTTES. We went into Joe Allen, a popular after-theater restaurant I'd been to once for a birthday party. I knew they had okay food and it was lively. I decided, as we sat down at a table with a blue-and-white checked cloth, that no matter how much I wanted to, I was not going to complain about how uncomfortable I was. And ... I made myself take off my jacket. Even though I felt like I was sitting there topless. I wasn't topless. But there was so much breast showing, I felt topless. And I felt like I was embarrassing him too, seeing as he wasn't used to thinking of me as having breasts. Well, maybe I was just projecting that. We both ordered burgers and then leaned towards each other onto the table as we waited for the food. I was sure my breasts were going to pop all the way out into the bread basket. I couldn't think of a thing to say. But it did occur to me, with some sense of victory, that there was no way he could think of me now as 'one of the guys.'

'So,' he asked, after the waiter had brought us two glasses of Cabernet, 'what did you think of the play?'

'The costumes were cute. Did you know it was fashionable for flappers to have small breasts?' I loved flapper fashion. The loose, comfy dresses, low-heeled shoes, cute hats. I once dressed up as one for Halloween.

'By the fifties,' I went on, 'you were supposed to have big breasts.' I definitely had breasts on the brain that night. 'But then in the sixties, thanks to Twiggy, you were supposed to be flat again.'

'Really.'

'At least in those days you were allowed to have some flesh. Now we're supposed to be incredibly skinny yet still have double Ds. It's crazy! In medieval times, believe it or not, large bellies were very in vogue. Something having to do with looking pregnant and the Virgin Birth and all that. There's always some way women are supposed to look.'

'I don't think men really care that much.' Tom was now looking around the restaurant. Shoot! I'd managed to alienate him. I knew ... I *knew* that I would not seduce a man with a feminist rant, even if I was impersonating a sex object. But I couldn't get myself to shut up. 'You know how they say no two fingerprints are alike? No two faces are alike? No two snowflakes? Well, no two breasts are alike either. Even on the same woman! Yet we're all supposed to aspire to some impossible ideal. Does anyone ever think they need a more attractive fingerprint?'

He smiled and shook his head and I was definitely getting on his nerves.

The waiter set down our burgers. I asked for a second glass of wine. Not the best idea. As a matter of fact, by the end of the meal, I had the general sense that I'd been talking quite a lot, though I couldn't remember what the hell I'd been saying.

The world was swaying quite a bit as we walked the few blocks to my apartment. I took his arm and leaned against him, the better not to hobble on the damn heels, and I was not doing a very good job of hiding my tipsiness what with all the giggling I seemed to be doing, and the truth was, I was petrified.

When we got to my building, we slowed down, and we both hesitated. Should I ask him up? Did he just want to go home?

'So ... uh ... what do you think? Should I come up?' he asked. 'Would you mind?'

'Of course I wouldn't mind.'

Mind?

We climbed the stairs. I feared Coco would be home even though I knew she wasn't. I unlocked the door. We walked in. I kicked off my shoes. Tom went to the bathroom. I double-checked to make sure she wasn't lounging around somewhere naked.

She wasn't.

The toilet flushed. I sat down on the couch. Then got back up again, because I needed to pee too. 'I'll be right back.'

It was such a relief to disengage the thong! As I sat on the toilet seat, I seriously considered the idea of walking out there in my jeans and T-shirt. Maybe he'd be relieved. I certainly would have been. But I fought off the temptation, pulled the thong back up, and went back out. 'Would you like something to drink?'

He was on the couch. 'Water would be good.'

I filled a glass for him, and one for myself too. We sat next to each other and drank.

Hydrated, we put our glasses down on the coffee table and reclined. Next to each other. He squinched closer to me. His arm came around me.

'So . . .' he said.

I was almost completely frozen. I couldn't even look at him. The only movement I could manage was to scratch the back of my neck.

'The way you look tonight,' he said, 'I wasn't expecting it. Don't get me wrong. You look great. But you didn't have to do it for me.'

'Really?' Because he only wanted to think of me as one of the guys? No, wait. His arm was around me. 'What about thongs?'

'What about them?'

'Do they turn you on?'

He shrugged. 'Personally? I like cotton briefs.'

'Really?' That almost seemed odd. 'And breasts?'

'What about them?'

'Do you think women with implants are more sexy?'

'Like Pamela Anderson? Those women look bizarre. Do you mind,' he said, 'if I stretch out? On the couch? I seem to be in a perpetual state of exhaustion.'

'Sure. If I can stretch out next to you.'

We both stretched out on the sofa. But I faced into the room, with my back to him, because it seemed too scary to be face-to-face.

He put his arm around my waist. 'Is that okay? It's more comfortable that way.'

'S'fine.' Fine? 'But . . . I do feel like I'm a little too close to the edge.'

'You can move back a little. I don't mind.'

I snuggled back up against him. Could feel his chin against the back of my head. The length of his body nestled against me. I felt so secure, right up against his soft warmth.

'Would you mind,' he asked, 'turning around and facing me?'

I smiled. 'Why?'

'I just thought we could . . . oh . . . you know . . . talk or something.'

I sighed, as if I was giving in. 'Okay.'

I turned around and faced him. Faced his throat, actually. Sort of hid my face there. He put his arm back around me. And I put my arm around him. It was very nice there, right up against him. Our bodies were still slightly apart, but I swear, there was a magnetic pull radiating between us.

Then he lifted my chin and kissed me.

He was a good kisser. Meaning his approach was gradual. Soft, light, dry kisses at first. Kisses that made me want more. Then firmer kisses eventually turning into wetter (but not too wet) kisses. It was so intimate, it was almost embarrassing . . . to be doing this . . . after having known each other . . . like friends . . .

He paused. Sighed.

'What is it?' Something was wrong.

'You're pretty amazing.'

'Me?'

'Yeah.' He started kissing me again.

I pulled back. I couldn't help it. I just had to have that explained. 'You think I'm amazing?'

'You're so cool, and confident. I've never known anyone like you.'

I had to exercise extreme self-control not to burst out laughing. 'You think I'm confident?'

'Yeah. Don't you know? It's intimidating. I'm just a small-town boy,' he said, only half joking. 'You're a big-city girl. Compared to what I'm used to, you're exotic.'

Exotic. Me. I liked that idea. It made me think how strippers are sometimes called 'exotic dancers,' which goes back to when they actually were from faraway places and their moves, and what they wore (and didn't wear), actually was part of their culture. It meant I could attract him without making any effort – just by being me.

'I've been wanting to kiss you since the first week of school.'

'So why didn't you?'

'I wasn't sure if you wanted me to. I kept inviting myself up to your apartment, and you kept saying no.'

'You only asked twice.'

'And you said no twice. I was afraid to ask tonight. Didn't want to get turned down again.'

'Still . . .'

'And I admit, I do like to take things slowly.'

We kissed again. His hand was exploring my body, going up my thigh, around my butt, down between my legs. The thong had shifted from the imbedded place it had been, and it felt so annoying, and I wished he would pull it out, give me some relief, but wasn't about to ask him to do that. If only he could read my mind. *Pull it out, pull it out, pull it out.* But his hand went back down my leg, proving once and for all that mental telepathy doesn't work. I was starting to feel quite turned on, though, and the thong pressing up into me was only making it worse (better?). Our lips locked in a nice, wet kiss, and I opened my leg over his hip and found myself rubbing against that friendly bulge there in his pants and felt like

I was going to have an orgasm right then and this definitely was better than my Kitty.

He had removed his hands from underneath my dress, and I took that to be a sign of his frustration – the dress was obviously getting in the way. So this was my chance to stop hiding myself – insecurities be damned. There was nothing wrong with my body, and it was about time I face up to it.

So I sat up straight and started to pull my dress up over my head – too quickly, I could hear Coco complain. But my impulse was to rush through this as if he wouldn't notice. Unfortunately, there was not too much give to the material, and I was having trouble getting it up past my shoulders, and it was squishing flat up against my face. I couldn't get the stupid thing off! I felt my own hot air against the cloth, which was right against my nose and almost suffocating me.

'Ummm . . . Ginger?'

'What?' I said through the dress. I could hear myself breathing. See my mother shaking her head in despair.

'Maybe we should stop.'

'What?' I kept the dress there for an extra moment, despite the indignity, because it seemed better than looking him in the face.

'I think we should stop.'

I pulled the dress back down. 'You want to stop?'

'Yeah. I just think . . . we should slow down.'

I adjusted the dress around my waist as casually as I could.

'Not,' he said, 'because I don't want to. I just think we should take our time.'

'Okay,' I said, in the most casual, I'm-not-feeling-rejected way I could.

'I guess maybe I'm old-fashioned, but cuddling, you know, it doesn't always need to end up in sex. I mean, I just generally like to wait until I really know someone, and, you know, I know it's going to be meaningful and special.'

Special? He sounded like such a girl! From a century ago! 'It's fine,' I said. 'Don't worry about it.'

'You aren't upset, are you?'

'No, of course not. It's nice you feel that way.'

Except, he hadn't waited for it to be 'special' with Tara, had he? I could still hear her taunt. *Who needs a vibrator if you've got the real thing?* But maybe she'd been lying. I would've asked him, but I didn't want to bring her up. It was more important to gather any shred of pride I could pretend I had.

'So . . . maybe you should head home,' I managed to say, 'before it gets too late?' I said it like a question, so that he could feel free to suggest the concept of staying overnight.

'Yeah,' he said, 'better get on that subway. Get some sleep.'

I walked him to the door, hugging my arms around my waist.

'You aren't mad at me,' he said, 'are you?'

'No. Of course not. Why would I be?'

'Just checking.' He kissed me on the cheek. 'Good night.'

'Good night.'

I shut the door. Went to my bedroom. Took everything off, got under the covers naked, arranged my head on the pillow, and told myself I had *not* made a fool of myself by throwing myself at him like a slut. That is, showing him I desired him.

chapter thirty-four

'Let me get this straight. You're upset because he said you were moving too fast?'

Ralph and I were walking to the deli. I'd been hoping to spend some
time alone with Tom during lunch, but Jean Paul made him and some of
the other guys set up tables in the dining room for the banquet the next
day, so there was no chance.

'Yes.'

'And he *wanted* to *cuddle*?'

'Right.'

'Okay, Ginger? Women *want* to cuddle, okay? That is the ultimate goal
of all women. To find a man who will *cuddle*.'

'So you don't think I should be annoyed? Or feel rejected?'

'I think you should have your head examined. Don't you realize that
you have found a treasure? Thank your lucky stars!'

'You don't think it means he just wants to be friends?' I couldn't bear
to bring up his alleged carnal relations with Tara. With little or no waiting period. Extremely doubtful that it had been special or meaningful.

But what if it had been? That thought was even worse.

'Ginger. I hate to tell you. But even friends don't kiss and cuddle. Do
we kiss and cuddle? No. We do not kiss and cuddle.'

'You know what else?' I volunteered, feeling encouraged. 'He said
women with implants are bizarre.'

'Either he's a really good liar, or you've found yourself the perfect guy.'

After school, Tom and I found each other in the lobby and took the
elevator down. His blue eyes were beaming at me. 'I had a nice time last
night,' he said.

'Me too.'

'Too bad I have to work tonight. There's a private party at the restaurant for the Association of Women Chefs. Maybe you want to drop by?'

'Oh, thanks for the invitation.' I almost told him I had to work too, but instead I used Tara as an excuse. 'I don't think she'd want me crashing.' I didn't want to explain my work consisted of selling vibrators after my mother's strip class.

I hadn't seen Coco since she got back from Vegas that morning. When I got home, I was all ready to congratulate the new bride and chide her for not calling. I found her in her bedroom, lying down in the dark.

'Mom?'

'We didn't do it.'

'What?'

'I called it off.'

I sat down on the edge of her bed. 'Why?'

'The morning Jack and I were supposed to go to the chapel . . . I was sitting at a slot machine feeding it coins. I was in this hypnotic stupor. I had to ask myself why I didn't feel more excited. The thing came up with three cherries. And I knew. I don't want to be married. I guess I just can't stand the idea of being tied down to one person.'

'I don't get it.' It depressed me to hear her say that. I was one person. Of course, she didn't mean me.

'I don't get it either.'

'Well. I'm sorry it didn't work out.'

She sat up and opened her arms for a hug. I moved over and gave her one.

'Ready?' she asked.

'Ready.' We lifted the trunk. Carried it down the stairs. Outside, it was raining. The city was drab and gray. This was the time of year I hated most, when fall turned into winter and there were months of bad weather to look forward to.

When we settled into a cab, I asked her, 'So how did Jack take it?'

'He ripped off all the buttons on my dress.'

'Not surprised.'

'I'm an idiot, right? Now I don't even get my face-lift.'

'Well, ya know, Mom? Being happy' – I nudged her in the arm – 'that's the best face-lift of all.'

'Ain't it the truth, huh?'

I was so surprised at this development, it didn't even click for me until the cab pulled up right up in front of L'Etoile that *this* was our destination. The private party Tom was talking about was the same party Coco was hired to work! Now I knew why Tara had been so 'good' about 'not telling Tom' about my mother's 'chosen profession.' She'd engineered this whole thing to try to humiliate me. And she was going to succeed.

'Mom,' I said, as I followed her out of the cab, 'do we have to do this?'

'Do what?'

The driver popped the trunk. 'I know the people who own this restaurant. People from my school work here.'

She laughed. 'Still ashamed of your old mom?'

'Mom, please! That's not the thing – '

'Good, then would you help me get this trunk inside?'

A voice inside told me to bolt. At worst, a few vibrators would go unsold. Still, I helped her carry the trunk in as if my fate had already been sealed. There was a sign up front: WELCOME TO THE ASSOCIATION OF WOMEN CHEFS! Underneath was a photo of about fifty women all lined up and smiling, wearing chef's hats. My future colleagues. Wonderful. The atmosphere was on the raucous side. The chefs had already been well fed and lots of wine had been poured. Excitement was in the air as the waiters moved tables aside to make space for my mother up front. Mr. Glass, a blondish man with reddish skin, wearing tan pants and a white polo shirt, came to greet Coco. 'What a treat this is! What a novelty! Thank you for coming!'

'My pleasure!'

'My daughter planned this event . . .' He seemed nervous. 'I just wanted to make sure . . . you aren't expecting my guests to, uh, actually take their clothes off, are you?'

'Oh, don't worry, my students are usually pretty modest, but I always put on a good show.'

There was lots of giggling and smiling and staring at my mom as she took her place in the front of the room. In fact, seeing as many women chefs are gay, this was bound to be an appreciative audience.

I could see Tom, along with four other line cooks, all men, closing down their stations as I set up my table. Every vibrator I set up on the table was like a stake pounded into my heart. *Please don't see me!* But Tara would make sure he would. I took a quick look around and saw her standing by the swinging door to the kitchen with a smug smile on her face.

Everyone quieted down as Coco started up. Since the room was large, I felt relatively invisible in the back, and everyone was focused on Coco while I set up my display. Soon after she began, I saw Tom and the other line cooks go to the back kitchen. Maybe Tom would leave. He had to be tired. Thinking of his bed in Astoria.

No. There he was. Leaning up against the wall next to Tara at the swinging door along with the other cooks. Of course. They weren't going to miss this. Tom had this grin on his face. A grin I'd never seen before. Like he was really looking forward to the performance, and it was gonna be a lot more entertaining than *42nd Street.*

Coco skipped a lot of the stuff, like hygiene, and cut to the chase. Yes, this was going to be more like a showcase for her skills. Lots of these women were from out of town, and this was like a girl's night out.

'You aren't a cheerleader,' she said. 'Don't dance to the beat. This is not choreographed. You make it up as you go along. The focus is on you and your body.'

Indeed, the focus of the entire room was on Coco and her body. I slid against the wall down to the floor and sat cross-legged on the rug.

From the floor, I could see Tom watching my mother. Ogling my mother, to put it more accurately. I tried to tell myself not to feel anything, not to take it seriously, not to take any of this to heart.

'You aren't just going to rip everything off and fling it in his face, right? No. There's an art to undressing, ladies. The first thing is your top. Take it off slowly. Finger the button. Look into his eyes.'

Tom was fascinated. Evidently, I'd neglected to treat him to the most favorite tourist attraction of all: small-town boy goes to the big city and sees his first stripper.

'Then, just as you're about to take it off, turn your back to him. Look at him over your shoulder. Slowly let the shirt . . . drop . . . to the . . . floor.'

Now she was wearing just a short skirt and a slinky black demibra. The women chefs were spellbound.

'Shoot him a look over your shoulder as if you're saying "Want me to take off more? You might get what you want. If you're good." '

The guy standing next to Tom screamed, 'I'm good I'm very good!' What a jerk. At least Tom wouldn't do anything like that.

But then Tom jostled the guy next to him. 'Whoo-hoo!' Leaned over and said, if my lipreading was any good, something like 'Wow, look at the size of those!' Put two fingers in his mouth and whistled. That's when my heart broke. I could almost feel it sear right down the middle.

Was this the same man who only the night before had told me Pamela Anderson was bizarre? Yes. Indeed. It was also the same man who wasn't interested in making love with me. Why should I be surprised? Compared to a hot dish like my mom, I was a side order of wilted lettuce salad.

'The skirt. Undo the zipper. Take your time. Wiggle your hips. Let it drop. Casually step out . . . and stroll away. Don't laugh, though. Ya gotta be dead serious, or you'll break the spell.'

I'd certainly botched that. As far as I was concerned, sex was a comedy routine with me as the punch line.

'Now you're down to your bra and your G-string.'

The whole crowd was getting rowdy, not just Tom. The women chefs were going wild. My mom was loving it. Soaking it in. 'He's dying,' she said dramatically. 'He's drooling. He's about to explode.'

Or, in my case, he's about to explain why he just wants to cuddle . . ..

'He has got to get a look at your tits. But you turn around, so your back is to him. Let one strap fall. Then the other. Now unhook your bra. Hold it out to the side. Drop it on the floor. Give 'im a look. "Whoops! Silly me. It fell." '

Tom was mesmerized. A big dumb grin on his face.

'Cross your arms over your chest. Now you turn and face him. Open your arms. *Voilà!*'

She proudly displayed herself. Everyone was hollering, Tom right along with them. 'Take it off!' he yelled out. 'Take it all off!'

How could he?

'Now, ladies, it's time to pop your G-string!'

Hold on. Was she going to strip completely? That wasn't part of the script. All this zeal from the crowd was goading her forward. Did she think she was back at the Pussycat Lounge?

'Play with it a little first. Pull the elastic off your hips, pull it up, pull it out. Feel it in your butt-crack, in your pussy, and let him think about how you're feeling that. If you want, sink to your knees, relax your butt down on the floor, and bring your knees to the side, like a mermaid. Then, roll back and bring your legs up in a V, like this. That way you can give him a good look at your crotch. It'll drive him wild.'

The guy next to Tom was beating his chest, fancying himself a Tarzan. At least Tom wasn't doing that. Oh, hold on, now he was.

'Stand up gracefully. Turn. Let him look at your ass. Bend all the way over with your legs straight and your back flat. That's right, you're gonna give him a nice straight-on view of your butt.'

As Coco spoke, she bent. The women were all standing there with their mouths hanging open. I didn't even dare look at Tom. Was she gonna do it? Was she gonna moon everyone? The crowd went wild, egging her on.

'And let it . . . ,' she said, the room . . . suddenly . . . absolutely . . . silent . . . , 'fall to your feet.'

The G-string fell to her ankles. There was her round little butt.

'Step out of it. Spread your feet and take a look at him through your legs.' She bent over. 'Peekaboo!'

Everyone cheered. Clapped. Tom put two fingers in his mouth and whistled again. Coco turned around, flipped her mane of hair back, took a deep bow, stark naked, then broke character and laughed while she put her G-string and bra back on. All in a day's work.

I had to escape.

I got up off the floor and tried to get to the door, to the street; Tara was too fast. She was pulling Tom by the hand, intent on heading me off.

'Ginger!' she hollered. 'Where are you going? Aren't you helping your mother sell the sex toys?'

Tom was looking puzzled, to say the least. Tara was babbling on. 'Can you believe that's her mother? They look like sisters, don't you think? I can't imagine what it would be like to have such a sexy mom . . .'

I wasn't going to rise to her bait. No need to fall into her trap. Just proceed out the door.

But then Tom chuckled and said, 'Wow, Ginger. When you said your mom was a dancer, I had no idea!'

'*Exotic* dancer,' Tara screeched with glee. 'Isn't it cool? Her mom used to work in strip clubs!'

'She's great,' he said.

'You certainly looked,' I couldn't resist saying, 'like you were enjoying yourself.'

'Well . . .' Perceiving he was heading for trouble, he shut his mouth.

'He is a red-blooded guy,' Tara added helpfully.

'She's obviously very talented,' Tom said, attempting to be magnanimous.

'I didn't think you were an implant man.'

'Lighten up, Ginger,' Tara said. 'He's trying to give her a compliment.'

'And thank you for making it possible!'

'You're welcome.'

Tom held his hand out to me: 'Ginger . . . ,' and tried to touch my arm, but I shook him off.

'Ginger!' It was Coco. 'Honey, I need you! Aren't you gonna give me some help over here?'

I headed for the front door. Tom followed me. 'Come on. Don't be mad. I was just going along with the crowd. It didn't mean anything.'

'You were into it!' It was pouring outside. I went out into it. 'Don't try to pretend you weren't!' The rain came down in hard mean splats. I so badly wanted him to tell me that he'd just been faking to fit in, and he saw nothing attractive about my mother or her talents.

'Of course I was into it,' he said, following me out the door. 'She's a professional!'

'How nice for you to benefit from her services!' I ducked my head and ran to wave down a cab.

'Hey, come on, what do you expect?' A cab pulled up. I was already soaked.

'Nothing. I don't expect anything at all.' I grabbed the cold, wet door handle knowing I expected too much. As Tara had just said, he was a red-blooded guy. You couldn't stop a force of nature. Before getting in the cab, I turned to face him.

'Did you sleep with her?'

'What?'

We were both getting drenched. 'Did you have sex with Tara?'

He looked down at his shoes. And then back at me. A little boy, caught. His hand in the cookie jar.

I got into the cab. There was a puddle on the floor. I looked up at Tom. 'I hope it was a meaningful experience.' I slammed the door shut.

'Where to?' the driver asked.

Unfortunately, the only place I could think of was home.

chapter thirty-five

*W*hen I arrived at school the next morning and saw Tom in the lobby, I was all set to deliberately look away from him. But I didn't have the chance, because he deliberately looked away from me. Then Kingsley strode past and avoided my gaze. Then Jean Paul told me to get my butt in the kitchen to make a cheese platter. Granted, everyone was tense because of the banquet that night and the world was not revolving around my troubles. But from the moment I got there, I wished I wasn't. Even Ralph was in a bad mood. I complained to him on my way to the walk-in. 'I'm really glad I spent all those thousands of dollars to have the opportunity to slice Swiss cheese for the investors.'

He snapped at me. 'Why are you so goddamned negative?'

Maybe I'd leave this place and never come back. That would show them!

After my cheese platter was done, Jean Paul had me join Tara piping out rosettes of butter. When he left the room, she said, 'This would encourage dairy consumption, don't you think?' I looked on the table in front of her. She'd piped two big breasts of butter complete with nipples. Ralph laughed. Even Tom laughed. She quickly scraped it off before Jean Paul returned and eyed us suspiciously. He passed behind me. I thought my rosettes were pretty good. My hands didn't even shake while he leaned over my shoulder.

'It iss time for lunch.' He scraped softened butter from the mixing bowl and flung it onto the table in front of me. It landed like a humongous splat of bird shit. 'Stay and do a hundred more. The rest of you, out!'

I was smoldering. More humiliation! It wasn't fair. I leaned over the table and did some more, but everyone was gone and it was totally absurd. After doing about fifty more, my back was aching. I straightened up, stretched my waist to the right, to the left, cracked my spine. Why was I doing this? Jean Paul would never know if I finished, and even if he did, he'd only see what was wrong, not what was right. There was no point to this pointless exercise, no point in going on at this school. He would never let me into the Master Class. I was wasting my father's money, so why did I even bother to come anymore?

I went to the refrigerator where my swan bodies were waiting to be filled with cream. The tray of necks was right underneath.

Underneath the necks, I saw Tara's tray of biscotti. She'd already baked them off. They just needed to be thawed out and served. Oh, the temptation. The temptation to take them and dump them into the garbage. That would feel so good. For about a moment. But really, who cared about her stupid biscotti anyway? Probably not even her.

I took out my own trays and slid them onto the table. They looked good. Professional. At least, I thought so. No one else would, though. Jean Paul would insult them, just like everything else I did. Because everything I did was intrinsically ugly, wasn't it, because it was done by me. Yes, I think I finally understood. That was the message. What was it Tom had said? *Of course I was into it. She's a professional!* I was just an amateur, though, and always would be. I started smashing the bodies to bits. Crushed each one using the palm of my hand. Scrunched them in my fingers until they were pebbly little bits and pieces. Then I took every single neck and pressed on it with my thumb till it cracked in half. How could I have let myself think, for one moment, that he would ever appreciate me? My eyes were stinging with regret even as I was indulging in my misery. My new recipe. Choux paste crumbs. Just add tears and stir.

I'd never been to my father's office before. The secretary didn't know who I was. She probably didn't know I existed. But I insisted on seeing him. She led me in. I sat across from him and balanced my knife roll on my knees. Between us was a huge modern wood desk that was layered with papers and folders and thick law books. It was not the time to think about affairs and betrayal. Not the time to ask how Emma was doing. It was the time to let him know I was a flop and a failure. A bad investment.

'I'm quitting school.'

He leaned back in his black leather chair – the kind with thick arms and a back that went higher than his head. 'You don't want to be a chef anymore?'

'No.'

'And what do you want to be?'

'I'm going back to the idea of getting a law degree.'

'Really.'

'I want to do some good in the world. Help other people.'

'Sounds idealistic.'

'Is that bad?' To the left of his computer was an eight-by-ten, black-and-white photograph of Leah. Next to that was a color snapshot of Emma.

'It's not easy.'

'You don't think I can?' And why should he? I'd backed away from law before. But this time would be different. I'd work really, really hard. Steel myself up to study like a fiend for the dry, boring, tedious classes. Make myself passionately interested in the constitution, the federal government, public policy . . . I would even make myself wear those stupid skirt suits.

'I thought you wanted to make pastries.'

'I did.'

'What happened?' he asked. 'You didn't get into the Master Class?'

Obviously I wasn't going to impress him by following in his footsteps. 'I want to help women who've worked in the sex business.'

This seemed to amuse him. 'Help them?'

'To get out. Recover. Find better lives.'

He leaned back in his chair. Crossed one ankle over the other knee, exposing a patch of skin between his sock and his cuff. It was white and hairy. 'And how do you think you'll do that?'

'Change the laws, for one thing.' I met his eyes. 'So the guys who go to them are just as culpable if not more so.'

He leaned forward. 'Forget about your idealism. Women who work in the sex business *like* it. If not, they get out. No one makes them do it. Sure, there are the self-destructive ones, but the laws won't help them.

They need counseling, and even that probably won't help. For the most part, these women are shrewd. Like your mother. She hasn't suffered, has she?'

I didn't know how to answer that.

'They don't need your help, Ginger. If anyone needs help, you do. What went wrong with cooking school, anyway? I paid a lot for your tuition. Now you want to quit in the middle of the semester? You're never going to succeed if you don't finish what you start.'

'The chef hates me.'

'Why?'

'I don't know! He has from day one.'

'Maybe you should ask him before you go and quit.'

'I tried to talk to him. It didn't help.'

'Then try again. Show him that you care.'

This was too much. 'What do you know about "showing you care"? I'm your flesh and blood and you never cared about me!'

'Excuse me?'

'You stayed away! Throughout my entire childhood!'

'I was staying away from Coco, not you. I couldn't be associated with a woman like that. What do you think it would've done to my reputation if people at the firm knew about her?'

'Nothing!' I was almost hyperventilating; it was so thrilling yet scary to be finally confronting him. 'They wouldn't have cared. They would've thought it was cool! That's what my friends always thought.'

'Don't try to lay this on me. You're upset about school, and that has nothing to do with me or anything I did or didn't do. So my advice – '

I sat erect. 'I'm not asking for your advice.'

'You took my money, young lady, you'll take my advice! Don't expect it to come easy. Nothing of any importance comes easy! It takes commitment!'

I stood up. 'Oh, yeah? If you're so big on commitment, what about your commitment to Leah?'

'What?'

'I think you know what I mean.'

I looked down at him from across the desk. He was silent, but his guilty face betrayed him. At least he had the decency not to deny it. 'If taking your money means taking your advice, I'd rather get a job churning out donuts at Krispy Kreme.' I turned and walked out. As I passed the secretary, I had a twisted half smile on my face. This had to be considered a partial victory. I'd finally had a fight with my father. I'd never felt more like I was his daughter. Too bad I also wanted to murder him.

'*d*on't you have the banquet tonight?' Coco was surprised to see me come home.

'I'm not going.'

'Why not?'

I just wanted to get to my room. She followed me down the hall.

'Ginger. What's going on with you?'

'Nothing.'

'Why did you take off last night?'

'I'm sorry!'

She followed me into my bedroom. I threw my knife roll on the floor. Took off my sneakers, got in bed with all my clothes on, and put a pillow over my head. I'd never had a lock on my door, and it was long over-due. On second thought, that would imply I was settling in for the long haul. What I really needed was another door in another building in an-other city . . .

'Fine,' she said, turning to go. 'But if you want to talk about it, I'm all ears.'

I took the pillow off my head. 'Did you know,' I blurted out, 'that Ben was unfaithful?'

She turned back around. 'What?'

'He cheated on Leah.'

'Really? Do tell.' She sat down on the edge of my bed.

'Maybe I shouldn't.'

'Come on, I live for this.'

I winced. She was joking. Sort of. And that's just what I didn't want to play into. Please her by hating him. But I felt the need to bounce this off her. Get her particular point of view. So I explained all about the diaries, and what he'd done, and how Leah had suffered. 'It just gets me so mad.

It seems like he didn't even feel bad about it. In a way, that's the worst part. He barely apologized to her. He basically said it wouldn't have been a problem if she never found out.'

'That is sort of true.'

'You're defending him?'

'I'm just not judging him.'

'You hate Dad for all sorts of reasons. For this you choose not to judge him?'

'Maybe she wasn't giving him any, and he had to find someone who would.'

'What if she wasn't giving him any because he was a lousy lover?'

'Then it was her job to teach him to be a good lover.'

'For some women,' I said, 'it's not so simple.' I was seething inside. 'It's not so mechanical. They need an emotional connection.'

'Are we talking about you now?'

Well, we certainly aren't talking about you. Thought, not said. I kept my mouth shut. There was no winning here. If she knew I let my feelings interfere with my desire for sex, she'd really feel like a failure as a mother.

'Jesus,' she said, taking my silence as a yes. 'I would've thought if I taught you anything in life, it's how to enjoy sex.'

'And anyway,' I said, 'you're blaming the victim! As if it's Leah's fault the "poor" guy had to cheat. Don't you think faithfulness is important? Doesn't it mean anything to be faithful?'

'There are two sides to the story. Leah wasn't perfect. I know you like to think she was, but she wasn't. So cut your dad some slack, okay? That's all I'm saying.'

Maybe she was refusing to judge my father because of her own past. Maybe she hadn't actually slept with her customers . . . but she'd certainly entertained scores of men. Married men. Men like my father.

Maybe she *had* slept with them. I never had been sure of how far she went. Never asked her directly. Never wanted to know for sure. But maybe it was about time I did know the truth.

'Mom?'

'Yes?'

'Did you ever . . .'

'What?'

'Have sex. With men. For money.'

Coco fluttered her eyelashes and spoke like a Southern belle. 'Why, I'm afraid I don't know what you mean!'

'Did you?'

She got up off my bed. Went to fluff her hair out in the mirror. I waited for her to speak. Didn't move. My ears seemed to stand at attention.

'It was always an option. You give a guy a lap dance. He tells you to call him. Maybe he's not bad-looking. Maybe he says he'll take you shopping. Make it worth your time. So you go out. Have dinner. Go to a hotel. Have sex. He gives you five hundred bucks. And you never see him again. Or maybe you do the same thing all over again. And again. And again.' She laughed. 'Lots of girls did it.'

'But did you?'

She groaned. 'You wanna know? Okay. There was one man. He was loaded, he was handsome, he was married, and he liked anal sex.'

'Too much information.'

'His wife refused to do it! That's why I'm telling you, you need to be flexible.'

'Thanks.'

'He spent a shitload of money on me.'

'That's nice.'

Her eyebrows were raised, her hip was jutting out, and she was grinding a stiletto heel into my old blue rug, waiting for me to say something disapproving. But I was so tired of being disapproving. It never seemed to get me anywhere.

'Look,' she said, seeing the distress on my face. 'It lasted about six months. After awhile, I realized it was making me feel like crap. I told myself absolutely no more of that, never again. Lots of the girls . . . I'd see them doing it for money on the side – eventually they'd self-destruct. I wasn't gonna go there. I had to draw the line, or I never would've lasted.'

Well. Okay. That wasn't completely horrible. And she was intact. Had come through more or less unscathed. Maybe Leah had been right. Maybe Coco really was a strong person. 'This is all so ridiculously backwards. I'm the kid. I'm the one who's supposed to be in rebellion. I'm the one who's supposed to have you disapproving of me. But how can I possibly earn your disapproval? By being an uptight prude? Great. That's lots of fun. Just what I want to be. It's impossible! You're an impossible mother to displease!'

She tried not to laugh. Maybe it *was* funny. 'You irritate me sometimes. You don't wear makeup. Or heels. And you really do need new bras.'

'Great. I'm rebelling against my mother by letting my breasts sag.'

She laughed. 'I'm sorry. I don't mean to laugh. You're so important to me.' She sat next to me, took my hand, and squeezed it. 'You know that, don't you?'

'I guess. But . . .' I felt my eyes tear up. Forced out the words. 'I never was as important as the men.'

'Are you kidding? Of course you were.'

I shook my head. The tears came.

'Ginger. Honey.' She put her arm around me. Gave me a hug. 'That was my job.'

'And you were a workaholic.' I made an unattractive snorting sound.

'You are the most important person in my life.'

The moment she said that, I knew it was true. In a sense, it was all I'd ever wanted to hear her say.

Now that she'd said it, I realized how scary it was for it to *be* true. The most important. That's a lot of responsibility. Where was Jack when I needed him?

'I know it wasn't easy growing up with me,' she said. She gave me a tickle in the ribs. 'When it comes to sex, I set the bar pretty high, huh?'

'Yeah. I mean . . . I'm hopeless. An amateur. I can't have sex without feeling emotionally involved. It has to mean something, or I just don't want to do it.' We were both half joking, but still, on some level, it was the truth, and I really did feel like I was admitting to being a wimp.

'Hey. If you want to go around having meaningful sex, that's fine with me.'

'Do you really mean that?'

'Yes!'

'You aren't just saying that?'

'Just don't be surprised when you get hurt. Sex with feelings is a risky business, let me tell you. God knows, I was never good at it.'

'So . . . you won't lose respect for me if I only have sex with someone I really care about?'

'Hey, look. If that's what you really want . . . I'll just have to deal with it. But I just have to say, honey, you take sex so seriously . . . and it doesn't have to be that way. Maybe someday you'll relax and have more fun with it, because, I'm sorry, but you don't know what you're missing.'

I sighed. It was annoying to hear that, but on some level I knew there was truth in there. And I did know what I was missing. I was missing Tom. I was missing the banquet. I was missing the chance to present my beautiful swans. I told Coco all about how I'd killed them off. 'Jean Paul will never let me into the Master Class now.'

'Do you have time to make something else?'

'He assigned things.'

'So?'

'The banquet is about to start.'

'Dessert comes at the end.'

'I can't just walk in there with my own dessert.'

'Why not? If you don't give it a shot, you're gonna go back there tomorrow, face all those people, and feel like dirt.'

'Dirt?' I stood up. 'That's it! I do feel like dirt.'

'That's good?'

I kissed her on the cheek. 'Yes!' I said, 'it's very, very good.'

This was a route I could take with my eyes closed. I ran down the stairs, down the block to the corner grocery, and headed straight to the cookie section. Grabbed two packages of Oreos. Next, the refrigerator for a tub of soft cream cheese and a stick of butter. Then what . . . yes . . . please god, let them have it . . . instant chocolate pudding. There it was, high up on the top shelf. Four packages. What else did I need? Back to the refrigerator. A carton of milk and heavy cream. Did I have time to whip it up? I looked at my watch. Not really. I grabbed a can of Reddi-wip.

Anything else? Think. No time to forget and come back. This was it. I went to pay.

The very same woman who'd worked behind the counter when I was a kid was behind the cash register. I'd never known her name. But there she was. Standing in the exact same spot, flanked by shelves of cigarettes, batteries, phone cards, condoms, and aspirin packets.

'How are you?' she asked.

'Good, thanks. How are you?'

'Good!'

That's what we always said. No variation. I considered asking her name. Hesitated. Why change the routine after all these years? On the other hand, why not? 'What's your name?'

'Name?' I'd startled her. 'Rose.'

'Rose. Hi. My name is Ginger.'

'Ginger!' she said. 'Good in tea, for when you have a cold.'

'Yes. And Rose is such a pretty . . .'

My brain clicked. I had a brilliant idea. 'Hold on a sec, I'll be right back.' I went out front to the flowers. Lo and behold, there were some decent bouquets of red roses. I grabbed a bunch and went back inside to pay. Before leaving, I handed one of the roses to Rose.

As I bolted down the street, I considered the risk of bringing a dessert like this to a fancy-schmancy banquet. But no one would have to know they were basically eating mashed-up Oreos. As Jean Paul said, presentation was more important than taste, right?

I flew upstairs and threw it all together. Oreos in the food processor until they looked like . . . dirt! Then blended the butter and the cream cheese. Whisked the milk with the pudding mixes till it was smooth. Folded the butter and cream cheese into that, and then into the Reddi-wip. Took a taste with my index finger. Yum. Now the fun part.

I alternated layers of Oreo dirt with the pudding mud. When I was little, sometimes I used to put Gummi worms in the dirt, but tonight, I was going to go for something more elegant. I carefully tore some petals off my roses and laced them around the perimeter of the cake. Then I took three more and laid them in the center. Had to refrain from going crazy and putting them all over the place. Better to keep it simple. Elegant. I stood back. Admired my work. Pretty! Coco came into the kitchen. 'It's gorgeous!'

I needed a good name, though. Dirt cake most certainly wouldn't do. 'Do you know the French word for dirt?'

'No. Garden is *jardin*, right?'

'Yes. That's perfect. Behold my new creation. *Mousse de Jardin.*'

*t*he school restaurant was all dressed up for the banquet. White table-cloths, floral arrangements, an ice sculpture of a dolphin. Tables laden with food lined the room. People made their way buffet-style to each one, loading up their plates. All the students were dressed in cleaned-up whites, serving food or just chatting up the guests. I felt self-conscious in my street clothes, but before going to change, I wanted to put my dessert out with the rest.

I made my way through the crowd, holding my dish out in front of me, wishing it would hide my jeans and my white sweatshirt that said LIFEGUARD on the back. Some of the advanced students, who seemed like celebrities simply because they were the chosen ones, mingled with the crowd of investors, mostly Japanese businessmen in dark suits or matronly-looking women in dresses from Talbots. Mr. Glass was talking to Mr. Knickerbocker. I was surprised, because I hadn't thought parents were invited to this. Was he an investor? Jean Paul was standing by the ice sculpture talking with Nancy Riviere, the guest pastry chef for next semester, the one I wanted so badly to study with. An attractive woman in her fifties, with short black hair and a dark tan, she was wearing a chic black pantsuit, silver chandelier earrings, and . . . I couldn't believe it . . . black Converse Hi-top tennis shoes. At that moment, I felt like my entire life was vindicated. I had to get into her class. I just had to!

Nigel Sitwell was sitting at a big round table in the middle of the room talking the ear off some matron who was obviously thrilled to be near his corpulent body. Behind one of the first tables in the line, Tom was slicing some roast beef and laying it on a woman's plate. Ralph was serving at the last table, the one with the desserts. So was Tara. I took a deep breath, approached, and before I could even set my *Mousse de Jardin* with the other offerings, Tara asked, 'What happened to your swans?'

'Crash landing. I made something else.'

'Love the petals,' Ralph said.

'Thanks.'

'Are they edible?' Tara asked.

'Try one and see if you get poisoned.' I turned to Ralph. 'I'll be right back.'

On my way to the locker room, I almost collided with Kingsley. 'Ginger. I heard your desserts were destroyed. Is everything all right?'

Jean Paul, Nancy Riviere, and Mr. Knickerbocker were all migrating towards the dessert table. 'It was nothing,' I said, and continued to the locker room. I pulled my clothes off, stuffed them into a locker, fumbled with the buttons on my chef's jacket, then raced back out to the lobby. Ralph was serving my dessert to Jean Paul, Mr. Knickerbocker, and Nancy Riviere. What the hell? A whole table of gorgeous pastries, and they wanted dirt cake? I approached with caution.

'What is this?' Mr. Knickerbocker was asking. He was impeccably dressed in an ice blue suit with a red bow tie. 'Can you eat the petals, or are they just decoration?'

'They are absolutely edible,' Ralph said.

'Fascinating.' Mr. Knickerbocker looked at Jean Paul. 'Is this your recipe? I've never seen it here before.'

Jean Paul looked at me and screwed his face up. I was sure he was going to yell at me about my swans, but maybe he didn't want to in front of Mr. Knickerbocker. While he hesitated, Nancy Riviere said, 'I can't wait to sample a piece,' and took a taste of hers. As she savored it on her tongue, I was dying. If I'd known she'd be sampling it, I never would've used the Reddi-wip.

'Hmmm,' she said. 'Who made this?'

There was a moment of silence. Time to confess. 'I did.'

She looked me over, her eyes settling for an extra moment on my lime green Kangaroos with orange trim.

'And what do you call it?' she asked.

'Mousse de Jardin.'

'Really,' she said. 'This tastes exactly like something my mother used to make. But that wasn't the name . . .'

Please, I thought, please don't tell everyone it's dirt cake. Did they have Oreos in France?

'I remember . . .' She got a far-off dreamy look. 'The crust was made with imported chocolate wafers that were available only from a little shop on the Champs-Elysées. The mousse was made with powdered bittersweet chocolate from Zurich. And of course, heavy whipping cream. Ah, yes. Really brings me back . . .' She smiled with a bit of chocolate pudding on her upper lip. And then, I could've sworn, she winked at me. '*C'est fantastique.*'

After cleaning up the kitchen and the dining room and wrapping up the leftovers for Meals on Wheels, we were dismissed. Jean Paul looked exhausted and didn't bother to ask me about the swans. I figured he'd enjoy informing me later that there was no way I'd be let into the Master Class no matter how much Nancy Riviere liked my *Mousse de Jardin*. I didn't bother changing into my street clothes and headed straight for the elevator.

I was walking down Fifty-third Street past the Museum of Modern Art thinking I really should go in there one day, when I heard a voice from behind.

'Don't you think you're being a little unreasonable?'

It was Tom. 'No.'

'Tara set it up,' he said, catching up with me. 'Believe me, the more I know her, the less – '

'It has nothing to do with Tara. It has to do with you ogling my mother.'

'I didn't know it was your mother!'

'It's not just because she's my mom. You can't imagine how it feels . . .'

'What.' He matched his pace with mine. 'Tell me.'

'I could never have that power over men.'

'You could if you wanted.'

'Well, I don't! And yes, I know, I'm contradicting myself.' We turned down Broadway. Sexy billboards looked down from the black sky. Every store used lights so bright you had to squint even in the darkness. All that 'glitz' just to sell porn videos or junky tourist crap like I LOVE NEW YORK T-shirts.

'Look,' Tom said, 'it didn't exactly make me feel proud of myself.'

'You could've left the room or turned away. You didn't have to get so into it.'

'Would you prefer I didn't have a sex drive?'

'Yes, I would. I'd prefer it if all men had no sex drive.' Except for the men I wanted – at the times I designated. 'The world would be a better place.'

'I don't think you really mean that.'

We were stopped at a red light. I stepped off the curb along with about five other people, anxious to press forward, but we all almost got clipped by a cab and backed up. 'I just don't want to feel like I have to be that way too.'

'You don't have to dress up like that. Or undress like that.'

'Yes, I do. Because sex appeal isn't a natural thing!' I was almost shrieking. 'It's a learned behavior! It's not enough just being a person, no, you have to master all these skills, or you won't be able to compete, and then no one will want you.'

'You don't really believe that, do you?'

The light turned green. I looked sideways at him as we crossed. 'Seems to me I was never able to get your attention.'

'You had my attention, it's just . . .' His voice trailed off in confusion.

'Look, if you aren't into me that way, fine. You don't have to make excuses. It's not like it can be forced.'

'It's not that! I just want to have a real relationship with someone before I jump into bed . . .'

'Fine. I hope you and Tara are very happy together.'

'I don't care about Tara.'

'Oh, right, that's why you jumped into bed with her.'

'Ginger – '

'You don't have to explain. Men just aren't attracted to women like me. That's how it is.'

I was almost home. We would get to the front steps. We would say good-bye. I'd go up to my room, get in bed, lie there and regret everything I ever said to him.

'Ginger, you have to believe me . . .' Again his voice trailed off. We were in front of my building. I paused on the sidewalk before turning to go up. He took my hand with both his hands. Funny how a small gesture like that can make your heart thump. 'I never felt anything for Tara. It's just . . . she kept throwing herself at me, and I guess I was sort of impressed with her because of the restaurant and all, but to tell you the truth, I don't really like her very much, and the more I got to know her, the less I liked her, and I don't know why I did what I did because . . .'

A woman in a pin-striped suit rolling a piece of luggage tried to pass. 'Excuse me?'

We moved up onto the steps. I didn't want him to lose his place. 'Because?'

He blushed, looked down at the step, then back at me. 'You're the one I care about. You're the one I want to know. You're the one I've sort of . . .' He cleared his throat. 'Fallen in love with.'

Suddenly, I felt a whole helluva lot better. 'Oh.' I allowed myself to breathe. Onion bagel.

'So . . . do you think you might be able to forgive me?'

I made a big show of frowning, like I'd have to think about it.

'I have a present for you,' he said.

I raised my eyebrows.

He reached into his backpack and gave me a box that was wrapped with tinfoil. We sat down next to each other on the stoop. I peeled off the foil and lifted the top. 'You got this?' It was the stainless steel pie cutter I'd seen at the restaurant supply store. 'For me?'

'Yep.'

'It's so beautiful. I love it. Thank you.'

'You're welcome.'

I kissed him on the cheek. He kissed me on the lips. And kissed me again. And again. And then it wasn't clear who was kissing who, and then it was most definitely each of us kissing each other. I decided that maybe public displays of affection weren't the worst thing in the world.

*t*he next morning, I slept really late. It was Saturday, and exceedingly quiet in midtown. That evening, I was going to Tom's for dinner. But there was the whole day to get through first. Coco was still asleep, and I was restless, so I decided to take myself out to breakfast. I left her a note, and headed to the diner.

I bought a *Post* from the newsstand next door, zipped up my down jacket, and dug my hands deep into the pockets. There was a chill in the air. Winter was definitely on its way. I got to the diner, pushed open the heavy glass door, bypassed the hostess, and sat down at the counter.

I scanned the menu as if some undiscovered treasure would call out to me, but of course it was the same old stuff. Should I get pancakes? A waffle? It was almost lunch. The soup of the day was chicken with rice. Boring. Maybe I should get what I knew I wanted. A hot apple brown Betty à la mode and a cup of coffee. Yes. That sounded good.

After the waiter took my order, I watched him get a cup and fill it from the rounded glass pot filled with dark, steaming coffee. He put it in front of me with two creamers. I took a sip while looking into the case of cakes and pies directly across from me. I focused in on the wall of mirrors that was behind the desserts, reflecting light on all their glory, and saw myself. I didn't look so great. Had barely taken the time to brush my hair and splash water on my face before coming in. Now I considered putting lipstick on, but it would just come off on my coffee cup. I hated lipstick on coffee cups. And who would see me? I stopped focusing on myself and took in the mirror's reflection of the room. I noticed a familiar figure. He was in a booth right behind me.

I swiveled around to make sure I wasn't hallucinating. Jean Paul.

I swiveled back before he might see me. What was he doing in a place like this? How would I eat knowing he was right behind me?

Maybe I would ask the waiter to pack up my brown Betty. I could eat it at home. Then I noticed something else in the mirror. Jean Paul was gorging on a huge, greasy, deluxe cheeseburger.

I swiveled back around. Had to see it with my own eyes. It was true. Mr. French Cuisine was chowing down on the most all-American of meals, and sipping from a tall glass of chocolate milk shake! I watched blood from the burger dribble onto his plate as he crammed the thick bun between his lips. He paused from his chewing. 'Bonjour.'

I smiled, at least I think I smiled – maybe I frowned – and then I swiveled forward without saying anything. After a moment, I swiveled back around. 'You know, quite frankly, I'm surprised to find you eating in a place like this.'

'Why?'

'You disapprove of this kind of food.'

'I have a reputation to protect.'

I swiveled back and opened up my paper.

'So,' he said, 'I don't suppose you know who destroyed your swans.'

I took a sip of coffee.

'I have noticed that you and Miss Glass do not exactly get along,' he said. 'You don't think perhaps . . .'

I looked at him in the mirror. 'I destroyed them.'

'Why?'

'Do you really want to know?'

'*Oui.*'

I got up from my stool and faced Jean Paul. 'You've had it in for me since the first day of school. I don't know why. I don't know what you want from me. You've made this whole experience miserable and I should probably just quit.'

I looked for the waiter. He was probably putting my apple brown Betty on a plate right that second. I'd have to ask him to transfer it to a plastic container. Oh, well. Jean Paul finished chewing and took a sip of milk shake from the straw. Every bone in my body wanted to walk out of the diner right then, but I also wanted to hear what he might say, so I forced myself to wait. Finally, after patting his mouth with his napkin, he spoke. 'If you quit, that would be too bad.'

'Because you're expecting the second half of my tuition payment?' I figured, let the school fight that out with the Sheriff. They'd never get it out of him.

'Because it would be a waste of your talent.'

'How can you say that when you've spent the entire semester making me feel like I don't have talent?'

'Do you think you have talent?'

'After spending the semester with you, I don't know anymore.'

He indicated the empty seat on the other side of his table. 'Sit.'

I didn't.

He went on. 'You are good. But you are a woman. That is what it will be like for you out there. Worse! In a real restaurant, they will destroy you, unless you can show them that you cannot be destroyed.'

'Maybe it used to be like that, but things have changed.'

'You are wrong. It hasn't changed that much, you will see.'

He took another bite of his burger. While he chewed, I wanted desperately to say, *So you do believe in me? You do think I'm good?*

But then I was glad I didn't, because he swallowed and said, 'If you are going to succeed, you must believe in yourself no matter what anyone else tells you. You must know, inside yourself, that you are to be valued, and to hell with everyone else and their goddamned opinions.'

'But when you're a student,' I said, 'you're hungry for praise.'

'You are too hungry. I saw that on the first day. Taste? Or presentation. You must have *both* to be the best.'

I couldn't believe he remembered that exchange. Had he been paying such close attention? 'I knew that.'

'Then why didn't you say so? I'll tell you why. You craved my approval too much. You needed me to say whether you were right or wrong. Many people, especially the women, they will quit as soon as they get a taste of the real thing. I am just trying to prepare you.'

'You don't seem to be preparing Tara.'

He pushed his plate away. 'Why waste my energy on someone who has no potential? She is useless in the kitchen. She will always be out front, the hostess, meeting and greeting. She will never be the creator of the food. But you?' He burped slightly into his napkin. 'You have real potential. Pastry is physically demanding work, but it is also delicate.

You can do both. You have the masculine and feminine side. That,' he said, 'is the magic combination.' Jean Paul leaned back in the booth as if it would make more room inside his stomach. 'The burgers here are really good.'

The waiter brought my apple brown Betty and set it down at my place at the counter. I sat down and dug up a piece of warm, cinnamony apple from the bottom, then added some ice cream from the top, and brought it to my mouth. The spicy warmth with the sweet cold was so good.

But I still had a nagging concern. I swiveled back. 'Now I feel bad that I destroyed my swans. They turned out very well, you know.' Not that I'd tasted one, but he hadn't either.

He shrugged. 'If it is the Master Class you are worried about, don't bother. I will be recommending you. As long as you don't make it a habit to destroy your desserts before they are served.'

'Thank you.' I swiveled back to my apple brown Betty. At first, I wasn't sure if I'd be able to enjoy it knowing he was right behind me. But I did. As a matter of fact, I pretty much wolfed it down. As I savored the last bit of ice cream on my tongue, I contemplated what I was going to do the rest of the day. It seemed like years before it would be time to go to Tom's. How would I fill up the afternoon? There was still Leah's bureau to empty out. I'd been planning on taking care of that. But I didn't want to go over there and run into Emma.

Or maybe I did. We couldn't stay estranged forever, even if she did think my mother was a whore. Someone had to keep her from being too much under the influence of the Sheriff.

I called on my cell phone, but no one answered. I decided to take a chance and head over.

Jean Paul was still sitting there working on a piece of strawberry short-cake. I gave him my *Post*, and said my good-byes. Just as I was about to head out the door, Coco walked in.

'You're leaving?'

'Guess what, Jean Paul is over there.'

'Where?'

'That guy at the first booth. Reading the paper. He says he's going to recommend me for the Master Class!'

'Congratulations! He's cute.'

'You think so?' I looked at him and wrinkled my nose.

'Do you mind if I go over and introduce myself?'

I shrugged. 'Since when do you ask my permission?'

Coco was already taking her leather jacket off and making sure her breasts were displayed prominently under her tight green sweater. 'Wish me luck.' She strutted on over and introduced herself. Jean Paul stood up, they both looked at me, I nodded encouragement, and turned to push the glass door. She had no idea what she was in for. But then again, neither did he.

I used my key to get in. Emma was on the couch watching TV. I said hello politely and told her I was finishing up with the bureau. 'Would you like to do it with me?' I asked.

She gave me a stiff 'no' without looking away from the TV. Just like old times.

I got a garbage bag and went back to the bedroom. It was a tall oak bureau, and there was still a tube of hair gel, some nail polish remover, and a jewelry box on top. I pulled open the top drawer. It was really a mess. Leah had junked together all sorts of odds and ends that she proba-bly should've thrown out but couldn't. A souvenir scarf from England with a picture of Lady Di on it, old floppy disks, extra nail clippers, glue sticks . . . The drawer underneath was more of the same. A Swatch watch still in its long narrow box. Family snapshots stacked inside envelopes. And a photo album with pink and red hearts all over the cover, still in its wraps.

I sat down on the bed and tore off the wrapping. The book still had its nice, new plastic smell. I slid each of the photos into a plastic slot. Al-most all of them were of Emma and Leah and Ben, but I was pleased to find a few nice ones of Coco and me, from my high school graduation.

Then I went to Leah's jewelry box and pulled out Emma's drawing. The one I'd found in Leah's underwear drawer my first day, with the two of them holding hands. I screwed the glue stick out, glad it hadn't dried up, and mounted the picture inside the front cover. Smoothed it flat. Nice.

I stood up. Blood rushed to my head from the sudden vertical move-ment. I stood for a moment waiting for the dizzy feeling to go away, hugging the album to my chest. Then I took a deep breath – surprised to find myself nervous at the idea of facing Emma with this – and made myself go out to the living room to present it to her.

She was still sitting there on the couch. There was a big, mean pimple on her cheek. You had to sympathize. I wondered how her supply of sanitary napkins was holding out. She was now watching a rerun of *Friends*.

'This album was in your mom's drawer,' I said. 'And there were a bunch of loose pictures. So I put this together.'

I handed it to her. She looked down at it. For a moment I thought she was going to reject it and hand it back to me without a word. But then I saw her nose get red, and the red spread to her cheeks, and I knew she was trying really hard not to cry.

I sank down next to her on the couch. She opened it up. Looked at the picture she'd drawn. And shut the book.

For a moment, I felt bad. I'd made a mistake. But then she leaned over and put her head on my lap, curled her feet up on the cushion so she was in a little ball, and lay there, still holding the album in her arms, and sobbed.

For like twenty seconds I tried not to cry too. I thought I should 'stay strong' and let her be the one who needed to be upset. But as I stroked her hair the way Grandma used to for me when I was missing Coco, I had to give in, and let myself cry along with her.

chapter thirty-nine

'*a*re you hungry?'

'Starving.'

'Good. Because I made a lot of food.'

I followed Tom into the living room of his one-bedroom apartment on the bottom floor of a small house on a quiet block in Queens. It had only taken about twenty minutes to get here from my subway stop in midtown. Tom met me at the platform and we walked together to his place. The main boulevard leading from the station was lined with Greek restaurants and the usual assortment of newsstands, fast-food places and a King Penny five-and-dime. We turned down a block with rows of small-ish houses from the forties with patches of lawn in front. It was surprisingly quiet. You could see the sky.

'An elderly couple lives on the top floor with their teenage son,' Tom was saying as he led me inside a small white stucco house. His place was simply furnished, very clean and freshly painted white. The table in the living room was already set, with two tall, lit orange candles flanking a vase filled with little yellow baby roses. 'They have fights upstairs like you wouldn't believe. He crashed a car last week and they almost threw him out. Would you like a glass of wine? Dinner is almost ready. I hope you like meat loaf.'

'Smells great.'

'I boiled some potatoes. I think they're ready to mash. You like the skins on or off?'

'Off.'

'Me too. And, of course, fresh peas. I shelled them myself.'

'You did? That's so sweet! Is there anything I can do to help?'

'Nope.'

I sipped my wine, watched him mash a pot of steaming potatoes, and told myself it was okay to let him do all the work – Jean Paul was not lurking in the shadows making sure I was staying busy.

When everything was ready, he led me out to the living room and pulled a chair out for me. 'They must teach manners in the Midwest.'

'Don't expect this all the time.'

I remembered when I had said that to him, when I was in the red dress. Was he putting on a show for me too? 'You don't have to do all this, you know.'

'Relax. I want to pamper you.'

He served the food while I sat there like a queen. A queen in Queens. I wondered if he had a queen bed. I could be a queen in a queen in Queens.

The food tasted so good, in a fresh and wholesome way. Even if it hadn't, it wouldn't have mattered because he made me feel so taken care of, because of little things, like the fresh cube of butter on a little glass dish with its own mini knife. The folded paper napkin under my fork. The plate he set down in front of me that had representatives from all three food groups. The way he looked at me with affection.

After we were done eating, I couldn't stand to be served anymore. I took the platter of leftover meat loaf into the kitchen.

He followed me in with the peas and potatoes. 'I thought we could take a walk into town and get some baklava.'

'That sounds nice.' I covered the meat loaf with Saran Wrap. 'But I'm having a craving. A meal like that calls for brownies, don't you think?'

'I think I may actually have some baking chocolate up in the cupboard.'

We got all the ingredients out. He watched while I melted the chocolate and butter in a double boiler. 'Do you like fudgy or cakey brownies?' I asked, when it came time to put in the eggs.

'Cakey.'

'Me too.'

'We're so compatible.'

I let him lick the bowl while I put the pan in the oven. Then I took the carton of eggs back to the refrigerator. It was crowded with all our leftovers. As I moved things around to make room, I wondered again if we would transition into lovers that night and how that might go. Would I be able to undress with confidence? Would I be able to pull off any of my mother's sexy moves? Or would I regress into my usual old modest behavior? He certainly did have lots of food in his refrigerator for a single guy. I was impressed that he had the energy to make things for himself after cooking at school and at work. I balanced the plate of meat loaf on top of a carton of half-and-half and a tub of cottage cheese. That accidentally set in motion a cantaloupe, which rolled off the shelf and landed on a pitcher of orange juice, which then cascaded all over the front of my pants.

'Oh, god.' I was soaked in sticky orange juice, and there was a huge puddle on the floor. Luckily the pitcher was plastic and didn't break. 'I am such a klutz!'

'Don't worry about it. Orange is your color. Or should I say scent.'

'Funny.'

'Maybe you should change into a pair of my pants.'

'They're probably too small on me.'

'Don't be ridiculous. I'll get you a pair.'

I followed him into his room. I didn't really want to have to find out if I had bigger hips than he did. 'You know, I'm so sticky. I should take a shower.'

'Sure.'

The bedroom was very pleasant. It was in the back, and it had a window that looked out on a garden. A couple would be very comfortable sharing this apartment in Queens that did indeed have a queen-sized bed.

Tom gave me a clean white bath towel and promised he would keep an eye on the brownies.

I went into his bathroom, hesitated before locking the door (as if he would just walk in there!), took all my clothes off, and got into his shower. The tiles in his bathroom glistened and the chrome fixtures were shiny. There was a little narrow window, and you could look out the side of the house and see a bit of the street while standing there under the spray. It was sort of novel to feel like you could spy on other people while you were naked. Except, it being Astoria and not Manhattan, there didn't appear to be another soul on the planet.

I was using his Suave cherry-scented shampoo and ruminating on how not suave I had been, when he called through the door, 'The brownies are ready. I'm gonna take them out.'

'Okay!'

As I dried off, I looked forward to my dessert with a tall glass of cold milk, which sounded especially good because I was thirsty from the hot shower. I pulled on his blue jeans, but they were tight. If I sucked in, I could get them zipped shut. Not too comfortable. Plus, the denim felt rough against my skin. I hated getting into clothing when I was still damp. So I took off the jeans and wrapped the thick white towel around my otherwise naked body. You really couldn't see anything, so there really was no big deal about walking out there naked with just a towel on. So. With the towel wrapped around my naked body, I stood in the doorway of the kitchen.

His back was to me. He was slicing the tray of brownies and moving them to a plate. He must've heard me come in, because he said, 'These smell great. I hope they baked long enough.'

'The hard part is to get the ones in the middle to cook through without overdoing the ones on the edges.'

'That is so . . .' he said, turning around, holding the plate of brownies, seeing me, in my towel, under which I was naked, 'true.'

'The jeans weren't really comfortable. Do you have any pajamas I could borrow?'

'Sure.'

He set the brownies down. I followed him back to the bedroom. He got cotton plaid elastic-waist pajama bottoms and a blue T-shirt from his drawer and put them on the bed. 'These should work.'

'Thanks.'

He was about to leave the room. Instead, he looked at me once more – as I stood there naked under the towel – then walked right up to me, put his arms around me, and gave me a hug. As he nuzzled his mouth against my hair and said, 'You smell good,' I really wanted to hug him back. But I was holding the towel up.

'It's your shampoo,' I said.

I realized that if I did put my arms around him, the towel would probably stay. After all, I was right up against him. His body would keep it up.

So I allowed myself to put my arms around him. And the towel, which was wrapped pretty tightly around me, did stay up. He was now looking into my eyes. And I was looking into his. I hesitated. But I had to ask. 'Tom?'

'Yes?'

'Did you turn off the oven?'

'Yes.'

'We wouldn't want to start a fire.'

'No,' he said. 'We wouldn't want to do that.'

That's when he kissed me. On the lips. I felt my towel loosen and unravel, so that it really just seemed like it was in the way. Part of me wanted that towel to drop to the floor so I could be right up against him, with his soft T-shirt against my breasts, his coarse blue jeans against my bare legs. But the towel stayed in place, held up between his body and mine. And when he stepped back, my hands automatically went to keep it up. Would he think I was too fat? Too hairy? Too tall? Too gawky? Was I still craving validation? Had I still not learned anything from my mom? Was I still the worst student in the class?

I let the towel drop to the floor.

Coco would've utterly disapproved of my method. No slow and gradual undraping here. But there was a footnote to her lessons that she'd never drawn attention to. None of those gimmicks were necessary if you were with someone who was already under your spell.

Tom gazed at me with admiration as he sank down on the edge of the bed to untie his shoes. 'You are so . . . beautiful.'

Even if I was going to stop craving validation, it was nice to get the compliment.

He took off his T-shirt, twirled it in the air, and tossed it to the side.

'You,' I said, 'are pretty cute yourself.'

He unzipped his pants and let them drop to the floor. At that moment, there were a lot of things I didn't know about my future. But there was one thing I did know. We wouldn't be having dessert.